VALUED BY THE VISCOUNT

Second Sons of London
Book Six

Alexa Aston

Dragonblade Publishing, Inc. is an imprint of Kathryn Le Veque Novels, Inc.
P.O. Box 23
Moreno Valley, CA 92556
ceo@dragonbladepublishing.com

Produced in the United States of America

First Edition September 2022
Trade Paperback Edition

ARE YOU SIGNED UP FOR DRAGONBLADE'S BLOG?

You'll get the latest news and information on exclusive giveaways, exclusive excerpts, coming releases, sales, free books, cover reveals and more.

Check out our complete list of authors, too!

No spam, no junk. That's a promise!

Sign Up Here

www.dragonbladepublishing.com

Dearest Reader;

Thank you for your support of a small press. At Dragonblade Publishing, we strive to bring you the highest quality Historical Romance from some of the best authors in the business. Without your support, there is no 'us', so we sincerely hope you adore these stories and find some new favorite authors along the way.

Happy Reading!

CEO, Dragonblade Publishing

Additional Dragonblade books by Author Alexa Aston

Second Sons of London Series
Educated By The Earl
Debating With The Duke
Empowered By The Earl
Made for the Marquess
Dubious about the Duke
Valued by the Viscount

Dukes Done Wrong Series
Discouraging the Duke
Deflecting the Duke
Disrupting the Duke
Delighting the Duke
Destiny with a Duke

Dukes of Distinction Series
Duke of Renown
Duke of Charm
Duke of Disrepute
Duke of Arrogance
Duke of Honor

The St. Clairs Series
Devoted to the Duke
Midnight with the Marquess
Embracing the Earl
Defending the Duke
Suddenly a St. Clair
Starlight Night (Novella)
The Twelve Days of Love (Novella)

Soldiers & Soulmates Series
To Heal an Earl
To Tame a Rogue
To Trust a Duke
To Save a Love
To Win a Widow
Yuletide at Gillingham (Novella)

The Lyon's Den Connected World
The Lyon's Lady Love

King's Cousins Series
The Pawn
The Heir
The Bastard

Medieval Runaway Wives
Song of the Heart
A Promise of Tomorrow
Destined for Love

Knights of Honor Series
Word of Honor
Marked by Honor
Code of Honor
Journey to Honor
Heart of Honor
Bold in Honor
Love and Honor
Gift of Honor
Path to Honor
Return to Honor

Pirates of Britannia Series
God of the Seas

De Wolfe Pack: The Series
Rise of de Wolfe

The de Wolfes of Esterley Castle
Diana
Derek
Thea

Also from Alexa Aston
The Bridge to Love

PROLOGUE

London—1809
Opening night of the Season

L ADY VANESSA HUGHES looked at herself in the full-length mirror, a gift from her parents on her eighteenth birthday last year. Mama had said, though extravagant, the mirror would come in handy as Vanessa readied herself for all of the events in her come-out Season. Unfortunately, she had not made her debut as planned. Her parents, who had both been feeling poorly, succumbed to a fever. They died within a day of one another, three weeks before the Season began. Consequently, Vanessa returned to the country for a year of mourning the two people she deeply loved.

It had been a lonely year for her. Not only had she been close to both her parents, but Mama had gone ahead and dismissed Vanessa's governess of many years, saying the woman was no longer needed since Vanessa would soon be wed. She had bid her governess farewell just before she and her parents traveled to London. Vanessa had been caught up in all the many dress fittings and was eager to make friends with the other girls making their debuts in Polite Society.

Instead, she had spent the last twelve months in the country while her brother, Vernon, remained in town. He had not come a single time, not even to spend Christmas with her. Since he was her only sibling and her parents had been only children themselves, the holiday season had been bleak. When March came, she had hoped Vernon would send for her without being prompted. She did not expect to have an entire new wardrobe created—since she had yet to wear a single gown made up for last Season—but she had hoped to come to town a bit early and get to know London. Her parents had always left her in the country with her governess when they attended the Season each year. Vanessa longed to make friends and, more than anything, hoped she would receive an offer of marriage. She intended to have many children and would give them equal attention, making sure none of them ever felt lonely or ignored.

When she did not hear from Vernon, she wrote to him—again. He had not responded to a single letter she had written him in the year she had been in mourning. Finally, a reply to her last correspondence arrived. He told her he would send the carriage for her. Eagerly, she went about packing, thrilled to finally see London for the first time. Hopefully, she would at last get to know her brother a little better. Vernon was four years older and had never spent any time in her company. He had once told her when she was nine and he thirteen that females were worthless creatures, only good for breeding heirs. After that, she had stopped making any effort to know him. They were both adults now, however, and they had lost their parents. She hoped their shared loss could bring them close. She also assumed that Vernon would introduce her into his circle of friends and that she might find her future husband among them. Although the more Vanessa thought about it, the less she wanted to wed a friend of her brother's if they all had the same low opinion of women as he did.

The maid standing nearby smiled at her. "You look right nice, Lady Vanessa. I'll bet you dance every number at tonight's ball."

"I hope so, too. Thank you for your help tonight. You may leave now," she added, and the maid quietly exited the room.

Vanessa went and sat at her dressing table and put on the pearl earrings which had belonged to her mother. Mama had passed them down to Vanessa on her sixteenth birthday. The pair was her most cherished possession, a link to her mother, who would never see her daughter wed and bear children. By wearing these earrings, Mama would be with her tonight and every night of the Season.

She had no other jewelry to wear. She had seen Vernon so few times since she had come to town. When she had asked him if she might wear a necklace or bracelet of their mother's, he had put her off. She smoothed her hair a final time and stood, nerves dancing in her belly, but they were the good kind of nerves. Yes, it was true that she was a little anxious about this evening but she hoped to leave tonight's ball having made a few friends and having caught the eye of a few kind, eligible gentlemen.

Vanessa descended the stairs and arrived in the foyer, hoping Vernon would be waiting for her. No, not Vernon. He had snapped at her when she had called him by his name when she first arrived in town, insisting that she refer to him as Stillwell. He had admitted that he never liked his given name, one he shared with their maternal grandfather whom they had never met since he died before either of them had been born.

Adams, the butler, was in the foyer, as well as a footman who was on duty by the door.

"May I say that you look absolutely lovely tonight, my lady," Adams told her.

"Thank you," she replied. "This is the gown that Mama had wished me to wear to the opening night of the Season." She touched a hand to one earring and saw the butler smile.

"I recognize the countess' earrings. I know it comforts you to have a piece of Lady Stillwell with you tonight. She and his lordship are truly missed."

Tears misted in Vanessa's eyes and she nodded. Adams had been with them for many years and her father even used to take advice from his butler. It had surprised Vanessa shortly after her parents' passing that Adams and Mrs. Adams, their housekeeper, were summoned to London permanently. Adams had floundered a bit with his explanation and then finally had asked if he could be honest with her. When she encouraged him to do so, he shared that the London butler and housekeeper had been let go and they were to take the couple's place, year-round.

When Vanessa asked who would serve as the butler and housekeeper in the country, Adams gave her a weak smile.

"It is my understanding we are not to be replaced, my lady. Lord Stillwell believes a country butler is unnecessary and he said you could take on the duties of Mrs. Adams in managing the household."

His words had shocked her but she was well prepared for the job. Mama had schooled her only daughter from an early age in the ways to run a large household and Vanessa stepped into those shoes, serving as de facto mistress and housekeeper of the country house. She managed the schedule of the maids and when they were to clean and where, as well as planning out the menus with Cook. She had done no entertaining, due to being in mourning. At least functioning as the estate's housekeeper gave her something useful to do.

"Do you know when Lord Stillwell might come down, Adams?" she asked, a bit nervous that her brother wasn't here awaiting her. It was half-past eight and the ball's receiving line opened at nine. She knew there would be a crowd of carriages descending upon their destination and she and Vernon—no, Stillwell—might have to walk a bit.

"Lord Stillwell is not at home, my lady," the butler informed her.

Shock rippled through her. If her brother had been out somewhere at dinner—or at one of his gaming hells—he would need to change into evening attire when he did return home. That would cause them to be late. Of course, Mama had always told her a receiving line could go on for a good half-hour and even closer to an hour. With this being the opening night of the

Season and so many in attendance, that would be their only saving grace.

If Stillwell arrived in the next few minutes.

"I think I will take a seat, Adams," she said brightly, trying to hide her worry. "I will most likely be on my feet most of the night. Either speaking with others or dancing."

"An excellent idea, my lady," the butler answered neutrally.

Vanessa sat in a chair in the foyer, her eyes constantly going to the grandfather clock as it ticked away the minutes. When it chimed nine, her heart sank.

She was going to miss the first ball of the Season.

Her insides churned. A host of emotions flitted through her, ranging from sadness to rage at her thoughtless brother. He spent a good deal of his time away from the house with his friends. He had mentioned being at his club a great deal but Vanessa also knew from overhearing servants' gossip that many nights Stillwell was at gaming hells or brothels. To think of him at one now when he should be doing his brotherly duty and escorting her to her first ball made her want to claw out his eyes. If Papa were still alive, he would have made certain Vernon wasn't neglecting his duties, whether it was to his tenants in the country or to his sister in town.

Yet what was she supposed to do? If she called him out for his negligence, would he even care? Worse, he might be enraged at such insubordination and send her back to the country.

Vanessa waited another five minutes and then decided to return to her bedchamber. The small glimmer of hope she had held on to had faded into nothingness.

She stood and Adams, who had lurked nearby, came toward her. "I believe I will retire for the evening," she said stiffly, hating the look of pity in his eyes.

"I am very sorry, Lady Vanessa. I know how much you were looking forward to this evening."

She smiled ruefully. "You have nothing to apologize for, Adams."

He bowed his head briefly and then his gaze met hers. "I would take away the hurt if I could, my lady."

"I know you would," she said softly. "Thank you."

She turned and crossed the foyer, reaching the staircase. Her hand went out and gripped the handrail tightly, needing the support because she found her whole body shaking. Whether it was from anger or loss, she couldn't say. As she trudged up the first few steps, however, she heard the front door opening and wheeled around, her heart in her throat.

Stillwell stumbled through the door, looking disheveled. He was obviously in his cups, his face flushed a bright red, and his gait unsteady as he moved into the foyer. Glancing up, he noticed her.

"Ah, Vanessa. Just the person I need to speak with."

She hurried down the stairs and came to him. "We are going to be frightfully late to the ball, Stillwell. Shall I summon your valet and have him help you change? Perhaps most of the traffic has died down. Mama always told me receiving lines were long and—"

"That won't be necessary," he interrupted, waving his hand as if he brushed aside the fact they were missing tonight's event. "Come to my study," he mumbled, turning his back on her and shuffling away.

Disappointment filled her and her gaze met Adams'.

"I will send coffee to his lordship," the butler promised. "Hopefully, it will help."

Vanessa nodded and then hurried after her brother, who had now reached the entrance to his study and stepped inside. She followed him into the room and closed the door behind them. She had decided to stand up for herself and speak her truth. The servants did not need to hear her dressing down their drunken employer.

Stillwell tripped and fell to the carpet. She raced to him and took his elbow, helping him to rise. Guiding him to a chair, she turned him around and he collapsed into it, closing his eyes. She stepped away quickly, the stench of liquor on him overwhelming her.

Moving to the seat opposite him, she sat and cleared her throat. "We have things to discuss, Stillwell," she said firmly.

His eyes opened and she saw how bloodshot they were. "I will do the talking, Vanessa," he said brusquely. "You will listen whether you like it or not."

His words—and their tone—sent a chill through her. She swallowed and clasped her hands in her lap, waiting for whatever news he was about to share.

"Fetch me a drink," he commanded.

"Do you really need one, Stillwell? It seems you have had quite enough already this evening. Enough to make me miss the opening ball of the Season and my debut into Polite Society."

He frowned deeply, his look so stern that she wished the floor would swallow her up. "Get me the bloody drink."

Vanessa stood and went to the crystal decanters that sat on a side table and poured brandy into a snifter. She brought it to him and saw he could not take it with one hand. She reached for his other and placed both of them around the glass. Taking her seat again, she stared at him.

She thought he would sip the amber liquid but, instead, he drained it quickly and indicated he wanted more. Reluctantly, she rose again and took the decanter to him, pouring from it since she was afraid to remove the snifter from his trembling hands.

Again, Stillwell tossed back the liquor and then the snifter dropped from his fingers to the carpet. He finally met her gaze and she couldn't tell what was hidden behind it.

"You wish to wed, don't you? That's what women want, isn't it?" he demanded.

"Yes, I do hope to meet an eligible bachelor this Season. I know he will need to ask you for my hand in marriage before I may accept his offer. You will also draw up the marriage settlements, much as Papa would have done for me if he were still alive."

Stillwell snorted. "Well, he isn't, is he? It's me. I am the one who is deciding your future." He paused. "It was decided tonight."

Cold fear struck her and if Vanessa had not been seated, she would have collapsed.

"What have you done?" she asked, her nails digging into her palms.

"I arranged a husband for you," he slurred.

"You did . . . what?"

"You won't have to bother hunting for one. It has all been arranged. He will come here tomorrow morning to meet you and we'll draw up the marriage contracts." He rubbed his temples. "Damn. Need to send word to the solicitor."

Vanessa shot to her feet. "How can I marry a man I have never even met?"

Her brother shrugged. "Well, you will meet him in the morning." He closed his eyes again.

And started snoring.

She marched to him and shook him violently. "No, you don't. You do not tell me I am going to wed a stranger and fall asleep."

"Huh?" He looked up at her sleepily. "Oh, I know him."

An odd look crossed Stillwell's face and a sinking feeling overtook Vanessa. "Do you owe him money?"

She knew he gambled recklessly because she eavesdropped on the servants, who couldn't stop gossiping about it. It was how she learned the circumstances in which the London butler and housekeeper left. They—and a good number of the staff—were paid sporadically. Or not at all. That was the true reason Adams and his wife had been summoned from Kent and why they had taken a few servants with them to London. Vanessa had assumed Stillwell was trying to cut costs.

When he didn't answer her question, she poked him in the shoulder. Hard.

"Ouch!"

"Tell me. Have you lost money to this man?"

This man who was to become her husband . . .

"Yes," he finally answered. "Your dowry will just cover my debt."

Bitterness filled her. "So, in essence, Stillwell, you are selling me to pay for what you owe."

"I suppose some might look at it that way," he said hesitantly.

"The one who is being sold most certainly does," she spat out. "Why? Who is this man?"

Vanessa dropped to her knees. "Please, Vernon. Do not make me do this. I am begging you."

Her brother raised haunted eyes to hers and she realized just how deeply in debt he must be. "I have no choice," he rasped. "If I pay him, he promised to keep the other creditors at bay."

"Who is he?" she finally asked.

"Lord Hockley. He has been wed before and already has his heir. You do not have to worry about providing one for him."

"But I want children," she said, her throat tight with emotion.

"Oh, he'll probably get them off you. He is very eager to couple with you. He wanted a beautiful virgin and I assured him you fit the description."

"He said that?" Disgust filled her. No gentleman would speak so coarsely.

Stillwell's head fell back against the chair. "He says a lot of things. He told me what he wanted to do to you."

Queasiness filled her belly. "I don't understand."

Her brother raised his head. "You'll learn soon enough." He shook his head. "Go to bed, Vanessa. Lord Hockley will call at ten o'clock tomorrow morning. Wear something pretty for him. Now, leave me."

Slowly, she rose and left the room, passing Adams who carried a tray with the coffee upon it.

"My lady?" he asked, worry creasing his brow. "You look deathly ill. How bad is it?"

Vanessa shook her head. "The worst it could be," she said dully, brushing past him and going to her bedchamber.

Little did she know that things always could be even worse than anticipated.

SHE AWOKE THE next morning having gotten little sleep. She rang for her maid and dressed with no conversation. She supposed the footman on duty last night had spread some of the gossip circulating through the household today, from Vanessa not making her appearance at the ball to the earl stumbling home in a drunken stupor. The loyal Adams would have kept quiet.

She doubted anyone would know her betrothed would be making an appearance this morning.

Or perhaps they had some inkling of what might occur. If Stillwell had remembered to send for his solicitor, a footman would have delivered the note and surmised why the man was being summoned to their townhouse.

The maid broke the silence. "May I bring up some breakfast for you, my lady?"

"No. I am not hungry. But thank you."

After the servant left, Vanessa paced her bedchamber. She felt what little energy she had drain from her and took a seat by the window. As the hour drew near for Lord Hockley to arrive, her nervousness grew. She didn't know if he might be one of the friends Stillwell had brought home previously. Her brother hadn't introduced her to any of them when she had passed them in the hallway. They, like he, had been imbibing heavily. At the moment, she couldn't recall what a single one of them had looked like.

A carriage pulled up in the square and she pulled aside the curtain, looking down as the footman opened the vehicle's door. She realized she was holding her breath as an overweight, older gentleman exited. He must be Lord Hockley's solicitor, with his white hair and huge belly. She stared intensely, waiting for Lord

Hockley to emerge. Was he a viscount? Or an earl, as her father had been?

Finally, another man descended the stairs, rather drab in appearance and looks and also old. She hadn't necessary wanted a handsome man as her husband but this one was truly a disappointment. Vanessa dropped the curtain back into place and settled into her chair, breathing in and out slowly and deeply, trying to manage her emotions.

After half an hour, a knock sounded and a maid ventured into the room. "My lady, you are to come downstairs. To Lord Stillwell's study."

Rising, she moved toward the door. The servant kept her gaze averted and Vanessa couldn't blame the maid for wishing to hide her pity.

She arrived downstairs, where Adams awaited. "This way, my lady," he said, offering her escort to Stillwell's study.

She followed him, her head held high, the beautiful posture her mother praised her for on full display.

Adams hesitated at the door, his hand hovering just above the knob.

"Go ahead," she told him. "I know what my fate is."

Surprise filled his face. "You are very brave, my lady." With that, he opened the door and announced her.

She entered the room and two steps in paused, having caught sight of their visitors. Up close, she realized she had made a horrible mistake. She had misjudged the clothing both men wore. The younger of the pair, approaching forty, was the solicitor.

The older one was her betrothed.

Bile rose in her throat and she quickly swallowed it as she took in her future husband. He was perhaps an inch over five feet so she would hover over him since she was five inches over five feet. His girth was tremendous for his height and he had heavy jowls that pulled the lower half of his face downward. The white hair was abundant, making him look even older.

Slowly, she continued toward them and her brother said,

"This is Lady Vanessa Hughes, my sister, Lord Hockley."

"I see that," he snapped. He studied her a long moment and then said, "Turn around. Slowly."

She did so, feeling his eyes bore into her, as if he were judging her like horseflesh.

"She'll do nicely," Lord Hockley pronounced. "Shall we go, my lady?"

"Go . . . where?" she said dumbly.

The nobleman's face darkened and he wheeled, his eyes narrowed. "You didn't tell her, Stillwell?"

"I thought . . ." Her brother's voice trailed off and he shrugged helplessly.

Lord Hockley turned to her. "I hope you aren't the dolt your brother is. The marriage settlements are now signed. I procured a special license for us this morning at Doctors' Commons."

"What is that?" she voiced, dread filling her.

"It means we can wed immediately and will do so."

"Today?" she asked, her voice wavering.

"Yes, today. That is what immediately would refer to." Lord Hockley shook his head. "I suppose you are a featherbrain. A maid can pack your things. They can be delivered to my townhouse. Come along," he ordered.

"With you. Now," she said dully.

He sniffed. Taking her hand, he placed it on his arm. "Yes, Lady Vanessa."

They left the room. She didn't bother looking back to tell her brother goodbye. He had betrayed her in the worst way and, to her, he was now dead. In the corridor, though, she found her voice.

"Adams, please see that Mrs. Adams packs my things. They are to be sent to Lord Hockley's townhouse at once."

"At once?" echoed the butler, surprise showing on his usually composed face.

Vanessa nodded, biting her lip, trying to keep from bursting into tears. "Goodbye," she told the valued servant, and accompanied her fiancé to his carriage.

Once inside, she found they couldn't sit on the same cushion because of his tremendous size and she moved opposite him. The other man joined them and sat beside her. He never introduced himself nor spoke a word. They reached their destination, only a few blocks away, and all three climbed out.

They entered a townhouse. The place which would now be her home. She looked about the foyer, dry-eyed. Tears would be for later, shed in private.

"They're waiting in the parlor," Lord Hockley gruffly said and he led them to a room off the foyer.

Inside were three people. Once again, she was not told who they were. Two of them—a man and a woman—favored one other quite a bit and were regarding her with hostility. She supposed them to be her new stepchildren. A third man looked on in amusement as the woman slipped her hand into the crook of his arm. Vanessa gathered he was this woman's husband.

"I am here, my lord," a voice said, and a clergyman hurried into the room. "Have you the special license?"

The solicitor produced it and the clergyman studied it a moment. "Very well then. Are we ready?"

Vanessa repeated the phrases listlessly, vowing to love, honor, and obey the man next to her. At least she learned his Christian name during the ceremony.

Horace.

He would be Horace the Horrible to her. She almost giggled at the nickname she bestowed upon him.

They were pronounced man and wife and Horace the Horrible moved to her. She realized he couldn't stand on his toes so she bent, allowing him to brush his dry lips to her cheek.

The clergyman and solicitor left. The married couple followed them from the room without a word.

"Wait up, Mathilda," the remaining man called. He hurried to the door and then turned and glared at her.

"No one can ever replace our mother," he snarled and then

he left.

The moment he was gone, her new husband burst into laughter. "Ah, my Milton is quite put out with me," he said.

"I assume he and Mathilda are your children. My stepchildren."

"They are," Horace the Horrible said. "He's jealous. I keep tight control over his finances. He isn't astute enough with numbers to be the successful gambler that I am. No, Milton is waiting for me to die and hoping I won't get you with child because it would mean he would have to support the brat once I am gone and he is Earl of Hockley."

He shook his head. "Ignore him. You may see him at some of the events we attend."

"We will go to the Season?" she asked incredulously.

"Of course, we will. I must show off my newest prize. I believe there is a ball tonight."

She couldn't imagine dancing with him.

As if reading her mind, he told her, "You will not dance, of course. You are a married lady now and will sit with the matrons. I gather from Stillwell that you know no one in London. Perhaps my daughter will take you under her wing and introduce you around."

Vanessa doubted that would occur.

He captured her wrist. "For now, we will go upstairs and christen the marriage bed."

She froze. She had been told nothing about what occurred between a man and a woman. Mama had kept putting it off until it was too late. The thought of this man touching her intimately brought terror to her.

"You are ignorant, I suppose."

She nodded, not finding her voice.

"Perhaps that is for the best since I do have . . . unusual tastes."

He led her upstairs, showing her where the countess' rooms were and then bringing her to his. She wondered how often she would have to perform her marital duty. He was so old and had trouble moving with his girth. She hoped he wouldn't want her very often.

Without warning, he punched her in the gut.

Vanessa doubled over, the breath gone from her. She fought for and finally wheezed, gasping for air. He allowed her to catch it—and then with both hands, ripped her bodice open.

Hours later, battered and bruised, she soaked in a hot tub and then dressed in silence in the gown her mother wished for her to wear as she made her foray into Polite Society. None of the marks showed, covered by the gown. When the butler came to escort her downstairs, she was suitably cowed, afraid to say a single word.

"Lady Hockley?"

She looked up and her husband offered her his arm. She took it, trying not to visibly cringe as she touched him, and he led her to the waiting carriage. No conversation occurred on their way to the ball. They joined the receiving line and her husband introduced her to their hosts before telling her he was off to the gaming room.

"You will join the other matrons," he instructed. "Speak to no gentlemen—or you will regret it."

Wincing at his words, Vanessa quickly turned away and wandered into the ballroom, not knowing a soul. She blindly moved through the masses gathered inside and found where she was to sit. As other women arrived, they took no notice of her. She tried to introduce herself once and the woman looked at her in disdain.

"Do you not realize you must be introduced to someone in order to speak to them?"

She recalled Mama mentioning something about that—but who could introduce her? She knew no one.

Vanessa sat silently, watching the dancers, thinking how she would never be a part of them. When supper was announced, she remained seated. Horace the Horrible did not come for her. Her fear of him now was so great that she sat alone and waited for the other matrons to return. They did, tittering behind their fans, obviously about her. She avoided their blatant stares, her gaze focused on her hands in her lap.

Her husband came for her near the end of the ball and claimed her. They rode in silence back to his townhouse. He escorted her to her bedchamber. She began trembling, knowing now what was to come.

"I am tired," he told her. "We can spend time with one another tomorrow." He gleamed at her possessively and she wanted to plunge a knife into his eye.

Entering her bedchamber, she spied her trunks and a maid sleeping in the corner. The servant awoke and helped prepare Vanessa for bed, ignoring the bruising and gently lowering the night rail over her head and down her body.

"Anything else, my lady?"

"No."

The maid left. Vanessa went to the bed, grateful she would be in it alone. She climbed into it and curled into a ball, pulling the bedclothes tightly around her.

Vanessa prayed either she—or Horace the Horrible—would die during the night.

CHAPTER ONE

Boxwell Hall, Sussex—August 1816

REED DAVENPORT, VISCOUNT Boxling, rose from his bed, still feeling restless. A restlessness had filled him for some time now. He had been the viscount for three years, come this Christmas, pulling his father's estate and financial holdings from the mire. It still bothered him after all this time that his beloved father had turned to gambling in the final year of his life. A few poor investments, coupled with a rare, dismal crop, and his father had panicked. Reed only wished he had known of this and been able to help sooner.

Instead, his father had lct his only son blithely while away his time in London, doing the sorts of things young gentlemen of his class did when they were carefree bachelors. Reed had spent both his university years and those before his father's death in pursuit of fun and pleasure. He had ridden and boxed. Gone to the theater. Indulged in a little too much drink at times. Most of all, he had spent time with the ladies. Numerous ladies. He was a handsome, charming man and knew it, as did all of Polite Society. He took great care in making certain his lovers were fulfilled and happy with their encounters with him.

But deep inside, Reed had always longed for more. He knew when he eventually became the viscount, he would settle into a more staid life. That had occurred sooner than he could ever have imagined. His father had passed on Christmas morning, with Reed, his sister, their stepmother and her two daughters at the viscount's bedside. When Reed had met with both solicitors and financial advisers regarding his father's estate, he had learned the magnitude of what had occurred and how deeply the hole his father had dug. He did not let a soul know as he tackled matters on the estate and worked on investments, small ones at first, which paid off quickly, and then gradually moving to larger ones. Now, he was more than solvent. It seemed he had the Midas touch as far as investments went and the family coffers were once again full. It would prevent him from having to make a marriage solely based upon the size of a woman's dowry.

He wanted a woman now. A wife. Someone who could be both partner and lover to him in this journey of life. He thought he might have found one in Louisa Goulding, but she only had eyes for Lord Danbury. Fortunately, Danbury awoke in time to realize the jewel he had in hand and the couple had wed. It was bittersweet to see them together, blissfully happy, but Reed did feel blessed to now call the couple his friends.

He had felt the stir of attraction to Minta Nicholls, as well, but the Marquess of Kingston, shy man that he was, had asserted himself when the time was right and made Miss Nicolls his marchioness. Reed was also on friendly terms with this couple, as well.

He now placed high hopes on the house party the Danburys were holding. The Duchess of Camden, known for her match-making skills, was helping Lady Danbury compose a very select guest list, hoping to match more than one person with a soulmate during the event. Though Reed understood the Duke of Woodmont and Miss Seraphina Nicholls, Minta's sister, would be the focus of Her Grace's efforts, he had made known to the duchess his desire to find a bride.

Reed had skipped the Season following his father's passing, not only mourning the man he had worshipped but digging his family out of the hole. He attended the following Season and found little luck, becoming quickly bored with the emptyheaded girls making their come-outs. This past spring, his second Season in search of a viscountess, had proven to be just as much a waste of time. After attending only a handful of events, Reed had stopped going to them altogether and returned to the country. He had privately met with the Duchess of Camden before leaving and told her of his despair.

He hadn't admitted to her that he sought a love match.

His own father had made two of those. The first was to Reed's mother, whom he had never known since she died giving birth to him. The viscountess had provided an heir, a daughter, and Reed, the proverbial spare. He had only been two when his brother, Leonard, died, at seven years of age, and Reed had absolutely no memory of his sibling. He was close to his sister, Pamela, who was three years his senior and a married woman with two of the most adorable children on the planet.

Reed was dotty over children and yearned to fill Boxwell Hall with his own brood. It was hard, however, to find a woman who didn't bore him and would be willing to have numerous children, as most ladies of the *ton* did their duty and little beyond that. To want a love match—as well as finding a woman who wanted a bevy of children—might prove to be next to impossible. Still, it was what Reed desperately desired.

He had watched his father being stoic for years and then finding love later in life for a second time. He had once told Reed that he married the first time for duty and was fortunate to have fallen in love with his wife over the course of their marriage. The second time, he married for the sheer joy of love when Reed was fourteen. He now had two half-sisters. Camilla was fifteen and Nicola was fourteen. They—and his stepmother—lived in the Boxling London townhouse for much of the year, only coming to the country for brief passages of time. In fact, they were coming right after the Season ended, when he would be traveling from Sussex to Essex for the upcoming house party. He hoped he could convince his stepmother to stay a bit longer this time since he was beginning to enjoy the company of Camilla and Nicola. They were both bright, inquisitive girls and he was quite proud of them. He knew in only a few years the pair would make their own come-outs and he would be responsible for approving their grooms and negotiating the marriage contracts.

Rising from the bed, he rang for Dall, his valet. Soon, Reed was shaved and dressed, sitting in the sunny breakfast room, one of his favorite rooms at Boxwell Hall. He smiled when Pamela and Drake, her husband, entered the room. They had left town and stopped to see him on their way home. They would be leaving this morning and he already missed them terribly.

"Good morning," he said cheerily, masking the glum mood which had settled over him. "Are you all packed?"

"We are and will leave after breakfast," his brother-in-law said. "Thank you for allowing us to stop for a few days, albeit uninvited. I know the children were happy to spend time with their uncle."

"You spent more time in the nursery than I have the past few days," Pamela said, chuckling. "Perhaps I should leave Pip and Eve with you for a spell. It would give Drake and me glorious time alone so that we might make a new baby." Her eyes lit with the mischief he loved so well. Though Pamela had only been a few years older, she had mothered him from the time they were young.

"Normally, I would leap at that offer but remember, I am leaving in a week's time for the Danburys' house party," he reminded her.

She studied him a moment and then asked, "Did you meet with Her Grace as we spoke of?"

Reed nodded. "The duchess is definitely aware of my fervent wish to wed."

"You left town so long ago. I will wager that you do not know the latest gossip," Pamela said.

"And what would that be?" he asked, not really caring but

happy to have his sister here.

"Rumor has it Lady Danbury was hosting her house party to help find a match for the Duke of Woodmont and Lady Kingston's twin sister, who recently arrived from North America." Pamela paused and grinned. "Those two won't need a house party because they found each other all on their own."

Surprise filled him. "What are you saying? Are they betrothed?"

His sister nodded. "More than betrothed. They wed. They won't even be at the Danburys' house party."

Reed whistled. "You don't say?"

"I do. It was the talk of town before we left. I suppose Lady Danbury and Her Grace made some adjustments to their guest list because of it. I had heard a few women in society turned down offers of marriage simply because they wanted their chance at Woodmont during the house party." She sighed. "I hope you won't find a group of disgruntled ladies when you attend."

Dread filled him. He was a viscount. A wealthy one, thanks to his astuteness, but his title was no match for that of a duke's. Still, the duke would not be in attendance. Reed hadn't bothered to ask Lady Danbury or Her Grace who would be coming. He was putting his trust in those two women, placing himself in their hands. He decided if they recommended one—or more—of the women at this party, then he would put aside his notion of marrying for love. After all, his own father had wed out of duty the first time and love had come to him and his bride. Perhaps history might repeat itself in this very same house with Reed and the woman who became his viscountess.

"You will have to write to me and tell me if you find a lady to your liking," Pamela told him.

His brother-in-law cleared his throat. "Marry when it's right, Reed," he advised. "You will feel it in your gut and your heart." He reached and took his wife's hand and squeezed it.

A pang of jealousy shot through him. He was happy that his sister had found the man she had. Drake was a good husband and father and had a sterling reputation when the pair wed.

Unlike Reed, whose days of sowing wild oats seemed to follow him. Though he hadn't had a mistress or even conducted a single affair since his time as Viscount Boxling, he knew the mamas of Polite Society still wagged their tongues a bit when he danced with their daughters.

"Thank you for the sage advice, Drake," he said breezily. "I will not get my hopes up too high regarding this house party. However, if the quality of guests is what I suspect, it will be my best chance to find a wife. Neither Her Grace nor Lady Danbury are ones to tolerate fools. The women they will have invited will all be special in their own way. After having spent so little time at *ton* events this year, I look forward to more in-depth conversations. My experience has been one of getting to know people quite well due to the intimate atmosphere and close proximity at a house party. I fully expect to come out of it engaged."

Pamela frowned slightly but said nothing. Reed regretted ever having told his sister of his desire to marry for love. Since she herself had done so, Pamela would think that was the only way it should be done.

He dabbed the napkin to his lips and said, "I am off to the nursery for a final session of play. Wait until all the luggage is onboard your carriages before you come and I have to hand over those precious little loves."

He excused himself and went straight to the nursery. His niece and nephew sat on the floor, blocks in front of them. When they saw him enter the room, both their faces lit with joy and they scrambled to their feet. He swept up Eve and twirled her about as she giggled. Putting her down, he grabbed Pip by the waist and then tossed him high into the air several times, his heart melting as the boy squealed happily.

Bringing his nephew back to earth, Reed went to the blocks and sat before them. "What are we building today?" he asked.

Both children plopped next to him and Eve responded, "A house. A *big* house," she emphasized.

"And who is to live in this house?"

"Me!" exclaimed Pip. "You." He pointed at Reed. "Eve," he said, indicating his sister.

"And Mama and Papa," she concluded.

"Then it must be a very big house if so many of us are going to live in it."

They spent the next few minutes stacking blocks, with Reed pointing out various rooms in their structure.

"This should be the library," he told them. "It should be one of the biggest rooms in our house because books are important and we'll have lots of them."

"Read!" Pip cried, getting to his feet and collecting a book, bringing it back and handing it to his uncle.

"You want us to read this one, Pip?" he asked playfully.

Pip nodded solemnly and Eve said, "I like this one."

"Then it is the one we shall read together."

He leaned his back against the wall as Pip crawled onto his lap and Eve snuggled close next to him. He loved the smell of these children. They smelled of innocence and happiness and he believed his best times were spent with them, which is why he longed for children of his own.

Reed began reading aloud to them, changing his voice for the different characters as Eve liked him to do. He prompted Pip on when to turn the page and as the last page appeared, he finished the tale and proclaimed, "The end."

Both Pip and Eve clapped in delight and Reed glanced up to see Pamela and Drake standing in the doorway. They both wore indulgent smiles.

"It is time for us to go home," Pamela called out. "Tell your Uncle Reed goodbye."

Eve wrapped her tiny arms about his neck and squeezed. "I don't want to go," she said stubbornly. "I want to stay here with you, Uncle Reed."

"Me, too," echoed Pip.

Reed glanced to his sister, who shook her head. "Here we do

all the work and you get the credit of being the favorite," she teased.

He came to his feet, bringing both children with him, scooping them up so he held one in each arm.

"I would enjoy having you stay but I am leaving Boxwell Hall," he told the pair.

"Where are you going?" Eve asked.

"I am going to see some friends and spend time at their house. They have other friends who will be there so I will get to meet new people and make new friends."

Eve looked at him a moment and said, "Are you going to get married like Mama and Papa?"

Already at four years of age, his niece was a smart one. "If I like any of these new friends, perhaps I will. But she would have to be very special," he added.

Eve nodded in agreement and then said, "Can we come to the wedding?"

He laughed heartily. "I would never dream of marrying without you and Pip there. Your mama and papa are also invited whenever that happy event takes place."

"Good," she proclaimed.

They left the nursery and he carried the children to the waiting carriage, kissing them both soundly on their cheeks and promising he would see them soon. Shaking hands with Drake, he then turned and embraced Pamela.

"I do hope you will find someone at this house party," his sister said softly. "I want you to be happy, Reed. All you have done is work, work, work ever since Papa died."

"I will be gone from the estate so I won't be able to work," he declared. "My job will be to seek a viscountess." He kissed her cheek. "I hope the next time I see you will be for my wedding."

"I will pray for that each day, my sweet brother. And for the right woman to recognize just how wonderful you truly are."

He led her to the carriage and handed her up. "Safe travels."

Reed closed the carriage door and stepped back. He waved as

they departed and stood watching until the coach turned from the lane onto the main road. Turning, he walked slowly back into the house and his study. He took a seat behind his desk.

And hoped when he returned to Boxwell Hall, it would be as an engaged man.

Love be damned.

CHAPTER TWO

Dower House, Hockley Hall

V ANESSA PACED THE drawing room, waiting for her stepson to make an appearance. She knew Milton was aware of the time of their appointment. He had been the one to demand it. At his convenience.

Naturally, he would keep her waiting.

She sat, nervous energy bristling through her. She had a good idea what this meeting was about. At the end of it, she would be out of a home.

Staring out the window at the small garden, she thought of how happy she had been living in the dower house for the past year. The most peaceful year of her life.

Death had a calming effect on her.

She looked back to her time with Horace the Horrible, starting with the rushed marriage. She hadn't even been able to go upstairs and change her gown for their wedding. When her things arrived at her new husband's house, her pearl earrings weren't among them. She had spoken to Stillwell at an event when she saw him, asking for him to send them over. He had told her the earrings belonged to their mother, which meant they were a part of the estate. Vanessa had tried to correct him and explain they were given to her as a birthday present. Her brother was having none of it. The one thing she had valued had been kept in his possession.

She had seen those earrings gracing the earlobes of the woman he wed only two months after her own wedding. He had not invited her and Horace the Horrible to attend. She had seen him and his wife at a few events the remainder of that Season but they had never spoken.

That Season seemed so long ago now.

Horace the Horrible had escorted her to many of the events that spring. But he had never touched her again after the nightmare of their wedding day. He remarked how disappointed he was in her. That she hadn't been worth the steep price he had paid for her. How her looks were average and that she had no appeal. He berated her, saying he couldn't get even get his cock to stand for her. Vanessa had been smart enough to keep her mouth shut but his words stung. Never the most confident person, her insecurities grew as they continued to attend *ton* events, Horace the Horrible abandoning her and no one speaking to her.

Ever.

She wasn't allowed to dance. The only person she did converse with was the maid in the retiring room during her few trips there. Vanessa sat in her chair and watched the dancers, night after night, wondering what it would be like to be out on a ballroom floor.

After the first Season, they had returned to Hockley Hall in Kent. The house was a bit gloomy for her tastes but her husband wasn't fond of the country and soon returned to town without her. When spring rolled around, he asked her if she wished to accompany him back to London. It shocked her to be given a choice and Vanessa had said no, that she preferred the quiet life of the country. He had left the next morning, not returning for months.

That had become the pattern of her years, Horace the Horrible gone from March or April until August. He would return for a week or so when the Season ended and then be off again, visiting his friends for long stretches of time. He never asked if she wished to accompany him—and Vanessa would never have volunteered to do so. She saw him sporadically during autumn and the winter, sometimes going for weeks at a time between visits. Then the cycle would repeat itself.

She wondered why he had bothered to wed her. She supposed, in part, it was to collect the debt Stillwell owed and would have been the only way to squeeze any coin from that cowardly, bloodless turnip. She couldn't help but wonder if Horace the Horrible frequented brothels in London, as her brother had, and if her husband hurt the women in them as he had hurt her.

She still had scars from those few hours alone with him.

In the end, though, the six years of their marriage had not been hard on her, beyond her wedding day. She rarely saw her husband and visits from his son were infrequent. The daughter had never set foot inside Hockley Hall since Vanessa's arrival. She had ignored her new stepmother that entire Season.

When Horace the Horrible succumbed to a heart attack last year, he had been in London. It was Milton who brought his father's body home to Hockley lands. He told Vanessa her presence wasn't required at the funeral, which brought her a sweet sense of relief. Milton also instructed her to relocate to the dower house during the service and burial, which would take place in the local village's cemetery. She had been allowed to take one scullery maid with her, who would prepare all her meals. Another maid came in to clean twice a week. Other than that, Vanessa was left on her own.

Her official year of mourning had passed swiftly. She read. Took long walks. Worked in the garden. Went to the stables and rode, something she guessed Milton had no idea she did. She played the pianoforte and found a flute in the attics when she explored them one rainy afternoon. She had brought the instrument downstairs and taught herself to play it through trial and error.

And she danced. Oh, how Vanessa had loved dancing. Her governess had practiced with her from the time she was young, acting the part of a gentleman to Vanessa's lady. Sometimes, she could get Papa to dance with her if he was in a good mood. He wasn't much of a dancer and stepped on her toes frequently but she didn't care.

At the dower house, when the scullery maid had gone to collect food at the main house or she went into the nearby village to visit her parents, Vanessa danced. She would sing aloud and move through the drawing room, pretending she was at a ball. Those times she danced were the best of all.

Yes, this past year of her life as a widow had been spent alone—but she had not once been lonely.

Fear gripped her, though, as she saw Milton riding up on his horse. As he dismounted, her gut told her this idyllic time now came to an end.

Vanessa herself answered the knock since no one else was here to do so. She took her time going to the door and opened it, seeing impatience upon Milton's face. No, Hockley's. He was now the earl in his own right and she must address him as thus.

"Good morning, my lord," she said, demurely lowering her eyes as she stepped back to allow him entrance into the house.

"Yes," he replied, not much of a greeting in her mind.

He strode toward the drawing room and she followed.

"Would you like some tea?" she offered, more to be polite than anything. She doubted he would take her up on it. If he did, he would have to wait for her to boil the water and steep it herself.

"No. None. Thank you." For a moment, he looked unsure of himself.

"Please, have a seat, my lord," she invited, indicating a chair and he took it.

Vanessa sat in the one opposite it, smoothing her skirts, her face blank. She would not start this conversation. Whatever he had to say, he would be the one who must begin.

"It has come to light that . . . that is, to say . . . that the dower house is needed."

She sat expectantly, not speaking. She could tell it surprised him, her not peppering him with questions.

"I have wed recently," he informed her. "My new mother-in-law will be coming to live with Lady Hockley and me. Well, by live with, I mean that she is have the dower house. I promised Lady Hockley so."

Vanessa would not make this easy for him. "I am to share it with her?" she asked sweetly. "Or would you prefer me to move back to Hockley Hall proper?"

When he didn't answer, she couldn't help but be wicked. "Or I suppose if you wish me to live in town year-round, I could go there. Of course, I know the countess' suite would be for Lady Hockley. As the dowager countess, I would only require a bedchamber and sitting room."

She knew he would be giving her none of those options.

"You see, that isn't going to be p-p-possible," he stammered.

"Which one? I am happy to live wherever you wish me to do so, my lord."

"None of those places," he said firmly, gathering his courage.

Doing her best to look nonplussed, she shook her head. "Then what do you mean, Lord Hockley? I am confused."

"You are to go," he said flatly. "I do not care where. You are an embarrassment to me. Why Father wed a woman three decades his junior is beyond Mathilda's comprehension and mine. And then he didn't even try to get a child off you! It was the talk of the *ton*. How he'd wed you and forced you to go to events where you sat, humiliated. Then he left you in the country for years. Why, it was hard to live down the gossip, I'll tell you. Fortunately, it did not matter to Lady Hockley. She was happy to become my wife."

She narrowed her eyes. "Then where, exactly, am I supposed to go, my lord? You are my family," she said pointedly, forcing him to hold her gaze.

"You have a b-brother!" he sputtered.

"One who has nothing to do with me. We have not communicated in years. No, Lord Hockley. I married into this family. As a widow, I am *your* responsibility."

Her firm tone had him squirming.

"But I made no promises to you."

"You are your father's son," she said, her voice low and now dangerous, knowing she was fighting for her very existence. She didn't have a farthing to her name. "You hold the title. You also hold all the responsibilities that were his."

"I don't want you here!" he roared, taking her aback.

In that moment, Vanessa knew she had lost the fight.

"I can give you a week. Then you will need to be gone."

"Where?" she asked harshly.

"To . . . find work, I suppose. You could be a governess. Or a companion. Make your way in the world."

"And what am I to live on until I find employment?" She stared at him long and hard and saw when he broke.

"I will pay for a ticket on the mail coach to London. I will also give you . . . twenty pounds. No, thirty. You can live on that until you find a position."

The die had been cast. Vanessa would soon be booted from her home. A life of service awaited her. She had the education to be a governess and was gentlewoman enough to be a companion. But somewhere in the back of her mind, she had held out hope that one day she could return to Polite Society. Find a husband. Bear the children she so desperately wanted.

Now, it would never happen. As before, a man had made the decision for her. Though now six and twenty and of legal age, the rest of her life had been decided for her.

"I want the money delivered to me today. And not thirty pounds. Fifty. I do not know how long it will take for me to find a position." She paused, her stare hardening. "We both know your father would not want me out on the streets begging. Fifty pounds, my lord, else I will drag your name through the mud and make known that you are expelling me from my home and absolving yourself of all responsibility toward me."

"Fifty. All right," he said, rising, his head bobbing up and down. "But you must be out a week from tomorrow. Else our bargain is off."

Vanessa wanted to tell him that a bargain was struck between two people. She had been told to be out in a week. That had involved no bargaining. As far as the amount owed to her, she considered that a compromise upon his part.

"Very well," she agreed, knowing it was the best she could do. "But I want that fifty pounds today. I will go into the village now and purchase the ticket for the mail coach to London to make certain that is in hand." She rose. "I will need that amount from you now."

She wanted to laugh, seeing the look on his face. He had no idea how much the fare to London was. She watched as he emptied his pockets and gave her what he had.

"Buy it with this," he said as he handed the pound notes over.

Without a further word, he stormed from the room and, moments later, she heard the front door slam shut.

She collapsed into her chair, tears brimming in her eyes. She had known what Milton wanted when he asked to speak with her. Yet part of her ignored it, hoping she was wrong.

Angrily, she brushed away the tears that began to fall and rose. She had someone she wished to see now.

Her dead husband.

Vanessa changed into her sturdy walking boots and left the house. Blackburn, the nearest village, was three miles from Hockley Hall but only two from the dower house. She walked thrice that on any given day in all kinds of weather, the outdoors being a place of refuge for her.

She set out, trying to clear her mind from any kind of thought, and concentrated on putting one foot in front of the other. If she didn't, she was afraid she might fall apart and wind up in a weeping heap on the side of the road. Along the way, the simmering anger built until by the time she had arrived at the cemetery next to the church, it bubbled over.

Making her way through the gate, she realized she had no idea where Horace the Horrible had been buried. She glanced about, thinking it would have to be a grand marker, and headed toward the largest, tallest stones in the yard. Sure enough, she found herself among dead Hockleys as she worked her way around, looking for her husband's burial plot. Finding it, she stood before it—and began to rage.

Her rant went on and on as she accused him of all the terrible things he had done. He had stolen her innocence. Made her feel worthless and undesirable. Shamed her. Scolded her. Ignored her. Died on her, leaving her without two farthings to rub together. The anger subsided and she collapsed on the hard ground, weeping, desperation filling her.

It would be impossible to crawl back to her brother. He would be even more unkind than her stepson, who seemed dominated by his new wife's wishes, or that of his mother-in-law.

She was alone. More alone than she had ever been in her life. For a moment, Vanessa considered ending it all. She had nothing to live for. No one who would care if she lived or died. No one would even notice if she were gone. At least she could be with Mama and Papa.

Or would she?

What she contemplated was suicide, a mortal sin. She would burn in the eternal flames of Hell if she took her life. And then the Hockleys and Stillwells of the world would have won.

She burst into fresh tears, her sobs crippling her body, causing her to feel ill and tired.

Then an arm went about her, comforting her, the scent of lavender wafting over her. Blindly, Vanessa blinked away her tears and looked to see a woman at her side with hair so blond it was almost white and eyes the color of sapphires.

"It is all right," the woman said. "Cry all you wish. I am here. I will stay with you. I will see you safely home."

Vanessa clung to the stranger, bawling, until she was spent and no more tears fell.

"Can you stand?"

She nodded and the woman helped get both of them to their feet.

"I am Lady Danbury," she said.

Her mouth trembled as she replied, "I am Lady Hockley. The dowager countess."

If Lady Danbury was surprised at such a young widow, she did not show it.

"Would you like my driver to take you home?" she asked, her tone gentle and her eyes kind.

Vanessa nodded. "I walked here. I should be getting home."

Even though home was about to be nowhere.

"Come," said Lady Danbury, linking their arms and leading her from the cemetery.

They arrived at a grand carriage and Lady Danbury said, "Where is your home?"

She wiped at her face. "I live at the dower house on Hockley lands." Glancing up at the driver, she asked, "Do you know where that is?"

"I do, my lady. I will have you there in no time," the coachman promised.

A footman handed them up and Lady Danbury insisted Vanessa sit beside her. As the carriage started up, she said, "Tell me as much or as little as you wish, Lady Hockley. But I believe you need someone to talk things over with." She hesitated. "Were you at you husband's grave?"

"Yes. It was the first time I had seen it. I was not allowed to attend his funeral."

The woman nodded. "Many women are kept away from funerals by male relatives. I suppose the new Lord Hockley insisted on this?"

"Yes, he is my stepson," she managed to say as more tears came.

Lady Danbury retrieved a handkerchief from her reticule and handed it to Vanessa, who wiped her eyes.

"Did you love him very much?"

The question took her aback. "No. Not a bit. I only met him on our wedding day," she blurted out, regretting having revealed so much.

Lady Danbury took Vanessa's hand in hers. "Then these are tears not of sorrow. But anger."

She nodded, collecting herself. "Yes. Some of it is directed at Horace the Horrible." She snorted. "My nickname for my husband. He was thirty years my senior." She swallowed, deciding to throw out the entire truth, knowing she would never see this woman again. "The rest of my rage was directed at my stepson. My mourning period has ended. He has ordered me to leave Hockley lands. He will bring me fifty pounds today and I am to go to London, where I will seek employment as a governess or companion."

Vanessa's gaze met the woman's. "I have no pride left, my lady, so I will ask you if you know of anyone seeking help for either of those positions."

"That will not be necessary, Lady Hockley." Determination filled the woman's vibrant blue eyes. "You will come home to Danfield with me. My husband and I are hosting a house party in a week's time.

"And we will find you a husband."

CHAPTER THREE

"**W**HAT?" VANESSA GASPED. "Are you mad?"

She glanced about quickly, thinking she had gotten into a carriage with a person who surely should be a resident of Bedlam.

The woman calling herself Lady Danbury nodded sagely. "I suppose you would think me mad. I am a stranger to you, Lady Hockley, though we live not far from one another. Danfield is four miles the other side of Blackburn, the opposite direction of where we now travel."

Lady Danbury gazed at her steadily, no pity in her eyes, which Vanessa appreciated.

"I realize that I am a stranger to you, so let me share a bit about myself if you would indulge me."

She nodded. She would hear what this woman had to say and then most likely never see her again. At least riding in the woman's carriage had saved Vanessa from a long walk back to the dower house.

"I understand where you might be skeptical by my offer. It sounds generous, I know. Too generous, in fact."

Her eyebrows rose with that statement but she remained quiet and Lady Danbury continued.

"I am the daughter of Sir Edgar Goulding, who has worked in the War Office for a good many years." Pride was evident in her voice as she added, "Papa also was a member of the Congress of Vienna. My mother passed, leaving me to serve as his hostess for many years. Because of the threat of spies and leaks within the War Office, he often held meetings in our London townhouse. I entertained the men who came for those meetings, teas, dinners, and even late night strategy sessions. I came to find I had a remarkable skill in evaluating people. I wasn't a typical daughter of the *ton* because of this and I learned much about our government. The war. Politics. And our economy—and how all of those are tied together."

Lady Danbury took Vanessa's hand in hers. "I believe I am a good judge of character and I see the potential for a friendship between us, Lady Hockley. Through my husband's four closest friends, who act as brothers of his heart and our extended family, I have gotten to know these men's wives. The five of us believe women are the stronger sex, not the weaker one, and we choose to use our positions in Polite Society to help others."

Lady Danbury's gaze drilled into Vanessa's soul. "You are in need of help, my lady. I am offering it to you. You have shared with me how desperate your situation is. In a week, you will lose your home. What harm is there in coming home with me? I am offering my friendship, along with shelter and an introduction to a good number of eligible bachelors who will be attending our house party in a week. What do you have to lose? Better yet, what do you have to gain?"

Vanessa was overwhelmed by this woman and her generous offer. "I have never truly been in society, Lady Danbury. I never made my come-out although I did attend several balls the year I was supposed to debut, sitting among the matrons."

Lady Danbury's brows arched. "They aren't the most friendly group, are they?" she asked.

Vanessa nodded in agreement. "Since I knew no one, I was not able to be introduced to anyone. After that first Season, my husband left me in the country and I was grateful for that." She pulled her hand from Lady Danbury's and clasped hers tightly in her lap. "I don't know if I even know how to act around the members of Polite Society. I have spent most of the last six years alone, with no friends and no family to support me."

Lady Danbury's face lit with a radiant smile and her eyes sparkled. "I had spent very little time among the *ton* myself," she revealed. "Papa always needed me for something and so I went to only a handful of events over several years' time." She paused. "Then I met my husband and we both wound up attending the same house party. Fortunately, he came to his senses and realized what a good countess I would be," she teased.

Lady Danbury laughed and her laugh was infectious, causing Vanessa to join in.

Lady Danbury grew serious. "I want to help you, my lady. Please, come home with me," she pleaded. "It will do you good to have someone you can unburden yourself to. The house party will be full of interesting people. My good friend, the Duchess of Camden, and I have created a most wonderful guest list. If a gentleman attending attracts your attention, then you would be able to encourage him. And if by chance the house party ends and you do not feel you are suited with anyone, I offer you our carriage to take you to London and will do my best to help you find a position you might enjoy."

Turmoil filled Vanessa, her thoughts coming so rapidly they were hard to collect and sort out.

"Why would you—a perfect stranger—help me in this manner?"

"Because I think Fate put us in one another's path. I was supposed to call upon the good reverend yesterday and discuss providing additional pews for the church. I had to reschedule our meeting because my daughter, Margaret, was running a slight fever and she comes before anything. She awoke this morning fever-free, in a wonderful mood, and I left her in the nursery, along with my husband."

"Your husband . . . goes to the nursery?" As much as her own father had loved her, Vanessa couldn't recall a single instance of

Papa being in the nursery.

Lady Danbury chuckled. "He and his friends—who call themselves the Second Sons—are men who are quite loving when it comes to their children. I know Polite Society's fathers have a tendency to ignore their own children but Owen and his friends are quite active parents. Come home with me and you will see that he carries Margaret around perhaps even more than I do."

The carriage began to slow and Vanessa realized they were approaching the dower house. She made her decision, an instant one, one which she hoped she would not regret.

"I appreciate the invitation you have extended to me, Lady Danbury, and I will accept with pleasure."

"I am delighted to hear that, my lady." The countess stared at her a long moment and then said, "My given name is Louisa. If we are to be friends and you will be living under our roof, I hope you would do me the honor of addressing me so."

Vanessa was touched by the friendly gesture and tears sprang to her eyes. This time, it was she who captured Louisa's hand in hers and squeezed it encouragingly. "My name is Vanessa," she told her friend.

The first friend she had ever made.

"May I come inside with you?" Louisa asked as the carriage came to a halt. "I can help you pack if you'd like. Then we could head straight to Danfield once that is completed."

"I cannot do that. I must wait for Lord Hockley to send the money he promised. If I am gone, it will give him an excuse not to give it to me. I received nothing after my husband's death and literally have not a single coin to my name."

Louisa nodded slowly, taking in what Vanessa had told her. "Then have your things ready tomorrow morning by ten o'clock and I will return for you with the carriage. May I bring Owen with me so that you can meet him?"

She supposed since Louisa asked, she should agree to do so though why an earl would want to take part in such a mundane errand was beyond her.

"Yes, please feel free to bring him with you."

The door to the vehicle opened and Vanessa said, "Thank you. I do not know what the outcome of my situation will be but I believe I have made a friend this day."

She embraced Louisa, not recalling the last time she had done so with anyone. Most likely, it had been when she had said goodbye to her parents that last time before their deaths.

Vanessa pulled away and Louisa smiled at her. "Take care, Vanessa. I will see you tomorrow morning."

A footman helped her from the carriage and she went into the house, going straight to her bedchamber and washing her face. She looked into the small hand mirror and gazed at her image for a long moment, studying the woman there. It certainly wasn't the young, naive girl she had been on that long-ago night of her come-out. She wondered at her advanced age if any of the gentlemen attending this house party would give her a moment's consideration. She decided it did not matter. The only opinion that did matter to her was her own. Louisa was giving her a chance to forge a new life. If she were meant to be a member of the *ton*, then something significant would occur at this house party, whatever it entailed. If her destiny lay in a completely different direction, at least she would have given the world of the *ton* a try.

Speaking sensibly, the week she stayed at Danfield would be a week she would not have to pay for a room in London while she looked for a position, which would help stretch her limited funds further. She remembered she had not gone to purchase a ticket on the mail coach and grinned, thinking she still had that sum she had squeezed from Milton. Every little bit might count. With having made a new friend in Louisa, who seemed to have a powerful circle of friends of her own, Vanessa might make a connection that would lead to a cherished position.

She went downstairs to the kitchen and told the maid, "Have a seat. I am going to share something in confidence with you and I hope you will not betray me."

The young girl's eyes widened. "Oh, no, my lady. I adore you. Working this past year at the dower house has been the happiest of my life."

"It is good to hear that but my time here is coming to an end," she revealed.

Vanessa explained how a new occupant, Lord Hockley's mother-in-law, would be moving in.

"Will you return to the big house then?" the servant asked.

"No, Lord Hockley has informed me I am no longer welcome there or at his London residence." Her throat thickened with emotion.

"That's awful!" the maid exclaimed. Then she looked at Vanessa with trepidation. "Whatever are you going to do, my lady?"

"That is what I wish to share with you. A friend of mine is sending her coach tomorrow and I will return and stay with her for a couple of weeks before I make my way to London. I don't want Lord Hockley to know this, however. Neither where I have gone nor when I left the dower house. He is no longer family and it is none of his business."

"I agree with you there, my lady. If I didn't work for him, I wouldn't give him the time of day."

"I don't wish for you to lose your position. I assume you will remain here to cook for his mother-in-law. All I am asking is that you do not share with him when I left. Stay here and keep to your same routine. Go to the main house for daily supplies and even into the village if you wish. Eat everything yourself and when he does arrive in a week's time with his wife and mother-in-law in tow, you can merely say I have already vacated the premises. He had wanted me to take the mail coach into London so let us leave him with that impression."

Vanessa studied the young girl. "Do you feel comfortable doing this for me?"

"I do, my lady. And I will fix you the dinner of your life tonight since it will the last one I cook for you."

"Then please share it with me," she said. "I am going upstairs now to pack so I will be ready tomorrow."

She left the kitchen, feeling good about her plan, and went to her bedchamber, pulling out all her gowns. She supposed they were all woefully out of fashion and would most likely influence others' opinions of her but she reminded herself it was only her opinion that mattered from this point on. She spent the rest of the afternoon folding clothes and placing them in her trunks, leaving a few out that she would give to the maid downstairs as a thank you for her service.

Catching sight of a rider out the window, she hurried downstairs and answered the knock which came soon after. It was a footman she recognized and he handed her a small pouch.

"Lord Hockley said to give this to you, my lady."

"Thank you—and his lordship," she replied.

He frowned, looking uncomfortable. "His lordship said to tell you to be ready to vacate the dower house next Tuesday."

Nodding, she said, "I will do so."

"I know this is inappropriate, my lady, but I . . . I am so sorry." Sympathy filled his face.

"It is all right," she assured him. "Thank you for coming."

Vanessa closed the door, fearing if she didn't she would burst into tears.

She joined the maid in the kitchen, talking with her as the finishing touches were placed on their meal. They shared a dinner of roasted pheasant, fingerling potatoes, and asparagus. When they finished eating, Vanessa excused herself and went to the drawing room, where she played the pianoforte and her flute.

The hour grew late and she retired to her bedchamber for the last time, taking the flute upstairs with her. She slipped it into one of her trunks, knowing Milton would never miss it. She removed her gown, petticoat, and chemise, having given up a corset when she moved to the dower house because she had no one to assist in dressing her.

Climbing into bed, sleepiness washed over her. She closed her eyes, knowing when she opened then again, it would not only be a new day—but a new, hopeful chapter in her life.

CHAPTER FOUR

V ANESSA HAD SPENT three days at Danfield and already felt a
part of the place. She had enjoyed spending time in Louisa's
company tremendously but her new friend also gave her ample
time to pursue her own interests and enjoy a bit of solitude. The
earl had proven quite charming and put her at ease immediately,
while the couple's daughter, Margaret, was a real treat. The girl
was a miniature version of her mother and had just turned a year
old the week before. Much of Vanessa's time had been spent in
the nursery in Margaret's company, playing with her for hours on
end. It reaffirmed to her that she was good with children. If the
house party did not result in an offer of marriage, she had decided
to pursue being a governess instead of a companion.

Things would change a bit today because two of the Second
Sons and their wives would be arriving ahead of the other
expected guests for the house party. Vanessa had learned the
group of five close-knit friends referred to themselves as Second
Sons because they had been the spares to their brothers, who
were the heirs. Each of the five, through a twist of fate, wound up
inheriting their titles but they still jokingly referred to themselves
as Second Sons.

Vanessa supposed the dynamic would change today with the
arrival of the Duke and Duchess of Camden and the Earl and
Countess of Middlefield. Louisa had shared that she and the

duchess were the ones who had composed the elite guest list for the house party. Their original goal had been to find a match for the fifth of the Second Sons, the Duke of Woodmont, who had recently returned from serving in His Majesty's army and was in need of a bride. Not only had they hoped to find a suitable duchess for him, but they also had wanted to find a husband for Miss Seraphina Nicholls, the twin sister of the Marchioness of Kingston. Ironically enough, the duke and this sister had found each other all on their own this summer and had wed rather quickly last month. Now, they were on an extended honeymoon with the duke's two nephews and would miss the party entirely, as would Lord and Lady Kingston. Lady Kingston was with child and still experiencing severe nausea. Her husband insisted they remain home as he waited on her hand and foot.

She had been ignorant of how a woman could experience nausea while she carried a child and had admitted as much to Louisa. Her friend had told her about the different stages of pregnancy and her own childbirth experience so that Vanessa would be more informed and feel more comfortable with the topic. Though she longed to ask about marital relations between a man and a woman, she could not bring herself to do so. Louisa and her husband seemed so much in love that Vanessa realized what had occurred between her and Horace the Horrible might not be what happened in every marriage. She couldn't picture the affable Lord Danbury behaving so monstrously to his wife. Louisa was certainly a woman who knew her own mind and would never have stood for the things Vanessa had experienced in the marriage bed on her wedding day. But to ask what did occur between a loving husband and wife was more than she could articulate, especially since their friendship was so new.

A knock sounded upon her door and Vanessa answered it. It was Louisa herself who stood there.

"My friends have arrived," she informed Vanessa. "The men are going out for a ride on the estate, while the ladies are gathering in my sitting room. Would you like to come and meet them?"

Vanessa had given this some thought and she said, "No, I don't believe I will do so, Louisa. They are your friends and have come early to catch up with you before your other guests arrive. I would only be an intruder to your gathering. I can meet them later at dinner this evening."

Louisa stressed, "You are more than welcome to join us, Vanessa. They will want to meet you." The countess paused and then added, "But if you wish to remain in your bedchamber for some quiet time, I understand."

"Thank you," she said, taking Louisa's hand and pressing it gently. "Enjoy your conversation with your friends."

Half an hour later, as Louisa sat in a chair reading, another knock sounded at her door and she rose to answer it. When she opened it, much to her surprise, a breathtakingly beautiful woman stood before her. She had hair the color of honey and sky blue eyes.

What surprised her most was the woman was heavy with child.

With arched brows, the woman said, "Good afternoon, Lady Hockley. I am the Duchess of Camden and have come to retrieve you."

Vanessa looked at the woman blankly. "Retrieve me?" she asked.

"Yes, that is exactly why I am here. Louisa has told us a bit about you and you should be with us so we can get to know you."

Before Vanessa could protest, the duchess gave her a pointed look. "I insist."

She knew no one turned down a request from a duchess and so she demurred. "Of course, Your Grace."

They started down the corridor and she asked, "How are you feeling, Your Grace?" since she knew Lady Kingston was with child and very sick.

The duchess laughed heartily and cradled her bulging belly. "I am in great spirits and good health," she shared. "I am not due to give birth until November and I am larger now than when I bore my son, Edwin. You will have to meet him. Louisa told us you have spent a good bit of time with Margaret, so I supposed you must love children. My Edwin is a year and another half and a delight. As for me, they are saying it will be twins."

"Congratulations, Your Grace."

In the one Season she had attended, Vanessa could not remember having seen a single woman with child. It seemed an unwritten rule of Polite Society was to stay out of sight the minute you began to show. Yet here was the Duchess of Camden, full of life, and ready to attend a house party. She decided this was one unusual woman. And she liked her. Very much.

They arrived at the siting room and she was introduced to Lady Middlefield, a tall, lovely blond with curly hair and bright blue eyes. As they sat, Lady Middlefield said, "I hope you don't find me bold, my lady, but I would be delighted if you would call me Tessa. Louisa said the two of you are already on a first-name basis and I believe we are all going to be fast friends."

"And I am Adalyn," the duchess said. "If you do not address me as such, I will be quite put out. Even cross." She grinned mischievously. "And no one ever wishes for me to be cross."

The other two women chuckled and Vanessa felt bewildered. Still, she maintained her poise and told them, "Please call me Vanessa."

They agreed to do so and the duchess said, "I understand you have not truly been out in Polite Society. I would advise you to only refer to us in this casual manner when we are alone together."

"I can do so, Your Grace." She paused and corrected, "Adalyn."

What followed was the most lively conversation Vanessa had ever been a part of. These three women were genuine and, despite their social status, very down-to-earth. At one point, she merely shook her head in wonder.

"Is something wrong?" asked Tessa.

"No," Vanessa told her, "everything is actually very right. I will be honest and tell you that I have led a very restricted life. I remained on my family's country estate with my governess while my parents went to town each year for the Season. There were no other children in the neighboring properties or our estate that I was allowed to play with and so my time was spent in the company of my governess. Later, when I came to town, I . . ." Her voice trailed off as her throat thickened with tears.

Adalyn reached out and took Vanessa's hand. "Please tell us," she encouraged softly. "We are your friends. We are here for you, Vanessa."

She began weeping softly, embarrassed to be doing so. The duchess continued to hold her hand until Vanessa quieted.

"I don't know what Louisa has shared with you about me," she began.

"Nothing about your background," Tessa said. "That is your story to tell us if you wish to do so."

It was as if she had permission and the floodgates opened. Vanessa told the group about the night of her come-out. Her brother coming home late and preventing them from attending the evening's ball. His announcement that he had already given her hand in marriage to another, thanks to his gambling debts. How she had met Lord Hockley the next morning and how he had already purchased a special license for them.

"So, I married Lord Hockley that very day and left my brother's household to go to my husband's." She shuddered. "It was a most unpleasant experience."

The room grew quiet but Vanessa did not feel as if these women judged her. Instead, she felt wrapped in the love of friendship, which helped her to continue.

"We went to that night's ball and Lord Hockley told me I was to sit with the matrons while he spent the evening in the card room. I had no idea about Polite Society's rules and when I tried to introduce myself, I was rudely told I could not do so."

Sympathy filled her new friends' eyes and Louisa said, "That must have been difficult. To sit there all night amidst strangers."

"It was like that at every event we attended," she recalled. "My husband never introduced me to a soul. No one took pity upon me. Obviously, I never danced. I sat, night after night, alone, watching the dancers. Balls were the only affairs we attended together."

"What a horrible experience," Tessa said. "I cannot imagine a more terrible entrance into society."

"It wasn't so bad after that," she shared. "Horace the Horrible left me in the country from then on." She paused, seeing their puzzled expressions. "Oh, that was my name for him. Horace the Horrible. I spent the next several years in the country while he remained in town most of the time. I never returned to London, nor did I ever go to a Season again. I was widowed a little more than a year ago and moved to the dower house on the country estate. My stepson came to me a few days ago and informed me that I would have to vacate the dower house for his new mother-in-law. He would provide a few pounds to me and expected me to find a position on my own."

Adalyn took her hand again as she gasped. "I know exactly who the new Lord Hockley is. Would you like me to ruin him for you? I can easily do so. He sounds horrid and deserving of ruin."

She saw the fierceness in Adalyn's eyes. "You would do that for me?"

"We would all do that for you, Vanessa. And anything else we can."

She shook her head. "No, I don't want that at all. I wish to have nothing to do with Lord Hockley, his sister, or his family."

"Louisa did tell us she met you at Horace the Horrible's grave," Tessa said.

She chuckled. "Yes. I had gone to rage at Horace the Horrible when Louisa discovered me and invited me home with her, poor orphan that I am," she said, trying to make light of the situation.

Adalyn released Vanessa's hand and said, "A house party is

just what you need. I have never attended one where there was not an engagement announced. Sometimes more than one."

The duchess studied Vanessa for a moment and said, "I will wager you don't even know what a house party is or how couples become betrothed."

She shook her head. "No," she said softly.

Louisa said, "Rarely do people get to know one another during the Season, due to the large number of balls. It is quite difficult to hold a decent conversation during all that dancing. Oftentimes, a couple may have danced half a dozen times and spoken to one another on a few other occasions—say at a garden party or rout—and they will find themselves betrothed."

"Marriages are usually made for political gain," Tessa revealed. "It is all about status in Polite Society. Love matches are rare."

"Oh, I wouldn't seek a love match," Vanessa declared.

"We all found love matches and you might, too," Adalyn said. "A house party goes on for many days, between one and two weeks. Because of the length of time and everyone living under one roof, you are thrown together with a small group of people in very intimate settings. Louisa and I have planned all sorts of activities to help those invited to become better acquainted. So you see, Vanessa, a house party is quite advantageous."

"But . . . I am old," she said. "Six and twenty. I do not know how many gentlemen might be interested in someone on the shelf as I am, especially a woman who has been wed before."

"That won't make a bit of difference," Adalyn proclaimed. "Louisa and I have been quite selective in the people we invited to Danfield. Everyone has been carefully evaluated. You will not be judged in the least for your past or lack of time in Polite Society. In fact, some gentlemen even prefer a widow since they come with some experience and maturity."

A hot blush scalded Vanessa's cheeks. She thought back to her one physical encounter with Horace the Horrible. She kept quiet, however. If she were lucky enough to make a match at this house party, she would endure whatever it took in order to have a child.

"We should tell you a little bit about some of the guests who are invited," Louisa said. "However, I think we should wait until Lord Boxling arrives."

"Who is Lord Boxling?" she asked, curiosity filling her.

"I have asked the viscount to come early to the house party," Adalyn revealed. "He is quite good-looking and most charming. Best of all, he is actively seeking a wife. He attended the Season two years ago and did not find anyone to his liking. He only came to a few affairs this past spring, confiding in me that he found the girls making their come-outs immature and silly. He is definitely looking for a lady of quality, grace, and maturity. I had asked him to arrive early to talk with him more about what he wishes to find in a spouse. Perhaps it will be beneficial to the both of you. I think I shall wait until Lord Boxling arrives and then meet with the both of you about the guest list."

After that, the conversation turned to children, with Adalyn and Tessa telling Vanessa all about their children, who had accompanied them to Danfield. She gathered from the conversation that was unusual, as others in the *ton* would have left their children behind with governesses or tutors.

"Why don't we go to the nursery now so that you can meet all of them?" Louisa asked.

The women adjourned and went upstairs. Little Edwin, Adalyn's son, was napping, as was Margaret, but Tessa's two children were awake and playing. She instantly fell in love with Analise, who was two-and-a-half years old and her mother made over. Tessa's youngest, Adam, was a sweet boy who was just learning to crawl. As she played with them, the other two awoke and all four women wound up on the floor playing with the four children.

Vanessa looked around and realized how happy she truly was, for the first time in years. She had made real friends with three amazing women and hoped her future might be bright.

CHAPTER FIVE

TREPIDATION FILLED REED as he glanced out the window, knowing he would reach Danfield soon. He had been summoned to arrive at the house party early by the Duchess of Camden.

No one in Polite Society ignored Her Grace when she issued a command.

He thought back to what Pamela had shared with him, knowing this house party might have some disgruntled ladies attending. With the Duke of Woodmont now wed and off on his honeymoon, the women invited to Danfield may not be so amenable to finding their match with any of the gentlemen present. He wondered who had been invited to the Danburys' house party and if any of them might be interested in a lowly, though wealthy, viscount.

His stepmother and half-sisters had actually arrived this morning from London, which allowed him to spend a few hours with them before he was off for the Kent countryside. Constance told him they would stay at Boxwell Hall for a month and then she had her own house party to attend just outside Bath. She asked if it would be agreeable with him if she left the girls at Boxwell Hall and promised to return for them and take them back to town with her by the end of September. Reed assured her the girls were always welcome to stay in the country as long as they wished.

While their mother went upstairs for a long bath, Camilla and Nicola had remained with him. Reed had taken them to the stables to see two new colts which had been born a few months ago. Both girls were mad for horses and were thrilled by the new additions in the stables. On the way back to the house, they had peppered him with questions about the house party he was attending, asking if he would come back engaged and if they could come to his wedding. He told them he had no idea what his status would be upon his return, having no clue as to who would be at Danfield.

Nicola had bet Camilla that Reed would return betrothed, while Camilla said Reed wouldn't wed until he was thirty. When he informed her he would turn thirty during the house party, her eyes had widened and she'd laughed, calling him an old man. He had chased her all the way back to the house, Nicola hurrying after them, teasing him that he would soon be too decrepit to catch either of them.

He smiled at the memory, thinking how fast the pair was growing up. They would make their own come-outs before long. He worried about men his age ogling their bosoms and trying to steal a kiss from them in the moonlight on a terrace. The thought positively chafed him.

Reed hoped none of the women invited for the Danburys' house party would be young. He had cut short his own participation in this year's Season because of the plethora of featherheads which filled the ballrooms of the *ton*. He wished Her Grace and Lady Danbury had taken that into consideration as they'd put their guest list together. In fact, it was one of the points Reed had emphasized to the duchess before he abandoned town and returned to Boxwell Hall. Her Grace had written down everything he had said.

It remained to be seen how much of that translated into a guest he might hit it off with.

The carriage slowed a bit and made a turn. He took a deep

breath, hoping to calm himself. He shouldn't be nervous. After all, he was a handsome viscount. Women flocked to him.

But in a secret place deep within his heart, Reed still hoped to find love.

His coachman pulled up to the drive in front of the house and stopped the carriage. A footman opened the door and Reed climbed from the vehicle, seeing Lord and Lady Danbury waiting for him. He went straight to them, basking in the warmth of Lady Danbury's smile.

Taking her hands, he kissed them. "Thank you for inviting me to visit with you at Danfield."

"It is so good to see you, Lord Boxling," she said.

He turned to the earl. "Good afternoon, my lord. Thank you for having me."

Danbury chuckled. "It wasn't any of my doing, Boxling. You know my wife and Her Grace are the ones who concocted the idea for this house party and created the guest list. I merely pay the bills and play host."

Reed laughed. "Women do seem to be in charge of more things than we give them credit for."

The earl's gaze turned to his wife, a fond smile turning up the corners of his mouth. "My wife is always full of sage advice. I have learned to listen to her and act upon it. Always." He took the countess' hand and brought it to his lips for a kiss.

Wistfulness rippled through him. Reed had witnessed small moments such as this with the Danburys and a few of their friends. They were not shy about demonstrating their affection toward one another though many of the *ton* scoffed at such public displays of love.

Reed found them quite romantic.

"Come inside, my lord," Lady Danbury said. "The Duchess of Camden is awaiting you, as is Lady Hockley."

Confusion filled him. He had met a Lord Hockley at the beginning of this past Season and hadn't liked him in the least. The man was full of himself and a bit dense. He didn't seem the type to be friendly with the Second Sons' crowd.

As they moved toward the door and entered the house, Lady Danbury said, "Lady Hockley is staying with us for a few weeks. She is a widow and recently out of mourning. Naturally, I was happy to have her here while our house party occurred."

That made a little more sense to him. He had gathered that Lord Hockley had not held his title for long. Lady Hockley must be the new earl's mother. Though the fact she and Lady Danbury had become friends surprised him.

He followed them up the stairs and looked over his shoulder, seeing Dall, his valet, and a footman carrying up his trunk.

"My valet is staying with me but I am sending my carriage back to Boxwell Hall," he said. "My stepmother and her daughters arrived only this morning and I promised them use of it while I am here."

"I will see that your horses are watered and fed and rested a bit before they make their return journey," Lord Danbury said, reversing direction. "I will see you for tea."

He left them and Reed continued along with Lady Danbury. They reached a door and she paused.

"I will let you talk with Her Grace now. When you are done, come to the drawing room for tea. You will probably need it to fortify you after being bombarded with information. I will see you shortly."

She smiled at him and then continued down the hall. He knocked lightly on the door and heard someone call out to enter.

When he did, two things struck Reed at once. The first was how large the Duchess of Camden was. He knew she carried a child but her belly had popped since he had last seen her at the end of April, when they had their private audience regarding his wish to find a wife. Four months later, she looked as if she might give birth at any moment.

But what struck him even more was the slender woman standing beside Her Grace. Lady Hockley. He moved toward the women, his eyes taking in the widow. He judged her to be about five and a half feet, with light brown hair that sported golden highlights, as if the sun had painted streaks throughout it. Her violet eyes, a deep color, drew him in, causing his throat to grow dry. He couldn't remember the last time he'd had such a strong physical reaction to a woman.

Perhaps never.

"Ah, Lord Boxling," Her Grace said, beaming at him. "How good of you to come."

He took her hand and kissed her fingers. "When the request comes to meet with the Duchess of Camden, it is not taken lightly. I hope you are in good health, Your Grace."

"Swimmingly so," she declared. "May I introduce you to my friend, the Dowager Countess of Hockley?"

Reed turned and took the hand of the beauty, gazing into those violet eyes. "It is certainly nice to meet you, my lady. Lady Danbury told me you are a widow. I express my condolences to you for the loss of your husband."

"Thank you, my lord," she said as he pressed his lips to her bare skin, experiencing a ripple of sensation running through him. He was grateful they were not meeting in a formal situation, where she would be gloved. Holding her hand and touching his lips to her bare skin was a sensual experience. It made him long to touch more places on her.

She was much younger than he had pictured. He assumed she was the present Lord Hockley's mother but that was far from the case. She must have been the earl's second wife, one he had wed when she was quite young, because he judged Lady Hockley to be in her mid-twenties. As he released her hand, his eyes quickly skimmed the ripe curves of her breasts and hips. His heartbeat sped up. Yes, physical attraction was obviously present between them. But Reed knew that could pass. What he yearned for was a deeper connection, one beyond the body. One of the mind. Of the soul.

Would he find it with Lady Hockley?

The next two weeks would tell the tale.

She lowered her lashes as he released her hand, hiding those magnificent violet eyes.

"Shall we have a seat, my lord?" the duchess asked. "I tire rather easily these days. It is twins, you know. At least that is the best guess of the midwife and doctor."

As they took seats, the two ladies on a settee and Reed in a chair closest to Lady Hockley, he said, "I extend my congratulations to you and His Grace. I believe you have a son already?"

Her face softened. "Yes. Edwin. You can meet him if you would like to. We brought him with us."

"He is here?" Surprise filled him. He didn't know of anyone who lugged children to house parties.

"Of course. His Grace and I would not think of leaving him at Cliffside, though it is only a few miles away."

Reed had heard the Second Sons were devoted to their children. "Have any others decided to bring children with them to Danfield?"

The duchess chuckled. "Only the married ones who have them. Lady Middlefield brought Analise and Adam and your hostess has little Margaret, who just turned a year old. I have high hopes to match my friends' children to my own someday."

During this brief conversation, the dowager countess had remained silent, her hands folded neatly in her lap.

Trying to draw her in, he asked, "Do you have children, Lady Hockley?"

The question seemed to startle her. "No. I . . . don't, my lord." She paused and then added, "But I have had a wonderful time playing in the nursery with the children here."

"I will have to join you there," he said. "I quite like children. I have a niece and nephew, Eve and Pip. There's nothing better than spending time with them."

Lady Hockley appeared bemused by his comments. "Surely, you believe a man can enjoy playing with children as much as a woman can?" he asked her.

"I have never spent time around children until I came to

Danbury this past week, my lord," she replied. "My impression was that the parents of the *ton* spend very little time with their offspring. However, I have witnessed it to be quite different with the Second Sons and their wives."

"Ah, so you are familiar with their nickname?" Then he added, "I am also a second son, but few know of it."

She cocked her head to one side. "Why not?"

"My brother died of a fever when I was only two. I am afraid I cannot recall him, much as I wish I could. With his death, I went from being the spare to the heir apparent."

"I did not know that, Boxling," Her Grace said.

"I have never shared it with anyone," he admitted. "When I went off to school, I was known as the heir. I saw no reason to correct others and tell them that once there had been a different heir to my father's title."

"Are you close with your other siblings?" Lady Hockley asked, seeming to warm to him.

"Yes. My older sister, Pamela, is mother to Pip and Eve. I am getting to know my two half-sisters in more recent years. They stay in town a great deal of the year with my stepmother, who is barely five years my senior."

He shared a little about Camilla and Nicola and then asked Lady Hockley about her own siblings. He realized it was a mistake when he caught the glistening of tears in her eyes.

"I have a brother. Lord Stillwell," she said stiffly. "We are not . . . close."

"It is a good thing, my lady, because he is a dolt."

Her eyes widened—and then she burst out laughing. Her laughter was rich and light at the same time, music to his ears. It made her eyes crinkle up with mirth and her ample bosom shake. Her laughter made her come alive.

And Reed wanted to kiss this woman more than any woman before.

He offered Lady Hockley his handkerchief and she dabbed at her eyes. "I apologize for my outburst, my lord. But . . . I have thought the same of Stillwell for years."

"No apology is necessary, my lady. If you are estranged from him, I say you are better off without him."

She grew quiet and he wondered what had occurred between the pair. The little he knew of Stillwell was unflattering. The man thought himself clever and worked too hard to impress others. Reed had heard Stillwell was an inveterate gambler who lost frequently at the tables.

A terrible thought occurred to him. Lady Hockley had been wed to a much older man. Reed wondered if that arrangement had come out of Stillwell's gambling. He wouldn't dream of asking her about her marriage, though.

He glanced to the duchess, who studied them both with interest, wondering if she meant for them to make a match.

"I am sorry we have left you out of our conversation, Your Grace," he said.

"Do not be concerned with that, my lord. I am glad you are getting along so well together. Lady Hockley does not know anyone in Polite Society and it will do her good to have become acquainted with you before this house party commences. Perhaps you might help look after her during the duration of it?"

"I would be happy to do so, Your Grace," he replied, wondering at the duchess' motives.

"Now that you have met, I would like to talk with the both of you regarding those on the guest list. I will admit that the original intent of this house party was to find the Duke of Woodmont and Miss Nicholls a spouse. They took care of that matter themselves and I am happy to report that they are wildly in love without any interference on my part."

She glanced from Lady Hockley to him. "That means my focus has shifted. I am interested in finding the two of you a perfect match. There will be eight others who are single and eligible and I believe you will find them all quite interesting. Once you have met everyone in attendance, I am more than happy to guide you in your decisions, as well as encourage those you are interested in to reciprocate your interest." She paused. "You might even wish to talk over things with each other. Sometimes, being around a group can be difficult because you might miss something. One or the other of you could point out certain things to each other. Lady Hockley will be spending a good deal of time with all the ladies and could offer you insight, Lord Boxling. The same could be true of you. You will do a few of those manly things with the other gentlemen and your impressions could aid Lady Hockley in deciding if any of them will suit with her."

Reed saw the twinkle in the duchess' eyes and believed she was deliberately giving them an excuse to be around one another even more.

"I think it a fine idea, Your Grace," he agreed cheerfully. "I would be happy to hear Lady Hockley's insight into the other women present. I also hope I could share my perceptions of the gentlemen guests with her. Hopefully, by the time this house party concludes, the two of us will have found a person who will make us happy."

"I don't need to consider happiness, my lord," Lady Hockley said quietly. "I merely seek a man who is interested in a large family. I have wished for children and that is my priority. As long as my future husband agrees, my personal feelings don't truly matter. I will say in my favor that I am extremely organized and skilled in running a large household. I would even be happy with a widower who already has children, as long as he is interested in having more."

She hesitated and looked to the duchess. "I know my age might be held against me, despite your reassurances, Your Grace, but I also have one drawback that will be hard to overcome. I have no dowry to offer a man. I understand that is a central part of the marriage process in the *ton*. Unfortunately, as a widow, I have no funds which were left to me upon my husband's death. I am sorry I forgot to mention this to you. I will understand if that drawback is so great that I should not attend the party. I would be happy remaining in my room for meals and simply playing with the children in the nursery the rest of the time."

Reed's heart went out to this vulnerable woman. She was beautiful and yet lacked in self-confidence, something which came naturally to him. He wondered about her marriage and how her much-older husband had treated her. He found it strange, too, that absolutely no provision had been made for her when she became a widow. That should have been established in her marriage settlements before she even wed. He would think on this and see how he might be able to look into the matter for her.

Before the duchess could reply, he said, "Dowries are important to some men and their families, my lady. However, I do not think the lack of one should keep you from attending this house party. I know Her Grace somewhat and have grown close to Lord and Lady Danbury. The type of guest they have invited will be open to a marriage, regardless of the lack of a dowry. Do not withdraw from the festivities for that reason, I beg you. Get to know those in attendance—and allow them to come to know you."

Reed saw her hesitation and so boldly took her hand. "Please, Lady Hockley. Give everyone a chance before you decide for them. You might be surprised."

Her fingers felt warm in his, causing his pulse to quicken.

"Do you truly think so?" Her gaze met his, a deep yearning revealed within them. He believed this woman had endured a difficult life and, despite her beauty, lacked in confidence.

He aimed to help her find it.

"I do—else I wouldn't have spoken up."

"You are right, Boxling," the duchess said. "I have asked gentlemen of quality to attend this house party. None of them are men who seek a bride with a generous dowry because their estates are run down and their finances poor. They have all expressed to me their desire to wed as soon as possible and they seek a woman with depth." She looked to the dowager countess. "You have no excuse to stay in your bedchamber. I expect to see you—and Lord Boxling—at every activity. Is that understood?"

Lady Hockley nodded meekly, the power of the Duchess of Camden squelching any objections she might have wished to raise.

Her Grace nodded. "I want to go check on Edwin before we settle down to tea. Would you keep Lady Hockley company for a few minutes, Lord Boxling?"

"Of course, Your Grace."

He stood and helped the duchess to rise as she said, "Come to the drawing room in a quarter-hour. We should all be gathering for tea by then."

The duchess left the room, leaving Reed to wonder if she left them alone on purpose.

CHAPTER SIX

V ANESSA WATCHED THE duchess leave the room, not able to hear her footsteps because of the blood pounding in her ears. Her heart beat wildly, as if she were a helpless creature caught by some prey.

And that prey was Lord Boxling.

The viscount was the most handsome man she had ever seen. During her lone Season of sitting on the sidelines, she had become a great observer, watching the men and women of the *ton* as they flirted and danced with one another. While she had seen a fair number of men with good looks, none of them were as striking and impressive as Lord Boxling, with his dark, wavy hair and expressive brown eyes. Even her charming host, Lord Danbury, and his friends, the Duke of Camden and Lord Middlefield—while all extremely nice-looking and possessing lovely manners—did not compare to the viscount.

Her attraction to this man terrified her.

She had no experience where men were concerned, at least in social situations. She had not spoken to a single man in Polite Society at *ton* events, other than her husband. They did no entertaining when he had his brief sojourns in the country. The only nobleman she had spoken with before she arrived at Danbury was Milton, her stepson.

Lord Danbury and his Second Son friends had put her at ease.

Perhaps it was seeing how happily wed the trio was that had allowed her to relax in their presence. But being with Lord Boxling now and having to make conversation with him was a frightening prospect. She believed she had nothing to offer him. That made her worry about the other gentlemen who would be attending the house party. What was she going to say to them? She was as dull as a church mouse. No one would give a fig about her.

Vanessa longed to retreat to her bedchamber and hide. Unfortunately, she had agreed to attend every event for the duration of the house party. If she didn't, she knew all too well that Adalyn would coming looking for her. Why, her new friend was so bold she might even halt an activity and keep others from participating until Vanessa appeared. That would be mortifying and draw attention to her that she would never invite.

Her best option was to go and try to be as unobtrusive as possible. She would need to speak some to the other guests. She might as well try now with this all-too-handsome viscount. If she could get through these next few minutes successfully, it would bolster her.

She glanced up and saw him studying her. A warmth filled her, much as it had when he took her hand for a moment, pressing her to get to know the invited guests. Simple, human touch had not been a part of her world for many years. Perhaps that was why she felt so overwhelmed by him.

He took a seat—but not the one he had sat in before. Instead, he replaced Adalyn on the settee next to her. Immediately, she caught the scent of his cologne. It had a warmth with undertones of orange and gave her quite a heady feeling, almost luring her toward him.

"Her Grace is certainly one to be reckoned with," Lord Boxling said. "She is highly thought of throughout Polite Society." He grinned. "But she is not someone that likes to be told no."

Vanessa couldn't help but chuckle at his observation. "I have experienced that firsthand. When she and Lady Middlefield arrived at Danfield, I thought to give them time alone with Lady Danbury since they are old friends. Her Grace was having none of that and marched straight to my bedchamber, demanding I join them so she could get to know me."

He laughed, a deep, rich laugh that caused goosebumps to sprout along her arms. "It sounds just like her."

"Mind you, I am not speaking ill of her," she said. "In fact, I have enjoyed getting to know her—and Lady Middlefield—since their arrival. Her Grace is very loyal to her friends. She is a blend of fierceness and kindness, which I never would have thought went hand-in-hand. Until I met her."

He nodded thoughtfully. "She is known for her loyalty as much as her matchmaking skills. If she is your friend, she is your friend for life. It seems she has taken you under her wing, my lady, and will always protect you."

"Why do you need her to make a match for you, Lord Boxling?" Vanessa asked, surprising herself for such an audacious question since it was not in her nature to pry, much less ask something so personal of someone she had just met.

"That is an excellent question, my lady."

He stared into space a moment and she wondered if he wanted to avoid her question altogether. She thought she should ask him something inane. Something safe. Just to keep the conversation moving along.

Before she could, he replied. "I have mixed emotions on requesting Her Grace to help me find my viscountess." He hesitated and added, "I hope you don't find this awkward, my talking about how I hope to find a bride among the guests coming."

She smiled. "Not if you don't find my asking you about it awkward."

He visibly relaxed. "My father was the greatest influence on me. He married out of duty and came to love my mother very much. So though they were not a love match originally, they became one. She died in childbirth while having me and he was alone for many years. When I was fourteen, he remarried. For love."

Vanessa found that idea intriguing. Though her own parents had been friendly with one another, she knew no romantic love existed between them. Her mother had talked to her of that very thing when she had begun to tell Vanessa about the Season and how marriages were arranged among members of the *ton*. Although she had protested her brother choosing a husband for her, sight unseen, she had always known she would wed the man of her father's choosing, out of her duty to her family. Love never entered her mind. She only wished for an amiable young man who wanted children.

"My parents became quite friendly and they loved me very much. They were not in love, however," she told him.

"I see," he said. "Though I never knew my mother, Father told me about her and his love for her. Then I witnessed his relationship with Constance, his second wife, and saw how affectionate they were toward one another." He shrugged. "I got the foolish notion that I, too, would make a love match."

"Are you disappointed that you have not found love?" she asked.

"More than that. Father left the estate in financial shambles. The man I had admired above all others showed me he had feet of clay. My disappointment in him proved to be quite bitter. Fortunately, I have made some prudent investments and our crop yield has proved fruitful for the last two years. It allows me the freedom to wed a woman with any size of dowry, large or small."

He raked a hand through his thick hair. "I have tried, really tried, to find love. It has been an unsuccessful venture on my part. Her Grace told me that I have been looking too hard, forcing the issue. She believes love will creep up on me when I least expect it."

The viscount sighed. "I have also been disappointed in the eligible women I have met. They might have been pretty but they are dull. I believe part of marriage is stimulating conversation and working together as partners. Building a family and sharing experiences. Frankly, I haven't met a woman I would care to do those things with. I know, however, that I need to wed and provide an heir for the viscountcy. I have known others who have dallied about, only to die young and leave no heir. Or the heir is someone who was not to their liking."

Lord Boxling nodded his head a few times. "That is why I have placed myself in the hands of Her Grace. She has a reputation of bringing people together who suit well. I hope I will be like my father and make a good marriage and find myself falling in love with my wife over time."

He seemed so earnest. So admirable. Vanessa wished for a moment that he would want *her* to be the one by his side. She didn't think that would be possible, though. He spoke of looking forward to meeting the other guests. She doubted he would ever consider her as his wife. A confident, attractive, elegant man such as Lord Boxling would need a lady of considerable looks and charm, one who could converse with others with ease. A woman who would be his equal in every way. One he would love and find his love returned.

Vanessa would never satisfy a man such as this. She knew she was worthless. Her husband had told her so.

"What are you looking for in your next marriage, my lady?"

His question startled her.

"I am not sure what to say, my lord."

His deep brown eyes pierced her soul. "Say what is in your heart," he urged.

She swallowed, deciding she would be honest with him and doubted she would ever repeat these words to another soul.

"My marriage was most unsuccessful, my lord. My brother arranged it to pay off his gambling debts. Lord Hockley arrived with the marriage contracts in hand and I was whisked away to our wedding ceremony."

She found she was trembling and Lord Boxling took her hand in his, bringing her comfort and steadying her.

"Had you known Lord Hockley long?" he asked.

"I had never laid eyes upon him," she admitted, shame filling her. "Stillwell told me of these plans the night I was to attend the first ball of my come-out Season. We never went to the ball. Lord Hockley arrived the next morning. We were married two hours later."

He laced his fingers through hers. She only saw compassion on his face, no judgment in sight.

"I have met the current Lord Hockley, whom I assume is your husband's son. That means that your husband was quite a bit older than you."

"He was," she said, her voice shaking as she thought of the time in his bed.

"You deserved much more, Lady Hockley. A man that old might find it hard to please his wife."

"He was set in his ways," she agreed. "He never thought once to please me in any way. He never bothered to learn a single thing about me. He did not introduce me to a soul, allowing me to sit with the matrons of the *ton* and observe the dancing at balls. No one spoke to me. No one cared about me. I had no one," she finished, her voice a whisper.

The viscount's eyes flashed with anger but his voice remained gentle. "I do not recall seeing you these past few Seasons. I would have noticed you."

"I remained in the country after that first year. My husband was . . . displeased with me."

Again, his eyes simmered with rage and her heart broke, thinking this man who had only just met her cared more for her than the one who had married her.

"It was nothing you did, my lady," Lord Boxling assured her. "You were merely a pawn used by two men. For that, I am sorry."

He lifted their hands, fingers still entwined, and pressed a soft kiss against her knuckles.

"Close the door on that chapter of your life," he advised.

"Start afresh at this house party. You will be with others closer to your age. You have already made a true friend in Her Grace, as well as Lady Danbury and Lady Middlefield." His gaze held hers. "Know you are a woman of value. One of worth. No matter what your dead husband said. Now, I will ask you again—what do you wish for in a husband?"

Vanessa swallowed. "I wish . . . for a man who would see me. Not ignore me. One who loves children and will give me many of them. I do not need fancy clothes or to take my place in a society which has already rejected me. I want a quiet life in the country, surrounded by peace and a growing family. I want to be a good wife and make his life trouble-free. Manage his household. Help care for his tenants. Help in whatever capacity I can."

Lord Boxling nodded, as if to reaffirm what she wished for might actually come true.

"I think you will make for a fine wife, Lady Hockley. You are caring and compassionate. You will handle your responsibilities with care and ease."

She bit her lip. "But I have nothing to offer a gentleman, my lord. My looks are average. My dowry nonexistent. I have led such a quiet life that I have nothing of note to speak to others about. I doubt I will draw the notice of any gentlemen at this house party."

He squeezed her fingers. "You have drawn my attention, my lady," he said firmly. "And I see you lack in confidence."

She flushed at his words, her cheeks growing hot. "I have no experience in social situations, my lord. I am more unsure than I thought possible."

"You need to believe in yourself, my lady. When I look at you, I see a beautiful woman filled with poise and grace. You have more to offer than you realize. But you are missing that conviction in yourself. Confidence can be a potent thing, Lady Hockley. And when you have it, you will be unstoppable."

She looked at him forlornly. "How am I to find it, my lord?"

"We can start like this."

And he lowered his mouth to hers.

CHAPTER SEVEN

R EED DID WHAT he had wanted to do the entire time they had sat beside one another.

Kiss her . . .

He pressed his lips to hers, finding them soft and pliant. He didn't rush the kiss. He couldn't. Without knowing the full story of her marriage—other than her admitting it was unsuccessful— he instinctively understood Lady Hockley was a damaged, fragile creature. One not merely lacking in self-confidence but one who had been hurt in some way. Whether through neglect or some type of physical or emotional abuse, it had resulted in her becoming a very vulnerable, emotionally frail woman.

He didn't know if he could solve any of her problems, which lay locked deep inside her. But what he could do was help her to feel worthy again. Vibrant. Wanted.

That was what this kiss would do. It would be the first step to assure her she was a woman of value and worth.

More than anything, he suspected it was her first kiss. If she had not made her come-out, she had experienced no stolen kisses by eager gentlemen. Many men her husband's age had trouble performing their sexual duties and Reed had discovered very few of them bothered kissing their wives. That kind of romance was usually reserved for mistresses and clandestine affairs with the wives of other men of the *ton*.

Because of that, he wanted this to be right. Perfect in every way.

And that meant not taking it too far.

Softly, slowly, he brushed his lips against hers. She wore no scent other than the clean scent of her skin. As a widow, she probably had limited access to any type of luxuries, and that would include perfumes. Still, Lady Hockley's skin smelled heavenly to him.

His hand went to cup her nape and steady her, as his other hand went to her waist and rested there, his thumb gliding back and forth, skimming her ribcage. He chose not to deepen the kiss but kept it simple, now stopping his lips and pressing them again to hers firmly. She made a soft sound in the back of her throat, dreamy and sweet, and he fought to keep from taking more than he should.

Reed would bide his time. He would only take a bit of her now.

But in the end, he would claim all of her for himself.

He broke the kiss, his lips hovering just above hers, and rested his forehead against hers. Never having done this with another soul, he found he rather liked the intimacy of the touch. They remained that way for several moments and then he lifted his head from hers, allowing his hands to drop from her waist and nape.

She looked dazed. If she appeared thus after such a sweet, tender kiss, it gave him a thrill to see the look on her face after she had been thoroughly kissed. And touched. Yes, her dead spouse had done her a disservice. He had led her to believe she wasn't attractive when the exact opposite was the case. Perhaps Lord Hockley had wanted to beat down the spirit within her in order to make certain she remained docile and under his thumb.

The little she had revealed shocked Reed. To have to wed a stranger because of gambling debts was harsh enough, but for her husband to deliberately drag her to *ton* affairs and never introduce her to a soul was abominably cruel. It would have beaten down any resistance she had to the marriage, finding herself adrift in a sea of judgmental members of Polite Society. They would been highly entertained, seeing her flounder as they watched in delight. Her husband burying her in the country is what had probably saved her sanity. If she'd had to face the members of Polite Society every Season, constantly rejected, it might have done her in.

Gazing deeply into her violet eyes, dark now with desire, he said, "That is a start. Do you feel more confident now, Lady Hockley? Do you feel as if you are desirable? Worthy of attention?"

She shook her head back and forth, not speaking. Finally, she said, "That kiss . . ." Her voice trailed off.

"I apologize for not asking if I might kiss you," he said. "But I wanted you to feel the spontaneity of the moment. Feel you were attractive and desired."

A blush stained her cheeks, making her all the more attractive. Reed fought the urge to kiss her again. This time, a real kiss.

"Mama used to tell me I was pretty," she told him. "But Lord Hockley . . . well . . . he was of a different opinion regarding my looks."

"Lord Hockley was a bloody fool." He cupped her cheek with his hand. "He was a sad, old man who did not know what to do with such a vibrant young woman."

Her face drained of all color and she turned away, leading him to believe the old earl had done more than abuse her with words. If that were the case, then he would have to take very small steps to build up her spirits and make her believe she had true value.

"We should probably head to the drawing room," he suggested, lowering his hand, feeling bereft at the loss of contact. Touching her smooth skin had him craving more. He longed to glide his hands up and down her bare back. Press his lips to her breast. Touch her in ways so intimate that she screamed his name as he brought her exquisite pleasure.

All in good time.

His mind had been made up. If this was why Her Grace had left them alone, then her plan had worked. Reed knew the duchess did not champion anyone lightly. She had chosen to do so with Lady Hockley. He would see it through.

Rising, he offered her his hand. She placed hers in his and again he was glad they were not at a ball and both of them wearing gloves. He liked the feel of her hand in his and reluctantly placed it upon his sleeve.

As they exited the room and moved down the hall toward the drawing room, he said, "We were so caught up in our earlier conversation that Her Grace never told us about the other house party guests. We will have to meet with her at another time and hear who will be calling at Danfield."

Vanessa tried to listen to what Lord Boxling was saying but it was almost impossible to do so. All she could think of was the hard forearm her fingers rested upon. The feel of his lips against hers. The heady scent of his cologne which she inhaled with each breath.

This was madness.

Yet she believed the viscount to have had good intentions. He had called her beautiful, trying to bolster her confidence. She hadn't believed him and he must have read so in her eyes. That had led to him kissing her. And for a few moments, she had felt desirable. She had become lost in the sensations. His soft yet firm lips. His fingers warm against her nape. The thrill that rippled through her each time his thumb brushed against her gown. Without gloves, that heat had seared her through the layers of clothing she wore.

Yes, for a brief while, Vanessa had felt as if she might be able to attract a gentleman's attention. Whether she could hold it or not would be left up to her. She asked herself if Lord Boxling had truly found her attractive or if he merely wished to strengthen the little faith she had in herself. Whatever the case, she had come alive with his touch. Felt the possibilities that existed in this house party. Hoped she could find a husband and begin a family.

They arrived at the drawing room and entered. She saw they were the last to arrive for tea. Lord Middlefield held a tart up to Tessa's lips, teasing her to take it. His Grace spoke with Lord Danbury, all the while holding his wife's hand. Louisa was pouring out the tea.

"There you are," Adalyn said. "Come and join us."

The men stood and greeted her. Lord Boxling seated her and then went to shake hands with each of them. He had an effortless, casual way that made him fit in with others. She wondered again why love had not come to him and hoped Adalyn would match the viscount with a woman who would be a perfect fit for him. She imagined herself one day, married at last, sitting and watching Lord Boxling and his wife dance the waltz across a ballroom floor. Their steps would be perfectly matched, as would their looks. They would gaze adoringly at one another. She imagined him catching sight of her and stopping, introducing her to his viscountess, telling her how they had met at a house party long ago. Or perhaps the woman would be a guest at the upcoming party and she would remember Vanessa. They would go in to supper together and catch up, telling one another about their families and what had happened on their estates.

And she would always remember this man had given her the very first kiss of her life.

Lord Boxling took a seat beside her and she found the settee suddenly too small for the both of them. He was tall but not incredibly broad, tending toward a more lean, athletic frame, though his well-fitted coat let her know he had large biceps. She doubted any padding was used, as she had discovered about her husband. Again, she flashed to their one time together, his naked, bony body and the awful things he had done to her and wanted done to him in return.

"Are you all right?" Lord Boxling asked, leaning close to her ear, his lips barely brushing the lobe, sending a shiver along her spine.

"I am fine," she lied, putting the nightmarish image from her mind. "But definitely in need of a cup of tea."

He turned and accepted one that Louisa handed over. "Take this. I will see to a plate. You look pale and most likely need something to eat."

Vanessa appreciated his concern as she sipped the hot brew. As always, a good cup of tea lifted her spirts.

Lord Boxling turned back to her, a plate in his hand full of tarts, biscuits, and a rather large sandwich.

"I am not certain I can eat all of that," she told him, accepting the plate and placing it upon her lap.

"I am as a growing lad and remain ravenous most days," he said, his voice teasing. "I will eat whatever you cannot finish."

The thought of him taking something from her plate seemed far too intimate. Vanessa sensed the blush spill across her cheeks as the viscount smiled at her.

She lowered her eyes to her plate, hoping none of the others present would see the hot blush which seemed to spread down her neck and up to her roots. Vanessa could not remember the last time she blushed—before today. Receiving attention from this man seated next to her was causing strange sensations within her. She seemed helpless to control her reactions to him.

As she sipped her tea, talk turned to Danfield and the other country estates these lords held. She was intrigued by how an estate ran though she had never had anything to do with the running of one. From what these gentlemen said, it was much like running a large household, a fine balance of managing things and addressing the needs of the tenants upon the estate. Horace the Horrible had a steward and because of that, the steward had managed everything. She would have liked to have become friendly with their tenants and seen to their needs but her husband had expressly forbidden her becoming involved with anyone upon the estate. She had been too cowed to question him, afraid if she disobeyed him, he would punish her as he had the one time they had coupled together.

She noticed her friends chiming in with enthusiasm, obviously knowledgeable about what occurred on their husband's lands. Adalyn, in particular, made some excellent suggestions, which Lord Boxling picked up. He asked her several questions and she freely shared her opinions.

Vanessa was proud to have made friends with these three women. They had a wide range of interests and it was obvious their husbands valued what they had to say. She also knew all three to be excellent mothers, having witnessed them with their children. She decided to aspire to be more like these women— traditional members of the *ton* and yet ones who seemed to break out of the mold set forth by Polite Society.

Lord Boxling asked, "When might we ride around Danfield, Lord Danbury? I would like to see for myself some of these ideas which you have implemented on your lands."

Their host said, "There is no time like the present, I believe. Dinner will not be for a couple of hours. If you would like to go now, Boxling, we can."

She wished she could go with them and see more of the estate. She had walked some of it, of course, needing to get in her daily walk, which she believed centered her. She had yet to ride, however, since she had arrived at Danfield.

Louisa spoke up. "Do you mind if Vanessa and I join you, dear? I know she has yet to see all of Danfield." Louisa turned to her and asked, "Do you ride, Vanessa?"

She nodded eagerly. "Yes, riding and walking are two of my favorite outdoor pursuits," she informed her hostess. Glancing to Lord Danbury, she added, "I would not wish to invite myself along if you would prefer it be only gentlemen, my lord."

Lord Middlefield said, "We rode the depth and breadth of Danfield when we came earlier this week. Frankly, I would rather stay behind instead of seeing what I have already seen and go to the nursery to spend time with Analise and Adam."

The duke nodded in agreement and said, "Why don't just the four of you go? We will hold down the fort here. I suspect Addie needs to lie down and rest a bit. I will join Spence in the nursery."

Lord Danbury rose, offering his hand to his wife, who took it.

"Then it's settled," Louisa said. "Give us time to change into our riding habits and we will meet you at the stables."

Lord Boxling came to his feet and offered Vanessa his hand. She placed hers in his, again feeling something which she had never experienced before.

"Thank you," she said quietly.

"I look forward to our ride, my lady," he told her.

Vanessa joined Louisa and they left the others behind in the drawing room, heading to their respective bedchambers.

Louisa said, "I am happy you wish to see more of Danfield. We are very proud of our estate and the work done by our tenants."

"I am eager to see it," she commented. "You, Tessa, and Adalyn seem to know a great deal about how estates are run. I had no idea. I did not participate in that after my marriage. Before it, it was not something my father ever encouraged from me."

"We lived in town year-round because of my father's work with the War Office," Louisa shared. "I did go to the country during the summers to visit Tessa and Adalyn, who are my cousins."

"I did not realize that."

"Yes, both cousins and dear friends. I have found a peace in the country which I never experienced in the city. Though I still enjoy going to town and taking advantage of everything there, my heart is and always will be at Danfield."

"I hope if I am fortunate enough to find a husband at this house party, he might be openminded enough to allow me to learn about managing a country estate. I have always found organizing the tasks to run a household something I am interested in. It sounds as if estate management is similar. You must deal with day-to-day matters, as well as be aware of the scope of things and plan according, whether it is by a week, month, or year."

"Or several years in advance," Louisa noted. She took

Vanessa's hand and squeezed it. "I have high hopes you will find your match here, Vanessa. In fact, I believe you and Lord Boxling would do well together."

The inevitable blush heated her cheeks. "I don't know about that, Louisa. I feel he needs someone much different from me."

"Lord Boxling once attempted to court me when I first stepped into society full-time, Vanessa. I found him a most delightful and amiable gentleman. I had met Owen previously, though, and my heart only had room for him. If Owen had not slipped into it, I believe I would have wed Lord Boxling. He is a fine man, full of integrity and good character. I hope you will give him your full consideration."

They reached Louisa's rooms and parted. Vanessa went further down the hall until she reached the bedchamber assigned to her. She entered and rang for a servant to help her into her riding habit. As she waited for the maid to appear, Vanessa changed from her slippers into sturdy boots, which would be more appropriate for their ride.

She wondered what Louisa had observed regarding her and the viscount and if the other two women also thought a match was possible between them. She knew Adalyn had left her and Lord Boxling alone deliberately so that they might speak openly with one another.

She grew warm recalling the kiss they had shared. She wondered if the viscount truly found her attractive or if he merely tried to boost her confidence. Regardless of his purpose, she would bask in the memory of that kiss for a long time to come. Having never been kissed, she found it to be a sweet and very sensual experience. She believed he held back, though, trying not to frighten her. She wondered how much more there was to kissing—and touching—remembering his warm fingers cradling her nape and his hand resting at her waist.

The maid entered the room and Vanessa explained she needed help getting into her riding habit. The servant retrieved it from the wardrobe and soon Vanessa was ready, donning a hat which had been a particular favorite of hers years ago, and one she wore every time she did ride. Moving along the corridor, she found Louisa waiting for her just outside her own bedchamber. Her friend linked her arm with Vanessa's and they proceeded down the stairs and out to the stables.

Vanessa decided to take the advice she had been given and remain openminded about what happened today, and every day, as the house party commenced.

CHAPTER EIGHT

T HE RIDE HAD proven exhilarating in more ways than one. Vanessa was able to see so much more of Danfield and was impressed with everything about the estate. The four of them stopped at various spots along the way and Lord Danbury would explain what he was up to with his tenants on that portion of the estate.

Though she enjoyed listening to what the earl had to say, she was ever aware of Viscount Boxling's presence. He rode beside her, only making a comment every now and then to Lord Danbury or Louisa. Never her. Yet she could feel the air crackling between them. Just being near him caused her insides to flutter insancly.

Vanessa supposed this feeling must be physical desire, something she had never experienced and never thought would occur. The physical aspects of a marriage were something she had locked away long ago from her wedding day, knowing that if she did find a mate at this house party, she would have to endure them again to get the children she wanted. Horace the Horrible had told her how undesirable she was and what a mistake he had made, overpaying for her. The few times he was in her company, he constantly berated her, telling her how worthless she was and what a disappointment she had been and would always be. It clouded the way she viewed herself and she felt as if others must feel the same way about her.

Yet Lord Boxling seemed to want her. The tender kiss had proven as much, his eyes dark after it. She also saw how happy her three friends seemed to be in their marriages and how much they loved their husbands. Surely not everything that occurred in the bedroom was as hideous as what Horace the Horrible had done to her. Yet she had no one to ask about those things. Though she liked and even trusted her new friends, Vanessa knew there was a line to be drawn. Certain subjects could never be brought up among them. Curiosity filled her, though. She wondered if she would have the same kind of physical response to any other gentlemen who would be guests at the house party. That remained to be seen. She did hope to meet with Adalyn again and learn a little about each of the guests before they arrived, preferably without Lord Boxling present. If he were present, she didn't know if she would hear a word Adalyn spoke.

They returned from their ride and Louisa told Vanessa that she would have hot water for a bath sent up to her bedchamber, reminding her what time dinner would be served. She went to her room to await the hot water. It had been a bit unnerving getting used to having meals with others present when she arrived at Danfield. She had opted for a tray in her room all those times she was alone in the country. The few instances Horace the Horrible had been present, meals with him in the dining room had seemed interminable. He sat at the far end of the table and she at the opposite end. They never exchanged a single word as footmen brought course after course. When her husband left to return to town, relief always washed through her.

The hot water arrived, several servants bringing buckets of it, as well as cool water to mix with it. A maid assisted her in removing her riding habit and Vanessa dismissed her, wanting time to soak in the tub in private. She remained lost in her thoughts until the water cooled and then she washed and rinsed quickly and toweled off with the bath sheet. She rang for a maid to help her dress again, thinking how many times a day she had been changing clothes, something very unusual for her. When she walked or rode by herself, she never bothered to change into a riding habit or different gown. She supposed this house party would be very different, with ladies changing for most every activity. Again, she thought her wardrobe lacking, knowing it was terribly out of date but having no choice. She hoped the ladies coming were of a quality that they would be kind enough not to mention it.

Vanessa made her way downstairs to the drawing room, where Louisa had mentioned they would be having a drink before they went in to dinner. She joined the others already present and immediately found Lord Boxling at her side.

Awareness filled her as he greeted her and she caught the spice of his cologne. A footman came by with a tray of drinks and the viscount picked up one for her and himself.

"You sit a horse beautifully, Lady Hockley," he complimented. "Have you always ridden?"

"I learned to ride as a young girl but I did quite a bit of it during my marriage since I spent so much time in the country. Riding—and walking—are two of my favorite pastimes."

"Perhaps we can stroll in the gardens after dinner if you would like. Lady Danbury has told me they are lovely."

She knew she would like it—but didn't know if she could trust herself to do so. Words her mother had spoken years ago came back to her, warning her that when her Season began she was never to be alone with a gentleman. Mama said the rules changed when a lady wed or if she had been widowed. Vanessa, as a widow, did not want to be taken advantage of, even if it was a handsome viscount doing so.

Lord Boxling escorted her into dinner and, for once, Vanessa wished a meal could go on and on. She had never had so much fun merely listening to others converse and she actually contributed some to the conversation herself.

When the meal did end, Louisa invited the ladies to the drawing room while the gentlemen stayed behind to partake in their port and cigars. She went along with her friends and walked with Adalyn on the way there.

"I would like to meet with you—without Lord Boxling—and discuss the guest list," Adalyn said. "We will find a convenient time tomorrow and do so," her friend promised. "I will also meet separately with Lord Boxling and do the same." Adalyn paused and then asked, "What do you think of Boxling?"

Her heart sped up. "He is very nice," she said, keeping her voice neutral.

Adalyn nodded. "You are wise not to tip your hand, Vanessa."

"What do you mean?" she asked.

"Lord Boxling will be but one of the gentlemen present. I know he has already paid you a bit of attention but it is good if you allow your feelings to remain a bit mysterious. I am not saying you should play hard to get but keep all your options open. In the end, your heart will tell you if he is the one for you."

"I worry still that none of the gentlemen invited will find me interesting. If that is the case, I will appreciate the opportunity you and Louisa have given me. It will let me know that I gave it my best effort and that seeking a position as a governess or companion is what I am meant to do."

They reached the drawing room and Adalyn took Vanessa's hand. "I don't wish to see you working for a living. Not that I don't think you would do an excellent job in whatever position you accepted. I see a different life for you, Vanessa."

They joined Louisa and Tessa and the three women enlightened her as to the type of activities that occurred at a house party.

When they finished elaborating on what was planned, she said, "I am astounded at all that goes on. We will be so busy. I am a little worried, though, because I have not played any of these lawn games of which you spoke."

"There are always others who have no experience with lawn games," Tessa shared. She smiled. "And there are certainly gentlemen who will demonstrate for you how to play them. It is all part of the flirtation that occurs at a house party. Ask Louisa."

Louisa pinkened slightly. She told Vanessa, "Owen and I came together during a house party. I told you previously that I had met him prior to attending it but it was during this time that we truly got to know one another. That is why I prefer a house party over the social affairs held during the Season. At a ball, you only dance with a gentleman once, else tongues wag. I always had to concentrate on the steps and the music and found it impossible to converse. Even at card parties or musicales, attention is devoted to that activity and sometimes little is said. A house party is infinitely more fun and very different."

She smiled at Vanessa. "I do hope you will find your match in the coming week."

The door opened and the four gentlemen entered. Vanessa wondered if Lord Boxling would recall he had asked her to stroll in the gardens with him after dinner. The thought caused her to grow warm all over.

Lord Danbury said, "I would enjoy hearing my lovely wife sing this evening." He looked to Vanessa. "Louisa has a beautiful voice. But during the house party, I doubt she will sing because she will wish for our guests to show off their talents to the others present."

Louisa turned to Tessa. "Would you play for me?"

"I would be delighted to."

Louisa, who had been sitting next to Vanessa, rose and went to the pianoforte. A moment later, Lord Boxling took her place.

"Perhaps we can take our walk through the gardens tomorrow afternoon. I do not want to miss Louisa singing for us. She has a true talent."

Vanessa hid her disappointment. She still would walk with Lord Boxling tomorrow. She turned her attention to her friends and thoroughly enjoyed the music. Louisa's voice was a rich contralto and Tessa played beautifully. They performed for almost an hour and then Adalyn yawned.

"Forgive me," she said, as she rubbed her belly with both

hands. "I think I will retire."

His Grace helped his wife to her feet and they said goodnight. The others all indicated they were ready for bed and Lord Boxling leaned over.

"Might I escort you to your bedchamber, Lady Hockley?"

She didn't know if she should let him do so or not but he had been a gentleman up to this point and so she told him, "Yes, please."

They followed the others down the corridor, taking a more leisurely pace, until no one else was in sight. When they reached her door, she paused.

"I suppose this is goodnight," he said softly.

"Yes," she said breathlessly, the blood pounding in her ears.

He bent and brushed his lips against her cheek. His gaze was intense when she believed he wanted to do much more.

He took her hand and brought it to his lips and tenderly kissed her knuckles. Warmth flooded her.

"Goodnight, Lady Hockley. I look forward to spending more time with you tomorrow."

The viscount opened the door for her and she floated into the room, closing it behind her. Leaning against the door, she closed her eyes, still able to catch the scent of his cologne. She touched her fingertips to her cheek, where his lips had been just moments ago and sighed.

Could he truly be interested in her? Or was he merely being polite?

Vanessa couldn't help but wonder if things would change once the other eligible ladies arrived. Most likely, they would be younger than she was. Prettier. Better dressed and no doubt have better connections in society. She was a widow of limited means, with no family to speak of. Having no idea what her brother's reputation was like after all these years, she hoped no one would ask her about her family. Not that Stillwell considered her family anymore. Her stepchildren did not think of her in that way, either.

A wave of loneliness washed over her. She was fooling herself. Her new friends were sweet, kind women and eternally optimistic to a fault but Vanessa knew she would have nothing to offer the bachelors attending this house party. They—and Lord Boxling—would see she was undeserving of their attention. She had no dowry, no social connections, and no experience in life.

Resolving to stay in the background, she would merely listen to the conversations around her and try to enjoy this week. It would be the last leisurely one of her life, the last time she pretended to be a part of the *ton*. Two weeks from now, she would be in London seeking a position. She would ask Adalyn to write a reference for her. Being a duchess, her recommendation would carry a great deal of weight and would hopefully impress the agency trying to place her in a position.

Resigned to her fate, Vanessa rang for a maid, grateful she at least had an education and would not have to work as hard as a servant to support herself.

The maid appeared and helped her ready herself for bed. Once she lay tucked beneath the bedclothes, Vanessa swallowed the painful lump in her throat and drifted off into a restless sleep.

CHAPTER NINE

REED ANSWERED THE Duchess of Camden's summons, going once again to the small parlor where he had met with her and Lady Hockley yesterday. He entered the room and couldn't help but think of the sweet kiss he and the widow had shared on the settee where the duchess now sat. If Reed had his way, he would show Lady Hockley there were many ways to kiss.

Starting this afternoon in the Danfield gardens.

"Good afternoon, Your Grace," he said pleasantly.

"Ah, Lord Boxling. You are right on time," she replied as he came and took her hand and kissed it. "I do think punctuality is important, don't you?"

Chuckling, he took a seat next to her. "You are speaking to a man whose sole purpose in life is to be punctual. If I am always on time, then others cannot gossip about me, can they?"

She smiled. "You think you are a topic of discussion, my lord?"

"I think during the Season, any bachelor finds himself being raked over the coals by all the doting mamas. Analyzed and evaluated and thoroughly vetted. Rather as you did in composing your guest list for this house party, I would say."

"You are far too clever for your own good, Boxling. You are also correct in assuming that Louisa and I took great care composing our list. Of course, I thought my primary objective would be to find suitable spouses for the Duke of Woodmont and Seraphina Nicholls. Little did I know they would do my work for me and find one another."

She pulled a handkerchief from her sleeve and patted her brow with it. "I get so beastly hot when I carry a child. Usually, my nature is cold and I find myself chilled and always wrapping a shawl about me. Things change when another little life grows within you." She rubbed her belly, smiling.

He smiled. "I am eager for a wife, Your Grace. I have told you that. I am also looking forward to that said wife being with child."

"I recall you have a fondness for your sister's children. She has two—or is it three?"

"Two, Your Grace. Eve is four and has me wrapped about her smallest finger. I find it hard to say no to her. Pip is two and lively as they come. They were at Boxwell Hall just prior to my coming to Danfield. If I had not already committed to this house party, I might have kept the both of them and sent Pamela and Drake home without their children."

She studied him a moment. "That says a great deal regarding your character, my lord. A man who loves children as much as you do will make for not only a good father but I believe a good husband, as well."

"I do wish to be a good husband. I . . ." He hesitated.

"Go on, Boxling. I am curious as to what you wish to say."

"My father wed twice. The first turned into a love match and the second was one from the start."

"I see. So, you have a wonderful example of what a good husband can be. Do you seek a love match yourself?"

"I had hoped for one," he admitted. "Now, I believe by putting myself in your hands that if you believe a lady and I would suit, that means we will definitely become friends. Love can grow from friendship, I believe."

"What are your impressions regarding Lady Hockley?" she asked, surprising him. Then again, the duchess was known for being blunt.

"I have a most favorable impression of her. I like her quite a bit, what I know of her. I fear she lacks self-confidence, though. She needs to believe in herself before she can commit to any future relationship."

The duchess nodded in agreement. "You are very wise, Boxling. That is an astute observation. Lady Hockley lived a sheltered life before her marriage. During her marriage, she remained that way, isolated from Polite Society."

"It has not made her any less interesting, Your Grace," he noted. "I find her quite refreshing."

"Enough to pursue her?"

He grinned. "I am already working on that, Your Grace, as well as trying to bolster her confidence."

"The Three Cousins are doing our part, as well," she replied.

Reed knew the duchess, Lady Danbury, and Lady Middlefield referred to themselves as the Three Cousins. They had been close since childhood and apparently even closer after they all wed.

"Keep with it," he encouraged. "I will be working from my end. My only fear is Lady Hockley may find another bachelor to her liking. Might I ask who will be in attendance?"

"I had called you here to discuss the ladies I had invited. I had thought two of them would be a good match for you. That was before Louisa brought Vanessa home with her."

"Brought her home?" he asked, confused.

The duchess grew serious. "This is between the two of us, Viscount Boxling. It is not to be shared with the others in attendance at the house party."

"I am happy to keep any confidence you share with me, Your Grace. I am pleased—even humbled—you would confide in me to begin with."

"Lady Hockley's year of mourning recently ended. She had been living at the dower house of her dead husband's estate. Her stepson, the new Earl of Hockley, informed her that he was ousting her."

"From the dower house?" he asked, wondering where Hockley intended for his stepmother to go.

"From every property he owned. He told her he would provide her with the funds to take a mail coach to London, where she could seek employment."

Fury filled him. "He what?"

The duchess looked gravely at him. "You heard me. That bloody bastard was going to throw her off his property and ignore his responsibilities to her."

"I will fucking kill him," Reed said, his voice low and deadly.

She smiled. "I like that about you, Boxling. It tells me all I need to know about you. Yes, I knew before you were charming and affable and intelligent. You scored further points with me because you believe in love and you yearn for children. You enjoy family and hold them in high esteem.

"But wishing to protect Vanessa?" Her triumphant look caused her face to glow. "You are the one for her. We just need to convince her of that. Be your charming self. Continue to spend as much time with her as you can. Kiss her several times to convince her of your desire for her. And once you are wed, you should meet with the Second Sons and see how you can bankrupt Lord Hockley. I know murder is on your mind but it wouldn't do for you to hang from a gibbet, now would it?"

Anger still coursed through him at the thought of Hockley wishing to dump Vanessa on a mail coach and be rid of her. That brought another question to him.

"How did she come to wed Lord Hockley in the first place?" he asked, wondering if Her Grace could add anything to the little Lady Hockley had shared with him yesterday.

"From what I understand, Vanessa's brother had mounting gambling debts. He owed a great deal of money to Hockley."

Disgust filled him. "He sold her to the old fool to pay off his debts?"

"Yes," the duchess confirmed. "Her dowry was to cover what he owed."

Vanessa had lived an awful life. Through no fault of her own, she had been the pawn of the men in her life. No wonder she had such little confidence.

"She will have a hard time trusting me," he said.

"She may," the duchess agreed. "You must convince her otherwise." She paused. "Do you love her?"

"I have feelings for her," he said cautiously. "It is like a fire when first started. The sparks are there. The embers are catching and beginning to spread that fire. But a fire that lasts—one which grows large and bold—must be carefully stoked and nurtured." He rose. "I will do this with Vanessa," he promised. "And I believe those flames will fan into love."

She smiled up at him. "You are a good man, my lord. Take care of her. You will have my full support and that of my cousins and their husbands as you woo her."

"We are to walk in the gardens now that my meeting with you has concluded. I have no wish to hear of the other women who will come to Danfield. The one I am meant to be with is already here. I plan to take full advantage of that time alone together."

"Kiss her senseless," Her Grace recommended. "I find that is always a good start."

Reed laughed aloud. "I will see you at tea, Your Grace."

He left the parlor and went to the library, where he had arranged for Vanessa to meet him. She had become Vanessa in his mind and heart. The woman he needed to save from all the wicked things that had befallen her.

Entering the room, he scanned it and found her in a wing chair that sat next to a window. She was engrossed in the book resting on her lap and he took a moment to study her.

He liked how the light coming through the window struck her hair, a rich brown which possessed golden highlights. His fingers longed to skim the curve of her nose and travel down the long, slender column of her throat. They would continue downward, cupping her full breasts. He yearned to look into those violet eyes as he touched her intimately, watching them turn dark with desire.

He already liked her a great deal and was physically attracted to her. He believed love would come.

For both of them.

"Lady Hockley?" he said, watching her as she looked up and smiled.

"Lord Boxling," she said, a catch in her voice. "I did not hear you come in. I was caught up in my novel."

She rose, closing the book. "It is written by Anonymous and called *Emma*. Have you read it? It is a recent publication."

"I have not—but I would enjoy hearing you tell me about it." He offered her his arm.

She set the book on a table and placed her fingertips on his sleeve. He liked the feel of her next to him, touching him. Her very nearness caused his pulse to race. If she had this effect on him by a mere touch, what would it be like when he had her in his bed?

They left the library and continued down a corridor until they reached a set of French doors leading outside. The August afternoon was warm. Thankfully, a slight breeze stirred the air.

"I believe the gardens are this way," he said, tucking her hand through the crook of his arm and leaving his hand resting on hers for the sheer pleasure of the contact.

They reached the gardens and entered them. Large trees mixed with a variety of blossoms. Abundant shade covered the path as they walked along.

"Do you have gardens at your country estate?" she asked.

"I do. I live at Boxwell Hall most of the year. My stepmother, whom my father married when I was fourteen, has no love of country life. She and her daughters live in the London townhouse a good portion of the year, only coming to Boxwell Hall for a brief respite after the Season and again for the Christmas holidays."

"How old are the girls? They would be your half-sisters."

"Camilla is fifteen. Nicola is fourteen. I didn't know them

well until the past couple of years. They were far more interested in their dolls and tea parties and had no mind to spend time with an older half-brother. Still, we are learning about each other now and I quite like them. Before I know it, they will be making their come-outs."

"Have you been the viscount very long?"

"My father passed away two Christmases ago. I was furious at him for a while."

"Why?"

He shook his head. "I idolized him from my youth. He was always larger than life. He taught me. Encouraged me. Filled me with confidence. And then he let me down tremendously."

Reed saw a stone bench. "Shall we sit a moment?"

They seated themselves and she asked, "What happened?"

"I learned during the last year of his life that he had made some poor investments. To counter them, he turned to gambling. Needless to say, he lost far more than he won and I inherited an estate that was very much in trouble."

"It must have been hard, seeing your father in a different light. You had worshiped him and you discovered he wasn't necessarily the hero from your youth."

Her hands were folded in her lap and Reed slipped his between them, lacing his fingers through hers. "You are perceptive, Vanessa."

She emitted a gasp. "My lord, you should not be so familiar. We barely know one another."

He gazed long and deliberately into those magnificent violet eyes. "And yet I feel as if I have known you a lifetime."

With his free hand, he cradled her cheek and lowered his lips to hers. Her fingers tightened around his as their mouths touched. He kissed her gently to start and then more firmly, his hand sliding to cup her nape. Then he used his tongue to outline the shape of her lips. She stiffened a bit but he kept the slow, steady motion going, moving along her full, bottom lip back and forth. A whimper escaped and he kissed her again before gliding his tongue along the seam of her mouth. Her lips parted slightly and he swept inside, tasting her sweetness.

Reed explored her thoroughly, leisurely, his heart racing wildly. He told himself to keep it as only a kiss and focused on her mouth. There would be time to explore other places on her. He knew he couldn't push too far or too fast or he would chase her away. Like a turtle, Vanessa would withdraw into her protective shell and be too frightened to come out.

Finally, he broke the kiss and let his heart speak.

"You are the one for me, Vanessa. You will have to decide if I am the one for you. Don't answer me now. It would be unfair to you to say yes. You never came out into Polite Society. You need to mix in it a bit, starting with this house party, and to know the bachelors who will attend it."

She gazed at him, dazed, unspeaking.

Reed kissed her again deeply, his hands framing her face, wanting so much of this woman. She wriggled a bit, her breasts brushing against his chest, lighting a fire within him.

Breaking the kiss, he told her, "When you know your mind, share your thoughts with me. I won't hover around you during the next week but know that I will always be nearby, watching and waiting if you need me."

He hoped he hadn't overwhelmed her but he wanted her to know going into this event that he had deep feelings for her.

"You say ... you believe ... that we are meant to be?" she asked, doubt in both her eyes and tone.

"I wanted you to know of my intentions going into this house party," he said. "I will fight for you if I need to. You are a diamond of the first water, Vanessa. Others will see your worth as they come to know you, as your new friends have."

She bit her lip, causing desire to flare within him. "I fear you will change your mind when the other ladies arrive. I doubt I will compare favorably to them. I lack in so many areas."

"You should not compare yourself to others. Because no one compares to you," he said, his voice tender. "Vanessa," he said, feeling that saying her name was like a caress.

He bent, touching his lips to hers again, meaning for it only to be a brief kiss and yet he was carried away by his growing feelings. They kissed several minutes, his arms going about her, bringing her close, wishing he did not have to let her go.

Finally, he raised his mouth. "I have done what I needed to do. I hope I have left a lasting impression upon you, especially with the gentlemen who will soon arrive who will wish to steal you away."

She looked so beautiful and yet so unsure. For a moment, he warred within himself, wondering if he was good enough for this fragile creature.

It didn't matter. He had to have her.

She was The One.

Finding his voice, he asked, "Shall I escort you back to the house? It must be close to teatime. You will probably want to change your gown."

An odd look flashed across her face. "What is it?"

Misery filled her eyes. "My wardrobe is so inadequate. I haven't replenished it since the come-out I never made."

Anger simmered through him. He hated what she had suffered. Marriage with a stranger, an older man who wound up ignoring her. No family or friends to support her through several lonely years.

And now she worried how others would view her.

"May I share a secret with you, Vanessa? Men rarely notice what a lady wears. It is only other women who care about those things." He caressed her cheek. "Just be your sweet self. You will garner attention from every single man in attendance."

Reed rose and helped her to her feet. "Think on what I have shared. That is all I ask."

They returned to the house and parted ways. He returned to the library, looking to find a bit of quiet before going to tea, where he found his hosts and two friends.

"Boxling, good of you to join us," Lord Danbury said.

"Did you enjoy your conversation with my duchess?" His Grace asked. "She told me she was meeting with you."

"We did meet. And then I walked in the gardens with Lady Hockley."

"She is a lovely woman," Lord Middlefield said. "My Tessa has taken to her. And Lady Hockley is wonderful with our children. With all of the children in the nursery, actually."

Reed took a deep breath and expelled it slowly. "That is good to hear—because I plan to have several of them with her. I am going to make Lady Hockley my wife."

CHAPTER TEN

V ANESSA PACED HER bedchamber, waiting for it to be time to go down to dinner. Her thoughts were still swirling after everything that had happened in the gardens with Lord Boxling. She stopped and closed her eyes, the sensations running through her again as she imagined his kiss. Kissing was very different from what she had expected. He had started gently again but the length of each kiss had increased, as had the firmness of his lips. And then of all things, he had used his tongue on her!

He was very clever with that tongue.

She had been surprised when he had first used it to touch her lips and then when he had slipped it inside her mouth, it had been heavenly.

One kiss had become another until she was lost in a maze of emotions and sensations. She still doubted that he truly wanted her as his wife. Perhaps he was one of those smooth-talking rogues Mama had warned her about years ago, only wanting to take his pleasure with her and then abandon her.

But Vanessa didn't think so. There was a goodness to him. A tenderness when he called her name. She didn't even know his Christian name, despite the intimacies that had occurred between them. Worse, she kept thinking about how he might actually use his tongue in other places on her.

Where did such wicked thoughts come from?

He claimed to want her. He said he had told her before the other guests arrived so she would be aware of that. Yet he also had promised not to hover too near her in order for her to get to know the other bachelors once they came to Danfield. Was that not gentlemanly? Or was it cleverness on his part, to make her feel desired. Would he dally with her and then turn to another woman Adalyn recommended to him?

She thought the next week was going to be exhilarating. Confusing. A week which might be full of fun and yet agony, if she truly had to make a choice between Lord Boxling and another man. Then the thought occurred to her again that she would not compare to the other women and Lord Boxling would forget his infatuation with her. Surely, what he expressed was his infatuation with her—and not love.

She did have feelings for him, feelings that she wished to explore in more depth. As well as kiss him again. How had she lived this long and not known the wonders of kissing?

She knew she should head to the drawing room. Earlier, she had been fearful of going to tea and seeing him so soon after their stroll in the gardens. She did not have to, however, because the Danfield butler had come and informed Louisa that the gentlemen were tied up on the estate and would not make it to tea. The butler had said they would be home after tea so that none of the fathers would miss time in the nursery with their children, where they went every day once teatime concluded.

Vanessa had thought to take refuge in the nursery but changed her mind, knowing so many others would be there. She had retreated to her room with her thoughts and finally readied herself for dinner. She prepared herself to see Lord Boxling and would do her best to treat him no differently than she had before.

As she entered the drawing room, her eyes darted about and found him to be missing. In fact, only Louisa, Adalyn, and Lord Danbury were present. She joined them and gradually the others appeared, including the viscount. She greeted him the same as she did the others and the entire group talked as one until the butler announced dinner was ready.

She was standing next to the Duke of Camden and he offered to escort her to the dining room. On the way there, he talked a bit about his son, Edwin, and how he was looking forward to the arrival of his other children in November.

"I will admit to you, Lady Hockley, I am a bit concerned about Addie," he shared. "The midwife believes she carries twins and I see how large she has become. Would you be my eyes and ears when I am not around and the ladies are involved in their own activities this week? I want to make sure all is well with her and she's not overtaxing herself."

"I can do that for you, Your Grace," Vanessa told him. "Adalyn has been wonderful to me. In fact, all the Three Cousins have been. Her health is of utmost concern to me. I will watch and see that she does not do too much."

"Thank you, my lady," the duke said. "If a time comes when I believe that my wife is attempting too much, I hope you will side with me and make certain she receives the rest she needs."

Once again, dinner was a lively affair, with several stories about the Second Sons as boys and during their university days. It made her wistful, thinking she never had friendships like those at a young age, only the companionship of her governess and her mother. She hoped, though, that her relationship with the women seated at this table would continue beyond the house party. In fact, if she were lucky enough to become betrothed and wed, she would look forward to attending *ton* events next Season, having these three to socialize with. They had spoken fondly of Lady Kingston and the new Duchess of Woodmont and Vanessa hoped she would also be able to claim a friendship with these twins.

The pattern from the previous evening emerged, with the men remaining at the table while the women went to the drawing room and settled in. Louisa then turned to Vanessa and said, "Owen shared something with me that I think the four of us should discuss before our husbands and Lord Boxling arrive."

"Of course, Louisa," she said. "This is your home. You should speak freely with us."

Louisa gave her a winning smile and said, "I hear that Lord Boxling has made his intentions known to you."

Heat filled her cheeks and she became tongue-tied.

Tessa, who sat next to her, patted Vanessa's hand. "Spencer told me the same."

Adalyn smiled triumphantly and said, "Ev told me, as well. Since we all know this, it means Lord Boxling made known his intentions to our husbands. How do you feel about this, Vanessa?"

She found her voice and said, "The viscount did not offer marriage to me in so many words. He did let me know of his interest in me, saying he wanted to do so before the other guests appeared."

"He will offer for you," Tessa said with confidence. "He is being a gentleman, though, and while making his interest known to you, allowing you a bit of freedom to meet the other bachelors invited to Danfield. I think it brilliant on his part."

"You know I think highly of Lord Boxling," Louisa said. "He is right. Keep an open mind as the guests arrive tomorrow and then compare them to Lord Boxling. I think he will come out quite favorably."

Her face still felt flushed and Vanessa said, "I hope it will not be awkward. All of you knowing this."

"No," Tessa said. "In fact, I believe it is a good thing. We love you dearly, Vanessa, and want the best for you. I know your plans had been to leave here and travel to London to seek employment. Now, it looks as if you'll have one offer of marriage—and others could follow."

The men joined them then and Vanessa sat silently as the conversation flowed, feeling Lord Boxling's gaze upon her.

Suddenly, the viscount suggested, "We should have more music this evening. I quite enjoyed hearing Lady Danbury sing and Lady Middlefield play for her last night. I was wondering if

Her Grace or Lady Hockley would care to entertain us this evening."

Adalyn chuckled, waving a hand. "I have never been much for practicing the pianoforte and would find it difficult to even sit at it now. My belly would probably be in the way of my hands trying to reach the keys." She looked to Vanessa and said, "I do believe you play, however. Would you care to do so for us tonight?"

Vanessa reddened, all eyes upon her now. She made a quick decision and said, "While I do play the pianoforte—not as well as Tessa, of course—I am more skilled on the flute."

"The flute?" Lord Middlefield said. "I don't believe I have ever heard a woman play one before. I would enjoy very much if you did so for us, Lady Hockley. Did you happen to bring yours to Danfield?"

"I did, my lord."

"Then we shall send a servant for it," Lord Danbury said, rising to ring for one.

One quickly arrived and Vanessa told her where the flute was located.

"Did you learn the pianoforte before mastering the flute?" His Grace asked her.

"As a girl, I took lessons on the pianoforte," she replied. "I am self-taught on the flute."

"You taught yourself to play an instrument?" Adalyn asked. "How delightful. When did you first take up the instrument?"

Sheepishly, she said, "About a year ago. I had moved to the dower house after my husband's death and decided to explore the attics one rainy afternoon. I found a flute there and brought it downstairs. It was quite a bit of trial and error before I caught on but I found I had a bit of a talent for it."

Her gaze connected with Lord Boxling and he said, "That is quite admirable, Lady Hockley. I know of no one who has taught themself how to play an instrument."

She warmed at his words. "I have only played for myself over these last months and never for a group such as this. I hope you will be kind when you hear my efforts."

"You will be wonderful, I am certain," Louisa stated.

They spoke idly until the maid returned and handed the instrument to Vanessa.

She took it and blew into it, testing notes before she began to play a piece. Then she closed her eyes, nerves flitting through her. She needed to concentrate on the music and try to forget everyone surrounding her.

As always, music filled her soul as she played. She became lost in it and only opened her eyes after she sounded her last note. For a moment, the room was still. Then applause erupted from those present. She accepted her friends' compliments humbly.

"You will have to play for our guests," Lord Danbury said. "That was quiet moving, Lady Hockley."

"All the ladies will be jealous of such a wonderful talent," Adalyn told her. "And the men will fall in love with your playing."

Vanessa lowered her gaze, feeling all of a sudden that everything was too much.

"We should turn in," Louisa suggested. "Tomorrow will be a busy day with all of the arrivals. A good night's sleep will be important and refresh us all."

They rose as a group and she found herself beside Lord Box ling as they filed from the drawing room. Gently, he took her elbow and held her back until the others had left.

"I was moved beyond words," he told her. "It was magical. You displayed such a wide range of emotions through your playing. Parts were whimsical. Mournful. Playful. Adventurous."

"Thank you," she said softly. "I am happy you enjoyed it."

"You made the flute speak for you. It was an enchanting experience listening to you play. You are quite talented, Vanessa. Thank you for sharing this part of you with us."

She wet her lips, words failing her.

He took her hand and slipped it into the crook of his arm and led her from the drawing room to her bedchamber. Pausing in front of the door, he took both her hands in his.

"Tomorrow changes everything with the others arriving. I am thankful I have been able to spend this time with you, Vanessa."

He raised their joined hands and tenderly kissed hers, his gaze never leaving hers.

"Goodnight," he said, his voice husky as he released her hands and turned to leave.

"Wait," she said, unsure why she called him back.

"Yes?"

"I . . . want more," she told him, her voice barely a whisper.

His lips turned up slowly as a smile lit his face and traveled to his eyes. His hands took her shoulders.

"Oh, so do I, Vanessa. Much more."

He lowered his head and his lips touched hers. Fire lit her blood as he kissed her. Her hands went to his coat and clutched his lapels, yanking him closer, their bodies touching, his hard and hot. His hands ran the length of her back, traveling up and down it several times before he wrapped them tightly about her and held her close.

The kiss was demanding. Insistent. She answered it, giving herself over to it. To him. To this moment. It was as if her blood sang in her veins, rushing through her as molten fire.

Finally, he broke the kiss, resting his forehead against hers.

"Goodnight," he said softly and stayed for a moment, no words necessary. Then he lifted his head and released her. "Pleasant dreams, Vanessa."

"What . . . is your name?" she asked breathlessly.

His lips twitched with amusement. "Reed. I am Reed."

"Reed," she echoed softly, liking the way it sounded. Looking up at him, she said, "Goodnight, Reed."

He grinned, looking boyish, and then he seized her once more for a long, powerful, drugging kiss. Breaking it, he stroked her cheek and then turned away.

She watched him move along the hallway, hearing him whistle. Every nerve was alive in her body. Every breath called out his name.

"Reed," she said to herself, feeling very satisfied.

And optimistic.

For what her future—their future together—might hold.

CHAPTER ELEVEN

G UESTS ARRIVED IN waves the next morning and until early afternoon. As the hosts for the next ten days, the Danburys personally greeted each carriage as it arrived. Vanessa's window, which overlooked the front of the house, allowed her to glimpse each of the guests. She had finally gotten names out of Adalyn this morning during breakfast, curious as to who would be at the house party. Fortunately, she memorized names quickly and found herself matching them to the faces that appeared, based upon Adalyn's and Louisa's descriptions.

Tessa told Vanessa that this house party was a little unusual compared to most. While they were often held to bring single people together and encourage the announcement of betrothals, no chaperones would be attending this particular one. Adalyn had been adamant about that, saying that too many pushy mamas forced their daughters to make decisions quickly. She did not want anyone to regret pairing off with someone, whether it was for the duration of the house party or for a more permanent arrangement. Therefore, no parents had been invited. The young women would be chaperoned by the already-present married guests—the Danburys, the Middlefields, and the Camdens.

"Adalyn's standing in Polite Society is great," Tessa explained. "I doubt anyone else would be able to get away with this except her."

Vanessa's friend had joined her and they sat at the window, watching each carriage pull up and its passengers exit their vehicles. With the names committed to memory and Tessa's guidance to remind her of their physical descriptions, Vanessa would be able to acknowledge every guest by name and not be worried after a flurry of introductions if she knew who everyone was.

First to arrive were the ladies. Miss Parsons and Miss Maxwell came together. Miss Parsons had brown hair and brown eyes and was the daughter of a viscount. She liked discussing politics and had a pleasant singing voice. Miss Maxwell's hair was a deep black and she, too, had brown eyes. Tessa said Miss Maxwell was reserved in nature and most likely the most intelligent guest invited, including all the men. Both misses were slightly plump and very pretty.

Lady Jayne Newton was next, a blond with blue eyes and a trim figure. She was a duke's daughter and smart as a whip. Tessa said Lady Jayne liked to flirt. A lot. Hearing that made Vanessa uneasy. The woman was quite beautiful and would naturally be attracted to Reed. It remained to be seen if Reed would also feel an attraction.

Vanessa prayed that would not be the case.

Last of the ladies was Lady Rosalie, with her golden curls and sweet smile. Tessa told Vanessa that Lady Rosalie played the pianoforte beautifully and was perpetually optimistic.

Again, jealousy flared within her as she saw these attractive women make their way into the main house. She knew her lack of confidence was to blame, as well as Reed not giving her a firm offer of marriage. He had claimed she was the one for him and yet doubt still flared within her.

But would he kiss her the way he had last night if he didn't mean for them to be together?

The four bachelors arrived in two carriages which pulled up one after the other, accompanied by a third which held their valets and luggage. Tessa said it was common for bachelors invited to house parties to travel together from London.

The first door opened and Vanessa knew it had to be Viscount Darton since he was the only blond among the group. Lord Darton had an athletic figure and was just under six feet. Adalyn had said he was mischievous as a boy and still so as an adult.

Following him was the Earl of Wakeford. An even six feet, he had brown hair and brown eyes and was known for being quite serious and intelligent.

The pair waited as the second carriage came to a halt and its door was opened for the occupants. First out was the Earl of Jackson, easy to spy because of his reddish-brown hair and boisterous laugh. Louisa had said Lord Jackson was quite funny and utterly charming.

The last of the guests was Viscount Thadford. He had hair black as a raven and blue eyes. Adalyn had said Lord Thadford was the most competitive in the group and would try to win every contest held during the house party. He, too, had an athletic build and was just under six feet.

"What do you think?" Tessa asked as they turned from the window. "Did any of these men leap out at you?"

"They are all rather good-looking," she admitted. "But I have never truly been impressed with looks."

"Unless it is a certain viscount with dark, wavy hair and eyes the shade of melted chocolate?" her friend teased.

Vanessa blushed to her roots. "Lord Boxling is very handsome," she conceded. "But it would take more than good looks to win my heart."

Tessa cocked her head. "Has he won it, Vanessa?"

She bit her lip. "He has definitely stormed the castle walls and wormed his way close."

"It is just the two of us. Do not answer if you are uncomfortable. Has he kissed you?"

Her body grew warm at the thought of Reed's kiss, his arms about her, his hands roaming her back. "Yes," she admitted.

"Was it what you expected?"

"I had never been kissed before so I had no expectations," she confessed. "Remember, I never made my come-out. The things other young ladies experience in a Season are foreign to me." She hesitated and then added, "But if a kissing contest were held? I am certain Lord Boxling would take the top prize."

Tessa laughed aloud and leaned over, giving Vanessa a quick hug. "I thought Spencer quite dashing and his character sterling— but his kiss convinced me that he was the only man for me."

"I am beginning to feel that way about Lord Boxling but I don't understand why he likes me."

Tessa sniffed. "You do not give yourself enough credit, Vanessa. You are kind. Talented. Beautiful. The viscount could do no better than you."

Despite her friend's encouragement, she still worried about how Reed would react to the other women now present. She decided if he were attracted to one of them, there would be nothing she could do. Her heart would break but she would know if one of the ladies turned his head, they were never meant to be in the first place.

"Come to the nursery with me," Tessa urged. "I want to check on Analise and Adam and spend a few minutes with them before the madness begins. Remember, Louisa wants to have all the ladies meet in her parlor at two o'clock so we may have time together before joining the men for tea."

"I would love to accompany you," Vanessa said and they left her room, heading for the stairs to go up to the top floor where the nursery was located.

Much to her surprise, when they reached it, Lord Boxling was there, Analise on his back as he lumbered around on all fours. The toddler had her hands fisted in his hair to keep her on his back.

"Go faster!" she demanded and the viscount loped along, little Edwin toddling after them, crying, "Me! Me!" as he begged for a turn.

As she and Tessa paused in the doorway, her friend turned

and quietly said, "I think all you need to know about Lord Boxling is right here, in this moment."

Tears sprang to her eyes. "I agree," she said softly.

Tessa swept into the nursery and Vanessa followed her. Adam, who was sitting next to Margaret in front of a group of blocks, caught sight of her. He held up his arms. "Mama!"

Sweeping him up, Tessa said, "How are you, my little love?"

He gave her a sloppy kiss in reply.

Vanessa moved next to Margaret and sat beside her. "Are you playing with blocks?"

Margaret, looking very serious, nodded. She picked one up and inspected it and then handed it to Vanessa. By now, Reed had reached the far side of the nursery and turned. Their gazes met and he smiled.

Her heart hammered against her ribs and she mouthed, "Hello."

"Let's give Edwin a turn," he told Analise, easing her fingers from his hair and helping her slip from his back.

"Fun," Analise proclaimed. "I like you."

"I like you," Reed told her as she ran to her mother and hugged Tessa's skirts.

Vanessa watched as Reed moved low to the ground, taking Edwin's hand and helping the boy onto his back. Then he gradually pushed up until he could move on all fours.

"Hang on!" he cried and Edwin grabbed hold of his hair as Analise had.

Reed made another trip the length of the nursery, passing her and Margaret, and saying, "I can give you a ride later if you'd like."

"Are you flirting with me, my lord?" she asked coquettishly, feeling young and free for the first time since her marriage took place.

"I just might be," he replied, continuing to cross the room as Edwin cried, "Go! Go!"

When he reached the far side, the nursery governess lifted up

Edwin. "It is time for Lord Boxling to have a bit of a rest. You children have worn him out."

Reed joined her and Margaret and stacked a few blocks, which Adam knocked over. Tessa had set him down and he went straight for the stack.

"It is his favorite game," Tessa explained. "We call it crashing blocks."

They played with the children several more minutes and then Tessa said, "We should be getting downstairs. Louisa and Adalyn will want you to meet the other ladies."

Reed quickly sprang to his feet and helped Vanessa and Tessa to stand. He held her hand a bit longer than necessary, squeezing her fingers and giving her a smile.

"I will see you at tea, ladies," he told them.

They returned to the staircase and went to Louisa's parlor. Both she and Adalyn were already there, along with all four of the guests.

"There you are," Adalyn said. "We hoped you would be joining us."

"We went to the nursery," Tessa explained. "You know how difficult it is to walk away from adorable children. Come, Lady Hockley. Let us introduce you to everyone."

Adalyn, being the ranking female in the room, did the honors. "I would like to introduce you to my good friend, Lady Hockley. She has been staying with Lady Danbury and agreed to extend her stay so that she might attend this house party."

Taking her time, the duchess made the introductions, telling Vanessa a bit about each woman. She immediately warmed to Lady Rosalie because of her sunny nature.

Miss Parsons asked, "Was Lady Stillwell your mother, by any chance?"

Surprised, Vanessa said, "Yes, she was."

"I remember her calling upon my own mama and taking tea. You favor her quite a bit. How is she? I haven't seen her for many years. Mama died when I was twelve."

"I am sorry for your loss," Vanessa said. "Both my parents have passed on."

"I am sorry to hear that," Miss Parsons said. "But it is a delight to meet you, Lady Hockley."

Miss Maxwell was quieter than the others but she seemed very nice. As for Lady Jayne, the woman was a true beauty and very friendly. Vanessa hoped to make friends with at least some of these women.

They spent a pleasant hour getting to know one another. No one pressed her about not being at recent Seasons when she said she preferred the country. She doubted any of them had encountered Horace the Horrible, who usually made himself scarce inside ballrooms and stuck to the card rooms instead. Lady Jayne and Miss Parsons offered their sympathies when they discovered she was a widow. She accepted their condolences, thinking Horace the Horrible's death was the best thing that had happened to her.

No, meeting Louisa and finding a temporary refuge was.

No—meeting Reed was definitely the best thing that had happened to her.

The ladies adjourned after the butler came in to remind them of the time, telling Louisa the gentlemen had gathered on the terrace.

"I thought we would hold tea outside this afternoon as a way to mark the beginning of the house party," Louisa told her guests.

They all rose and Vanessa noted the four newcomers were two to three inches shorter than she was, making her a bit self-conscious. She cleared her head of her doubts, the ones which told her she was not good enough to be a part of this company and those which whispered in her ear that Reed would soon leave her behind for one of the women she had just met.

Stepping into the sunshine, she paused a moment, allowing it to warm her face. She saw the large group of men separated into three clumps and then noticed the bachelors smoothed out into a single line to make introductions more streamlined.

Lord Danbury joined his wife. "I will allow you to do the honors, my love, since you know the guest list far better than I. Women plan these intricate affairs—and men pay for them," he joked, causing everyone to chuckle.

Vanessa realized how expensive something like a house party must be. The Danburys had invited ten single members of the *ton*, as well as having the Camdens and Middlefields present, along with their children. Everyone but Vanessa had brought lady's maids and the men would all have their valets, not to mention the nursery governesses for the children. With fourteen adults and more than double that number in servants, feeding such a large group for a week and a half would grow expensive. Then there were whatever activities that they might participate in. Hosting this party would cost Lord Danbury a pretty penny.

"Thank you, my darling," Louisa told her husband. "I think it is best to introduce the entire group to one another and then we can split off for more intimate conversations."

Vanessa hoped the pale yellow gown she had chosen would be looked upon favorably by these gentlemen. Despite Reed saying men didn't pay attention to such things as women's fashions, she believed there were some who did.

Louisa had the ladies line up as the gentlemen had and she walked from one to the next, giving their names and sharing a few specifics about them. When she came to Vanessa, her smile broadened.

"And last, this is my wonderful friend, Lady Hockley. She was widowed last year and after having spent her entire marriage in the country, she is eager to make a return to Polite Society. Lady Hockley is fond of fruit tarts. She plays the flute better than any of God's angels. And she is kind and loyal beyond measure. You will appreciate her even more when you make her acquaintance."

Vanessa had to blink away tears at the sweet introduction. Louisa took her hand and squeezed it briefly before heading to where the men stood. Again, she went down the line, introducing the men by their rank and titles, and telling a few things about them. Viscount Darton enjoyed boxing. Lord Wakeford was interested in archaeology. Lord Jackson enjoyed racing. Viscount Thadford liked rowing and fencing.

"Tea is now served," Louisa said airily. "I've had tables of four set out. Take any seat you choose, but let us have two ladies and two gentlemen to a table. We will try and rotate after half an hour so you might get to know others."

Vanessa didn't know if she should immediately go to a table and hope others would join her or if she should hang back and wait for an open spot. In the end, it was decided for her—by Lord Thadford.

The handsome, dark-haired viscount made a beeline toward her. "Lady Hockley, would you care to join me at a table?" His smile was dazzling as he added, "And I refuse to take no for an answer."

Taking her hand, he placed it on his sleeve and led her to the closest table. Soon, they were joined by Lady Jayne and Lord Wakeford.

And so the house party began.

CHAPTER TWELVE

R EED WAS IN a foul mood as Dall dressed him for the evening.
He regretted having told Vanessa he would give her
some space during the house party. Instead, he wanted to cover
her like a blanket and hide her from the others.

Tea, for him, had been a disaster. For her, however, he
watched her blossom as she began to come into her own. For a
moment, he wondered what kind of woman she would have
come to be had she had the typical Season and wed someone after
it ended.

He had watched the four bachelors as introductions were
being made, since he had no interest in any of the women
present. He thought Lord Thadford and Lord Jackson to be the
most interested in Vanessa and he had been proven correct about
Thadford, who had immediately gone to Vanessa and asked her
to sit at his table for the first round of tea.

It was a clever idea of Lady Danbury's to move her guests
around and she did so each half-hour until all had been able to sit
with one another and learn a bit more about each other.

For his part, Reed hung back as the others took their seats.
Finally, he stepped to Lady Rosalie, a pretty blond with a sweet
smile. He had asked her to join him and since two of the tables
were occupied by the other eight Danbury single guests, he had
seated her with the Duke and Duchess of Camden. Lady Rosalie

had appeared to be slightly intimated at first but, if anything, the duke and duchess quickly put her at ease and Reed believed she enjoyed the first round of tea and talk. He did his best to be a good guest and asked a few questions of her, answering hers in return.

When Lord Danbury asked for them to switch around, they did and Reed found himself at a table with Vanessa, Miss Parsons, and Lord Jackson. Vanessa's cheeks were already flushed with excitement and no shyness was ready as the four of them spent a lively time. Then it was time to switch again and reluctantly he left her, giving surreptitious glances to the table she moved to. By the time tea ended, Reed knew he was in trouble. It seemed of the five women present, Vanessa and Lady Jayne would prove to be the most popular. It did not surprise him. Miss Maxwell was very reserved and Miss Parsons, obviously a bluestocking. Lady Rosalie seemed a bit immature. It was going to take every bit of self-discipline he had to keep from sweeping in and carrying Vanessa away. He knew, though, that it was important not only for her to socialize with others close to her own age but gain a bit of confidence and polish in the process. He had meant what he had told Her Grace—that Vanessa must believe in herself before she committed to a relationship with him.

Or anyone else.

That is what Reed worried about. Despite the kisses they had shared and his growing feelings for her, he was frantic that she would find one of these other bachelors more appealing to her than him. Though he was handsome, affable, and carefree and women adored him, he had been on this side of the coin, losing out on Louisa. To not be chosen by the woman he now wanted as his viscountess would be a crushing blow. Reed realized, however, that if Vanessa decided she suited with someone else more than she did with him, that he would have to respect her wishes. More than anything, he wanted to see her happy.

It struck him that he was in love with her because her happiness was more important to him than his own. It would crush him to see her go to another but he loved her enough to want the best for her.

Dall finally finished fussing with Reed's cravat and he dismissed the valet. It was time to go downstairs and he did so, making his way to the drawing room. When he entered, he counted ten others already present.

Vanessa was among the missing.

He joined a group consisting of Lady Rosalie, Lady Jayne, the Middlefields, and Lord Wakeford. He had been acquainted with the other four bachelors, having done some sowing of wild oats with both Thadford and Jackson. Of the women present, Lady Jayne was the only one he was familiar with. She had been the darling of this past Season, a vivacious duke's daughter whose striking looks had drawn the eye of every eligible gentleman and most likely many of the married ones, as well. Reed had danced once with Lady Jayne but it had been a lively Scotch reel and so no conversation had been possible at that time. He had dismissed her as simply another featherhead of the *ton*, knowing she would capture the attention of a high-ranking peer and wed quickly. It had surprised him to see her at this house party and he believed she must have been one of the women holding out for a duke, the Duke of Woodmont, in particular.

She had proven to be a good conversationalist during their limited time at tea, surprising him, and as he joined this group now, he listened to her tell a story, her storytelling skills on display. If he had not fallen for Vanessa, this woman would certainly have been an interesting candidate for a wife.

Each time he saw movement at the door, he waited to see if it was Vanessa making her entrance. That didn't happen. More and more came and worry filled him. He hoped nothing had gone wrong and that she had not fallen ill. Moments before the butler announced dinner, she entered the drawing room, wearing a gown in a pale shade of blue. Quietly, she joined a group not including him and, moments later, they began pairing up to head to the dining room. Reed found himself escorting Lady Jayne.

"Where is your country estate?" she asked him.

"It is in Kent but practically at the border of Sussex and Kent and Essex. It did not take me all that long to reach Danfield. And what of you, Lady Jayne? Your father must have a good number of estates, being a duke. Where did you spend a majority of your time growing up?"

He listened with half an ear as she spoke and then she fell silent. He looked to her.

"You haven't been listening to me, my lord," she chided gently. "I believe your attention is focused ahead. Perhaps on Lady Hockley?"

"I must apologize, my lady. My attention did wander. That is inexcusable."

She gave him a smile. "No apologies are necessary, my lord. I liked Lady Hockley from the moment I met her this afternoon. If you are interested in her, my advice is to pursue her because I believe she is going to prove to be quite popular at this house party."

"I hope I have not offended you, my lady," he said as they entered the dining room.

She chuckled. "On the contrary, Lord Boxling, I would prefer knowing where I stand with a gentleman. If it is truly Lady Hockley you wish to get to know better, I will aid you in this pursuit."

"You are most generous, Lady Jayne," he told her.

Locating her name card placed before her seat, he helped her to get settled and then found his own card near the center of the table. Reed found himself sitting between the two misses, with Vanessa directly across from him. He watched Lord Jackson seat her and then her gaze met his.

Her smile was only for him, causing his heart to race.

If he had thought the previous dinners with some of the Second Sons and their wives proved interesting, throwing a diverse group into that mix led to even more fascinating conversations. Throughout the many courses, though, he would find himself looking to Vanessa as if they shared some secret. Reed determined to sit with her whatever activity was planned after dinner.

Lord Danbury claimed their attention as the last course ended and said, "My wife has planned for there to be dancing this evening."

Lady Danbury added, "Dancing is always pleasurable and a good way to end our first evening together at Danfield."

Reed only wished someone would be able to play a waltz because he would claim Vanessa for it. The idea of another man's arms about her so intimately caused a frisson of jealousy to filter through him.

"We have some talented people from Blackburn, our local village, who have come to play for us tonight," Lady Danbury said. "Although we are few in number, we will go ahead and move to the ballroom now and be able to enjoy dancing there without the usual crowd."

Though Reed longed to escort Vanessa there, he had no way of getting to her. He knew good manners dictated that he turn to the woman on his right and escort her to the ballroom. He did so, leading Miss Parsons to the ballroom, where he saw a quartet of musicians setting up, tuning their instruments.

Her Grace addressed the group. "There will be a mix of dances and we will only be here for an hour," she told them. "I know some of you are weary after your travel to Danfield and we do have several activities lined up for tomorrow."

She told them what was in store for the next day and, by then, the musicians appeared ready to begin. He continued being a gentleman by asking Miss Parsons to partner with him for the first dance and she agreed. He noticed Lord Jackson, who had brought Vanessa to the ballroom, did the same.

Reed enjoyed dancing but had always found London ballrooms too crowded for his taste. Tonight was different, with their group being less than two dozen, and plenty of room was available to them. They danced a reel, followed by a country dance. He partnered with Lady Jayne on it. By now, two footmen arrived with trays of cold lemonade and he fetched one for himself and Lady Rosalie. He wound up standing with her, along with Vanessa and Lord Thadford. Of all the gentlemen present, he was most worried about Thadford. The viscount was intelligent and outgoing and seemed to have taken a shine to Vanessa.

Knowing he needed to make some kind of move, Reed said, "I have barely seen you since this afternoon's tea, Lady Hockley. Perhaps you might wish to partner with me for the next dance."

A blush tinged her cheeks and she said, "Thank you, Lord Boxling. I would be happy to do so."

Lady Danbury, who had joined their small circle, turned and winked at him. Reed wondered what that meant and watched the countess as she signaled to the musicians, tugging on her right ear. He knew she was up to something and leaned closer.

"Thank you," he said quietly. "For whatever you just did."

Mischief sparkled in her eyes and she whispered, "I will make certain it is a waltz."

They finished their lemonade and footmen collected the empty cups. Their hostess told them the dancing would commence again and Reed moved to Vanessa's side.

"I hear the next dance is to be a waltz," he shared.

Her face lit with a smile and he thought her the most beautiful creature on earth.

"Oh, I love to waltz."

Confusion filled him. "But . . . I thought you shared with me you had never been allowed to dance at *ton* affairs."

She flushed and told him, "I practiced dancing before I made my come-out. Yes, it is true that I was only able to watch the dancers during my only Season, but may I share a secret with you?"

Reed nodded, wondering what she might reveal.

"I dance every day in private. Especially during this past year of widowhood. There was only one scullery maid at the dower house with me and so I would go into the drawing room, close the door, and pretend I partnered with a handsome, young lord. Of course, I have never truly danced with a partner other than my governess, but I have danced with abandon this past year."

She gazed at him intensely. "I look forward to finally having my first true partner tonight."

She wet her lips and Reed exercised self-control. More than anything, he longed to take her in his arms and capture her mouth with his. He could not do that, else she would be ruined. He would have to settle for this waltz with her. A bit of pride ran through him, knowing he had given her her first kiss and now partnered with her in her first waltz. He intended to be her first in many other things—and her last, as well.

The Duchess of Camden said, "If you will find a partner, it is to be a waltz. We will do a few more dances after this one."

Reed offered Vanessa his arm and led her to the center of the vast ballroom. He didn't bother to see who else had partnered up, his sole focus on this lovely woman before him.

He took her hand in his and placed the other on her back, stepping close so that he could feel the heat of her body. Once again, he smelled her clean scent and reveled in it. He noticed she wore no jewelry and decided when they wed, he would shower her with both perfume and jewels.

The strains of the waltz began and he stepped off with her. Dancing had come naturally to him and he saw the same was true of Vanessa. They moved together like flowing water, fluid as they turned and whirled as one.

It was the most exhilarating dance of his life.

When the music came to a close, Reed reluctantly let his arms fall from her. She gazed at him with such happiness that he knew that happiness was reflected in his own eyes.

"Thank you," she said earnestly. "Dancing that waltz with you was like every dream I have ever had coming true. I feel a bit like Cinderella, the girl from the French fairy tale. My governess used to read it to me. I would daydream about attending a ball and dancing with and marrying a handsome prince." She blushed.

"I am sorry. I did not mean to imply—"

"I may not have formally asked for your hand, Vanessa, but I have told you that you hold my heart," he replied, letting the meaning of his words wash over her. "I am doing my best to let you mingle with the other bachelors here without interfering but I am rather annoyed by the attention you are receiving from them."

A slow smile turned up the corners of her mouth. "You are irritated by that?"

"Yes," he said gruffly. "In fact, I may have to whisk you off to some dark corner and kiss you again to remind you of my feelings for you." He paused and then added, "I want you to follow your heart, Vanessa. Whether it leads you back to me at the end of this house party or to another man."

Her eyes grew large. "And if I return to you?"

"Then we can plan the date of our marriage."

He saw hope fill her eyes—and what he believed was love.

"Let us rejoin the others," he said, leading her toward the other guests who were assembling for a cotillion.

Reed saw Lord Darton eyeing them as they approached. Vanessa joined the line of women and he the line of men. After two more dances, he had partnered with all five women present and Her Grace declared the evening to be at an end.

He said his goodnights to those present and watched Vanessa as she joined the group of single ladies, who exited the ballroom as a group.

Lord Darton walked out with Reed and said, "You and Lady Hockley performed the waltz quite well together. Have you danced often with her? I cannot recall you being at many *ton* events, Boxling, and I don't ever remember seeing her at one."

"It was our first time to dance together," he said guardedly, wondering the direction of their conversation. "I only attended the first two weeks of this past Season. From what I understand, Lady Hockley was still in mourning at the time. Her Grace told me that this house party is the first outing for Lady Hockley since her mourning period ended."

Darton sighed. "Well, she is quite attractive. I can see you are smitten with her and wanted to tell you I won't stand in your way. But if I were you? I would keep a careful eye on Thadford. I heard him telling Wakeford to stand down where Lady Hockley was concerned."

"Thank you for sharing that," Reed said, his fears about his old friend confirmed.

Tomorrow, he would have a talk with Viscount Thadford—and make it perfectly clear that he planned to wed Vanessa once this house party concluded.

CHAPTER THIRTEEN

V ANESSA AWAKENED EARLY, surprised at how deeply she had slept. Her dreams had been vivid.

And all centered around Reed.

Perhaps that is why she fell asleep so easily, knowing her future was now secure. There would be no traveling to London and locating an employment agency. No waiting to be paired with an employer, praying for the right position. She wouldn't have to travel from family to family, as positions came to a close and new ones were sought out.

Instead, she would become Viscountess Boxling, wed to the most handsome man in London Society. Oh, she realized Reed had far more depth. It wasn't just his looks she was attracted to. He was honorable, intelligent, and perpetually cheerful. She was eager to learn everything she could about him. Vanessa couldn't wait to meet the niece and nephew who had captured his heart and also wished to get to know his young half-sisters.

It still amazed her how much her life had changed—and for the better—ever since she had met Louisa at Horace the Horrible's gravesite. If Louisa had not stopped and asked Vanessa to come home with her, then she never would have been introduced to Reed.

The man she was falling in love with.

She had been telling the truth when she'd told him she felt

like Cinderella. Yes, she had always imagined herself dancing at a ball with a handsome prince. Last night in Reed's arms showed her reality could be far better than any fairy tale. Again, she had to thank Louisa for taking her in when Vanessa was at her lowest point. Perhaps they could name their first daughter after her friend. After all, Reed thought quite highly of Louisa. It was a beautiful name.

She basked in the idea of holding Reed's babes in her arms. Of him sitting with her, even holding them himself. She had already seen him in the nursery and knew he would enjoy playing with their children. Vanessa prayed she would be able to give him many of them. Filling Boxwell Hall with the sounds of children laughing and playing would be a dream come true as she watched over these children with the best man she had ever known.

Of course, she wouldn't say anything to the other guests at the house party regarding his plan to make her his wife. At some point, she would have to get the Three Cousins alone and share it with them, though. They would be so happy for her. All three thought highly of Reed and she could see the two of them joining the social circle of her friends.

Her future had never looked brighter.

She rang for a maid and washed as she waited for one to appear. Once she was ready, Vanessa went downstairs. Louisa had told everyone a buffet would be set up each morning in the breakfast room beginning at nine and concluding at ten-thirty. The room had numerous windows and faced the east, allowing a good deal of the morning light to pour through its windows. Since it seated twenty-four, it had enough space to accommodate everyone at Danfield. Louisa had also said breakfast could be brought to bedchambers if that was preferred. Vanessa doubted anyone other than Adalyn would choose to eat upstairs. Her friend said it took her extra time to get moving in the morning as she continued to increase and she preferred eating in her bedchamber as she took her time in getting ready. The Duke of Camden was downstairs, though, at the beginning of the buffet and she joined him.

He handed her his plate and took another for himself. "Did you enjoy the first day of the house party?"

"Very much so, Your Grace," Vanessa replied. "I have a knack for remembering names and am already familiar with all the guests. I thought serving tea outside on the terrace was a nice touch and the dancing was a nice way to break the ice and get us all involved with one another."

He smiled as he spooned eggs onto his plate. "My Addie knows people. She and Louisa have worked hard at planning a variety of events for each day so that no two days look alike."

"How is she feeling this morning?"

"Huge. Her words, not mine," he explained as he set a rasher of bacon on his plate. "We had no idea she might have twins. They don't run on either side of our families. The midwife told me—and Addie's doctor agreed—that she might have to take a long rest in bed the last month or more."

"Oh, she will dislike that," Vanessa said. "I haven't known her long at all but she is always in motion."

"If I have to lock our bedchamber door and block the way, I will make certain she stays in bed."

His words surprised her. It led her to believe the pair shared a bedchamber. Her parents had not done so and Mama had told her it would not be expected. She and Horace the Horrible had separate chambers, for which she had been grateful.

"I see you look a bit surprised," the duke said as they reached the end of the buffet. "Yes, Addie and I sleep together each night. Not many couples of the *ton* do. She only uses her rooms to dress and bathe. I would not have it any other way. The last thing I want to know before I fall asleep is that I hold the woman I adore in my arms. I also want to wake next to her each day and have my duchess be the first thing I see."

She smiled. "You ae quite the romantic, Your Grace."

He grinned. "I am, aren't I?" He glanced over her shoulder and then his gaze met hers. "And if I am not mistaken, you have a good man interested in you who is most likely the exact same way."

Looking over her shoulder, she saw Reed had entered the breakfast room. "Lord Boxling is very nice," she said, biting back her smile.

The duke chuckled as he led her toward the table. "Boxling was quite adamant that he intends to wed you, my lady. I believe he is already in love with you."

Her cheeks stung with heat and she quickly took her seat, busying herself with placing her napkin in her lap and then concentrating on buttering her toast points and doctoring the tea a footman brought to her. When she finished, she glanced up and saw mirth in the duke's eyes.

"May I sit with you?" a deep voice said and she looked up, seeing Viscount Thadford standing there.

"Please join us, my lord," she told him, wishing it had been Reed instead. The breakfast room had four large, round tables which seated six apiece and Lord Thadford now took the last open spot.

Miss Maxwell turned to Vanessa. "Are you going riding this morning, Lady Hockley?"

"Yes, I enjoy riding very much. Will you do so?"

The woman shook her head. "I had a bad experience on a horse years ago and have never gotten into the saddle again. I think I will stay here and write a few letters. I was hoping you might join me in the parlor to do so."

She liked Miss Maxwell and said, "Perhaps we can spend some time together after the ride. I would like that."

"So would I."

Vanessa finished her breakfast quickly. She never ate much in the morning, not being particularly hungry, and only ate toast and tea. She remained at the table, however, enjoying the conversation. His Grace and Lord Thadford discussed a recent bill passed in Parliament and Miss Maxwell chimed in, totally disagreeing with both of them regarding the bill's potential.

Having had no access to newspapers during her years in the country, Vanessa felt woefully out of touch with current events and listened carefully, gleaning what she could.

Lord Danbury said they would leave the stables at eleven, which was in an hour, and anyone wishing to ride should be there earlier in order to find a horse and be in the saddle. It was only then that she realized she was the only one who had worn her riding habit to the breakfast table and supposed that had been a faux pas on her part. It seemed a waste to wear a gown to breakfast only to change from it and discard it for the rest of the day.

All of the women left, whether to go and change into their riding habits or, like Miss Maxwell, go to the parlor to talk or write letters. Vanessa decided to go ahead to the stables, hoping she could ride the same horse she had when she had taken a tour of Danfield.

"Are you ready for the stables, my lady?" Viscount Thadford asked. "I can escort you there now if you wish."

"Yes, thank you," she said and they left the table, Reed's eyes upon them.

She liked that he watched her. And that he looked away as they passed.

Because she had seen the twinge of jealousy in his eyes.

Oh, she didn't want him to be miserable. Far from it. It was simply a wonderful feeling to know this incredible man wanted her and was a bit miffed that she was in the company of a handsome lord. Vanessa would make sure to steal a few moments alone with him later today and let him know that he was all she could think about. How much she needed him. How much she wanted his kiss.

As they made their way to the stables, Lord Thadford asked, "Might I ask a personal question of you, Lady Hockley?"

Unsure where this might lead, she responded, "How personal, my lord?"

"I wondered if you are interested in having children," he said bluntly.

"I very much would like to have children. Several, if at all possible," she answered honestly.

"I am of a like mind," he told her. "Oh, I will admit that it has taken me time to arrive at that conclusion. I had not given marriage—much less children—much of a thought until I came into my title last year. I inherited it from an uncle, who was my father's older brother. He never had any of his own and I knew I would one day be his heir. He served as a father-figure to me since my own father died when I was only five years of age. My uncle saw to my education and allowed me to run a bit wild as a young man." He paused. "Most of that was done with Lord Boxling. We have spent many a time deep in our cups or in gaming hells."

This struck her as odd. Reed seemed so responsible to her. She hadn't pictured him as being irresponsible but perhaps he had been before his father's death.

"You seem disappointed," the viscount said.

"I suppose it is a rite of passage for men to do such things before they decide to settle down," she said. "From what I know of my brother, he has spent more than enough time in gaming hells."

"Who might your brother be?" he asked, curiosity in his tone.

Regretting that she had said anything, she said stiffly, "Lord Stillwell. We are estranged, however. I have not spoken to him since shortly after my marriage when I was nineteen."

The viscount whistled low. "Stillwell, you say? It's a good thing you do not communicate with him. From what I gather, he owes every merchant in town and has racked up numerous gaming debts."

"Gambling is what led to our estrangement," she said. "I would rather not speak anymore of Stillwell, my lord."

"I can certainly understand why."

They reached the stables and she asked the groom that met them if she could have Moonlight saddled for her morning ride.

"Of course, my lady. And for you, my lord?"

"Might I stroll through the stables and see which horses are available?" Lord Thadford asked.

"Of course, my lord," the groom replied.

"Do you know much about horses?" he asked her.

"I ride frequently but I don't know anything more than the next person," she told him.

"Come with me as I look for a mount."

"All right."

They entered the stables and the groom pointed to the left. "You might want to look down that way, my lord. Once you hit the end, turn left. I think you'll like the horseflesh you see there."

"Thank you," Lord Thadford said and slipped Vanessa's hand through the crook of his arm.

She found no excitement rushing through her at his touch, another indication that Reed was for her.

They went to the end and moved to the left, pausing at three stalls and admiring the horses within. Vanessa reached up and stroked the nose of the last one, telling him, "You are a beauty, my friend."

Then suddenly, the viscount's hands were on her waist and he pulled her toward him. Before she could protest, his lips were against hers, kissing her. Again, she felt absolutely nothing and simply waited for him to finish.

He broke the kiss and gazed deeply into her eyes. "You were wed before. Did you enjoy kissing your husband, my lady?"

Vanessa frowned. "That is a very personal question, my lord." One she had no interest in answering.

His hands remained on her waist. "You did not respond to my kiss. Are you still in love with the memory of a dead man?"

Frowning, she tried to pull away but his fingers tightened on her waist. "I wish to leave," she told him. "Now."

"Give me another chance," he said, lowering his lips to hers once more.

This time, he kissed her more firmly and she started to protest. That only gave him the access he wished for and his tongue slipped inside her mouth. Kissing him felt entirely wrong. In that moment, any doubts she had about Reed fled. Whether they wed or not, Reed would always be the only man for her.

She brought her hands to the viscount's hard chest and pushed as she turned her head away, breaking the kiss.

When a moment had passed, she turned back to look him in the eye. "I do not seek a friendship—or anything beyond that—with you, my lord," she said firmly. "Please be so good as to release me."

He sighed. "I feared as much. It's Boxling, isn't it?"

Before Vanessa could reply, the viscount was ripped away from her and she heard a growl and saw a blur as a fist smashed into his face. Lord Thadford crumpled to the ground.

She looked up and saw Reed glowering down at the man.

"Oh, dear," she mumbled, afraid she would have to step in and keep Reed from beating this man to a pulp.

Then of all things, Lord Thadford began to laugh. Loudly.

And Reed joined in.

Thoroughly puzzled, Vanessa watched as Reed reached out a hand and Lord Thadford took it, being pulled to his feet. Already, one side of his face looked to be swelling.

"You really want this one, don't you, old friend?" Lord Thadford said.

"More than I can ever say," Reed said.

Lord Thadford dusted himself off and looked to her. "My lady, you will have to work hard to keep this one in line." He smiled. "But in the long run, I believe he will be worth the effort you put into him. Now, if you will excuse me, I need to see about putting a cold compress on my cheek and eye." Looking to Reed, he added, "I believe I was bloody clumsy and tripped in the stables."

"And smashed into a stall." Reed shook his head. "Terrible thing to do."

Lord Thadford shrugged. "I hope I will be invited to the

wedding, Boxling."

"Count on it, Thadford."

She watched as Lord Thadford strolled away, as if he hadn't a care in the world.

Turning to face Reed, she asked, "What on earth was that all about?"

He yanked her to him, causing her to go breathless, his hands spanning her waist. "You," he said. "Thadford and I go back a ways."

"To your days of sowing wild oats?" Vanessa asked.

He gave her a sheepish grin. "Yes. He mentioned that?"

"He did," she confirmed.

"Well, the oats have been sown and settled nicely. It seems both Thadford and I have settled down and are ready for brides and children." His thumbs slowly moved back and forth, causing a frisson of pleasure to run through her. "And now he knows I have staked my claim. He won't bother you again, sweetheart."

She liked being called sweetheart, hearing it in his low, tender rasp.

"Did he kiss you?" Reed asked, looking at her imploringly.

"He did." Deliberately, she added nothing else.

"And?" he finally asked, breaking the silence.

"And nothing," she told him. "I felt absolutely nothing."

Reed grinned. "So, your heart did not race? Butterflies did not explode within your belly? Your breath did not catch?"

She grinned back. "None of the above."

"Good."

He slipped his arms around her, pulling her into his embrace as his mouth crashed down on hers.

CHAPTER FOURTEEN

REED HAD KNOWN Thadford would make a move on Vanessa and hadn't been able to stop himself from following them to the stables. He had been delayed by a stable hand in the yard who asked him a few questions. By the time he wound through the stables, he had seen Thadford kissing Vanessa and only saw red as his anger boiled over.

He couldn't blame his friend. Vanessa was easily the most attractive woman at the house party and Thadford was, like Reed, ready to settle down and start a family.

But she was his—and it was time the world knew it.

There was nothing gentle about the kiss they shared. It was a brutal kiss, one marking her as his, branding her as the woman he wanted above all others. She clung to him, matching him in the war of tongues, as he made her his.

When he finally broke the kiss, his heart beat so fast it slammed against his ribs.

"You are mine," he said. "I thought I could give you the freedom to flirt with the other men present. Laugh a little with them. Have a bit of fun." He shook his head. "I can't. I don't want you to want them. I want you to want *me*."

"I do," Vanessa said breathlessly. "I just find it hard you want me as much as I do you."

Her words heated his blood and his lips found hers again.

They kissed for a long time and everything about the kiss told Reed he had come home. He had kissed his fair share of women from the time the wisps of hair tickled just above his upper lip. None held a candle to Vanessa. She was an incandescent beauty, both inside and out.

He broke the kiss. "I told Her Grace I wanted you to find who you are. That you needed to believe in yourself before I thought you could believe in the idea of the two of us. But I realize now that I believe in you—and us—and that is enough. I love you, Vanessa. Oh, God, I can barely begin to understand how very much I do love you. And I know my steadfast love will give you the assurance you need. I have already witnessed you blossoming these past few days. I see so much potential ahead for you."

He framed her face in his hands. "Tell me that you can learn to love me."

"I already do, Reed. You are correct in observing that I lack in confidence. I think in truth it is mostly a lack of experience. I led a quiet life as a child and a secluded one as an adult. This past week being at Danfield, making friends, seeing I have worth, has helped me to have faith in myself." She smiled. "I can only see that growing, thanks to you. To know that I have your love—your support—makes me feel as if I can move mountains. Horace the Horrible took a young, naïve girl and berated her so that she had no belief in herself.

"But you have made me see myself in a different light, Reed. You have allowed me to see the potential within me. For that, I will be forever grateful."

Vanessa smiled at him, a smile so genuine that he felt ten feet tall.

"And I know it seems impossible, but love for you has already filled my heart. It will only grow as the days and weeks and years go by and we build a family together."

She tugged on his coat, bringing his lips to hers. They shared a tender, sweet kiss, one sealing the bond between them. Reed knew their future together would be bright and full of endless love and devotion.

He broke the kiss and pressed his lips to her forehead. "When might we tell the others? That is, if Thadford hasn't already let the cat out of the bag."

She thought a moment. "Not everyone will be riding this morning. We should tell the group. Actually, I would like to tell the Three Cousins first."

"I had already told the three Second Sons I intended to wed you," he admitted. "Perhaps as our host, we might allow Lord and Lady Danbury to make the announcement at dinner this evening."

"That would be lovely," she agreed.

"How soon would you wish to wed?" he asked. "I am happy to go to London and obtain a special license for us."

"You would do that?"

Reed smiled, kissing the tip of her nose. "I would do anything for you, Vanessa. Do you have a preference on where you would wish to wed?"

"No. I have no family. I don't consider Stillwell kin anymore. He hasn't spoken to or seen me in years. I have no intention of informing him of our upcoming marriage."

"I would like Constance and the girls present, as well as my sister and her family," he told her. "We could see if they could come here and we could wed at Danfield. I know you would want Her Grace at the wedding. As large as she's grown, I doubt His Grace would wish her to travel to Boxwell Hall, even though it is only a few hours away."

Her palm touched his cheek, bringing a delicious warmth to him. "That sounds perfect. I will ask Louisa about it when I tell her and the others."

"I will write to Constance and Pamela once this morning's ride is over and dispatch the messages to them. Or perhaps I should wait until we firm things up with Lord and Lady Danbury."

"We should ask to speak with Lord Danbury once we finish

our ride," she said.

"I agree." He kissed her again. "Others should be arriving soon. I suppose I need to choose a mount. Have you done so?"

"Yes, I told a groom of my choice. I rode Moonlight the other day when the four of us went out and was comfortable on her."

He slipped an arm about her waist. "I cannot wait to buy you your own horse. I want to shower you with clothes and jewels and everything good in life."

"I don't need anything but you, Reed," she said. You are the good in my life."

"If you don't stop saying things such as that and looking so delectable, there won't be a morning ride."

A shadow crossed her face and it made him wonder again about how Lord Hockley had treated her.

He touched his fingers to her cheek. "You know you will always be safe with me, don't you?"

She nodded. "I do."

"Good."

He heard voices and they returned to the front of the stables, where he asked a groom to ready the horse he had ridden previously. Soon, others had gathered and grooms were bringing out saddled horses.

"Let me say a word to Lord Danbury," he said. "In fact, he is with Lady Danbury now. We should take them aside now."

Reed led Vanessa to their hosts and said, "Might we have a private word with you?"

He saw understanding flash in the earl's eyes. "Of course, Boxling."

The four of them moved away from the others who were gathering for the ride and Reed said, "Vanessa has agreed to marry me."

Lady Danbury squeaked and took her friend's hand. "Oh, I knew this would happen but I didn't know it would occur so soon."

"Naturally, we would wish for the two of you to be present at the ceremony and also wish for Her Grace to attend. In her present condition, she would not be able to travel far, however."

"You're right about that," Danbury said. "Ev is already hovering over her like a protective mother hen." He paused. "You should hold the ceremony here."

"That is what we hoped for," Reed answered. "I would like to have my sister and her family attend, as well as my stepmother and her two daughters." He grinned. "Both Camilla and Nicola—and even my niece—all were assuming I would become engaged by the end of this house party. They will be pleasantly surprised that a wedding will take place at it."

"How soon do you wish to wed?" Louisa asked. "We will need to get word to your relatives and give them time to arrive, as well as make preparations here at Danfield."

"And you'll need a special license," Lord Danbury reminded. "I would see to that immediately. Why don't you take my carriage today into London since yours returned to Boxwell Hall? Go now."

"That is most generous of you, my lord," he said. "I think I will go write to my family quickly and if you could have those notes delivered for me, I would appreciate it."

"Tell them to come as soon as they can," Lady Danbury said. "Vanessa, we should skip this morning's ride and start on wedding plans. Tessa was keeping Adalyn company this morning while we were going to be out. You know Adalyn will want a say in the festivities."

"Vanessa and I discussed having you make the announcement at dinner this evening, my lord," Reed said.

"I can do so." Lord Danbury glanced around. "I think everyone is here. I'll take care of the ride, my love. You start handling everything else."

Reed returned to the house with Vanessa and Lady Danbury. They parted from him and he went to his room, writing brief letters to Pamela and Constance, announcing his engagement and telling them he would be marrying at Danfield as soon as possible, urging them to come as soon as they could.

Taking the letters to the butler, he asked they be delivered at once. He left for the stables and found the Danbury carriage already waiting for him.

"Good morning, Lord Boxling," the coachman greeted. "I hear we have a trip to Doctors' Commons this morning. If you will board the carriage, I will have you in London in no time. We will see that you get your special license and then stop at his lordship's London townhouse and trade out the horses before we return to Danfield. I will have you back here by teatime today, my lord."

"Thank you," he said, climbing into the carriage.

The trip to London went quickly. To save time, the coachman dropped Reed at Doctors' Commons and went to the Danbury townhouse to handle the switch in horses.

It took him just under two hours to complete the business at hand. Seeing his name and Vanessa's scrawled onto the special license brought a special thrill. Yes, he had wanted to trust in the Duchess of Camden and leave the house party betrothed. Secretly, he hoped it would be a love match but had known he couldn't insist upon it. Instead, he would actually be married by the time the house party concluded.

And to a woman he found himself loving more by the minute.

As he returned to Essex and Danfield, Reed fantasized about all the things he wished to do with Vanessa in their marriage bed. He still believed she had experienced some unpleasantness in that regard with Horace the Horrible. He chuckled. Even he was thinking of the dead Lord Hockley as Horace the Horrible. Vanessa would not have hung such a moniker on her husband if he had not been deserving of that nickname. Because of it, he knew he would have to temper his passion and go slowly with her. If what occurred in lovemaking frightened her, he did not want her hiding those feelings from him. He wanted to share with her all the beauty of it. If Hockley had been too rough with her, he would be gentle. He doubted the older man had ever thought to pleasure his young wife, only himself.

Vanessa had learned to respond to Reed's kisses. He knew her to have a passionate nature which she had yet to understand. He planned to liberate her from her past and the poor experiences she had undergone. He would love her completely, always making certain she was taken care of before he was. Reed had thought himself to be an unselfish lover in the past but it would be even more important to continue to be so now and in the future. Slowly, he would help his beloved to relax and fully partake in every aspect of lovemaking. Until then, he would see that her satisfaction came above all else.

True to his word, the coachman had him back at Danfield about half an hour before tea was to be served. He was glad he returned from London when he did because the skies darkened above him as he stepped from the carriage and thanked the driver.

"My pleasure, my lord. And may I offer my congratulations to you?"

Reed grinned. "You may."

"A trip to Doctors' Commons can mean one of two things—a wedding needs to occur quickly to quell any gossip—or a gentleman cannot wait the three weeks for the banns to be read because he is so in love with the woman he is making his wife." The coachman smiled. "I can tell it's the latter with you and Lady Hockley. The staff adores her. She is kind and full of gratitude for the smallest task they perform for her."

"Lady Hockley will make for an excellent viscountess," he said and left the stable area to return to the house just as the first droplets of rain began to pelt him.

As he entered the foyer, he was greeted by the butler, who told him tea would be held in the drawing room due to the weather.

"Lord Danbury is in his study and wishes to speak with you, my lord," the butler added.

"Then I will go straightaway to him."

When he reached the study, he rapped on the door and heard a voice call, "Come." Entering, Reed found Danbury, Middlefield, and His Grace within. The bond between these Second Sons seemed tight.

"Ah, Boxling. Do come in," his host said. "Perhaps since you are now here, we might partake in a celebratory drink. You have nothing to tell. I am afraid I've been as much a gossip as a fishwife and these two already know of your plans."

The duke offered his hand to shake, as did Lord Middlefield.

"Can't say I am surprised," His Grace said. "My Addie has a talent for placing couples together. She told me the moment she left you and Lady Hockley alone that first afternoon that you were a perfect match. She went straight from your meeting to the nursery, where she found me, and proclaimed the house party would already be a success because the first couple had been thrown together and took to one another like ducks to water."

"I knew she deliberately left us alone," Reed said. "But she actually knew from that short meeting that we would suit so well?"

"She did," His Grace confirmed. "I shared that with these two and we have all been watching you and Lady Hockley like hawks. It seems Addie was right, as usual."

"Tessa and I couldn't be more pleased for you," Lord Middlefield said. "My wife is an excellent judge of character and she thought highly of Lady Hockley from the moment they met."

"Louisa felt the same," Lord Danbury added. "You might as well get used to seeing us frequently, Boxling. With our wives all being close friends, you will be thrown together with the Second Sons frequently. That will include Lord Kingston and the Duke of Woodmont, two cousins who are dear friends of ours. It is too bad you were your father's heir and not a spare as the rest of us were. I suppose we can make you an honorary Second Son."

"Actually, I was the spare," he revealed, sharing with them the story of his older brother dying when Reed was two.

"Then that settles it," Lord Danbury declared. "There will be no honorary to your membership in our elite, self-created club. You *are* a Second Son."

Touched, he said, "I am honored to be among such a group of honorable men. I realize I am riding the coattails of my future viscountess and it is she who is granting me entrance into such an esteemed band of brothers."

"Good Lord, Boxling is quoting Shakespeare to us now," His Grace said. "I believe *band of brothers* is from Henry V?"

"It is, Your Grace," Reed replied, "I have always been fond of Shakespeare."

"Well, if you are going to be a true Second Son, then you must act like a Second Son. I am Ev," the duke said. "This is Spence and Owen."

"I am Reed—and very happy to be your friend."

Vanessa had already brought a richness to his life. Now, he added these fine men to a select group who called themselves friends.

Reed couldn't wait to share this news with her, as well as tell all the house guests they were betrothed.

CHAPTER FIFTEEN

V ANESSA AWOKE FEELING refreshed. Yesterday before tea, Lord Danbury had asked if he could announce her betrothal to Reed during teatime, telling her that the secret couldn't stay that way for much longer, with her fiancé having been gone most of the day, causing people to talk. The servants were doing the same since the earl had sent messengers to both Boxwell Hall to inform Reed's stepmother of the news and also to his sister. She had agreed as long as Reed was present.

When he returned before tea began, she quickly told him what was planned and he agreed the sooner they spoke of it, it would allow the others to pair up. They had received many congratulations and she believed everyone present was truly happy for them. When asked when the wedding might occur, Reed informed them it would take place sometime during the house party. He was merely waiting for word of when his family would arrive so they would know how to proceed.

After dinner, they remained inside since the rain had not let up since it began late afternoon. They played indoor games, such as spilikins, charades, and several word games. Some had been men against the women, while others had teamed up and challenged another group. The evening had been most enjoyable and ended perfectly, with her fiancé escorting her to her bedchamber and giving her a tender goodnight kiss.

She rang for a maid, who brought hot water, and readied herself for the day. Louisa had told them they would attend a picnic, which would include archery. Since she had never held a bow and arrow, Vanessa didn't know if she would sit out the competition or not.

Going down to the breakfast buffet, she joined the Three Cousins.

"I don't know if Lord Boxling has told you," Louisa began, "but I did receive word from both his sister and stepmother. They will arrive separately sometime tomorrow afternoon. I think the next day might be too soon to hold the wedding ceremony. What do you think of the day following it? That would be Saturday."

For a moment, she lost the ability to speak. The idea of being wed in three days' time was a bit overwhelming. Then she found her voice, knowing it meant she would be starting the rest of her life with the man she loved.

"As long as Reed is amenable—and you think your staff can have everything readied by then, Saturday sounds lovely," Vanessa said.

"What is happening Saturday?" Reed asked, slipping into the seat next to her and lacing his fingers through her hand.

"Our wedding," she told him. "If the date is acceptable to you."

"My only objection is having to wait that long," he teased. Looking to Louisa, he said, "But I do know that our hostess needs time to plan everything accordingly."

"Your relatives will arrive tomorrow afternoon," Louisa said. "I think that Saturday would be a perfect day for a wedding. It would give our guests a chance to celebrate with you, while the house party would then continue through a week from today."

"Have you discussed a honeymoon?" Adalyn asked.

Reed chuckled. "The ink is barely dry on our special license, Your Grace. We only now have a date for the ceremony. I suppose Vanessa and I will need to talk about where she might wish to honeymoon." He turned to her. "Where would you like to go? Would you care to see Italy? France? Other parts of England?"

Her heart already knew without being asked. "I wish to go straight to Boxwell Hall. I want to see my new home. Meet your staff and tenants. Settle into life there." She paused. "With you," she said softly, feeling the love swell within her.

His fingers tightened on hers. "If that is what you wish, I can easily make that happen. Remember, though, that while Constance is leaving for Bath to attend her own house party, the girls will be left in my—our—care."

She smiled. "I don't mind that a bit. I am eager to meet them."

"They are just coming into their looks. Both were in a bit of an awkward stage the previous couple of years. There was lots of tripping and gangly limbs. But they are bright and fun-loving and very dear to me." He raised her hand and kissed it. "And they will adore their new sister-in-law."

Her cheeks grew hot from his gesture but she saw her three friends looking on with a smile at his tender gesture.

Others continued to enter the breakfast room and go through the buffet. A few planned to go riding after breakfast. Louisa had arranged a calligraphy lesson for those who did not plan to ride. She reminded her guests of this and that the picnic and archery would commence at one o'clock on the front lawn.

As people began to drift from the breakfast room, Adalyn said, "I think we four should retreat to Louisa's parlor and see to the details of the wedding."

"I don't want others to feel left out," Tessa said. "I will go to the calligraphy lesson and allow the three of you to meet. You are the planner, Adalyn, and Louisa will know what she can ask of her staff."

They told Tessa goodbye and went to Louisa's parlor. Adalyn immediately took charge, which didn't surprise Vanessa in the slightest.

"You want the wedding to be what you picture," her friend

said. "The details should be firmed up before Lord Boxling's relatives arrive tomorrow. With a sister, a stepmother, and two half-sisters on the cusp of womanhood, they will each have opinions. I know you, Vanessa. You will want to please them because they love the viscount dearly. But weddings are for the bride. *You* are the one who needs to be happy with the arrangements."

"Frankly, I don't know what I want, Adalyn," she admitted. "My first wedding happened so quickly, it was over before I blinked. And there was no wedding breakfast at all. Horace the Horrible's son and daughter were witnesses, along with the daughter's husband. They all left immediately after the brief ceremony."

Her mind flashed to what occurred directly after that and her stomach lurched, worried again how that experience would affect her time with Reed in their marriage bed.

"Then let's forget that altogether," Louisa suggested. "This is the true wedding of your heart with the man you love. What do you want? Name it and we will make it come true."

She thought a moment. "I think I would like the ceremony to be held in a church. A small chapel."

"That is easy enough. The village church in Blackburn will do. Owen certainly gives enough money to the place. I will send for the clergyman now to firm up those details."

She rang for a servant and when a footman appeared, she told him to go to Blackburn and bring Reverend Smythe.

"That's taken care of," Louisa said. "He will be here shortly. What else?"

"If it is not too much to ask, I would like the church to be decorated with a few flowers. Perhaps from your garden," Vanessa said. "Any blooms will do. I just am partial to a little color."

"Let me summon our head gardener." Again, Louisa rang for a servant and asked that the head gardener be brought to the parlor.

"What about after the ceremony?" Adalyn asked. "Would you like a wedding breakfast?"

"Yes, I would," she said.

They discussed the menu items, tossing a few ideas back and forth, and had decided upon it when the gardener showed up. Louisa told him about the wedding and how the bride wanted fresh flowers decorating the chapel.

The man congratulated Vanessa. "Let's talk about what is in bloom now, my lady. Then you can decide what you wish for us to cut."

After a few minutes of discussion, with the gardener sharing what was flowering in late summer, they decided upon bouquets of hydrangeas in a dusty rose, calendulas in soft lilac, and dahlias in bright fuchsia.

"I'll take care of everything, Lady Danbury," the gardener promised. "Me and the missus will decorate the chapel early Saturday morning with what the staff cuts late Friday afternoon. I'll also be sure there are bouquets mixed with those flowers for the tables used during the wedding breakfast."

They thanked him and then spent a half-hour with Reverend Smythe, who arrived next. He discussed a few particulars of the ceremony but mostly agreed with Vanessa to keep the vows traditional.

When he left, Adalyn said, "That only leaves the wedding breakfast menu to discuss with Cook."

"I can do that," Louisa said. "Why don't the two of you go to the end of the calligraphy lesson? I will see you at the picnic."

The rest of the day passed quickly. Vanessa enjoyed the picnic and actually participated in learning to shoot a bow and arrow, courtesy of her fiancé. Several of the other ladies had no experience with archery and so they paired up quickly with the gentlemen. She caught several flirtatious glances between Lord Thadford and Lady Jayne and wondered if a blossoming romance had begun between the pair.

That evening after dinner, Louisa had tables set up in the

drawing room and most people participated in card games, whist being the popular choice. Once again, Reed walked her to her bedchamber, with a rather lengthy detour to the library. He kissed her so thoroughly that her entire body heated with desire.

"Only three more nights and then you will spend all your nights in my bed," he whispered in her ear.

Vanessa hoped he wouldn't think her worthless as Horace the Horrible had. Her mind told her that her husband hadn't loved her and that because Reed did love her, things would be different.

One more long, drugging kiss and he escorted her to her room.

"I hope you will like my family," he said. "My sister, in particular. Pamela was as much sister as mother to me. She is a good mother to her two children, as well."

"I know I will like her. I only hope she will like me."

Reed cradled her face in his large hands and kissed the tip of her nose. "She will more than like you. She will adore you. Almost as much as I do." He kissed her lips softly. "Pleasant dreams, my love."

The endearment touched Vanessa. She felt so cherished by this wonderful man.

"Goodnight," she told him, too shy to say anything else.

THE NEXT MORNING after breakfast, Vanessa joined Reed and all of the single houseguests in walking to Blackburn. Louisa stayed behind with Adalyn, who couldn't walk that far.

"This will give me time to make certain all the arrangements are finalized for Lord Boxling's family," Louisa told Vanessa. "And to work on the wedding breakfast menu with Cook." She smiled mysteriously. "I also have a surprise but I will tell you about that later."

"I wonder what that is about," she said to Reed.

"It must be related to the wedding. I wouldn't worry about it if I were you. With the Three Cousins planning everything, based upon your choices, the event will run smoothly Let's enjoy our morning walk and seeing a bit of the village."

She had never been to the village. Horace the Horrible hadn't expressly forbid her from going but he had told her he did not want her mixing with others in the country while he was gone. Consequently, she had never even attended church, much less stopped in any of the shops. She was curious about what they would see.

It was four miles into Blackburn, which wasn't a great distance to her since she enjoyed walking frequently. Louisa had insisted that carriages from Danfield would be sent into the village for them to ride back to the estate and both Lady Rosalie and Miss Maxwell decided they would ride into Blackburn instead of walking. When they announced this, both Lord Darton and Lord Wakeford agreed to accompany the pair. They would all stroll through the shops and meet up at the inn for some refreshments before returning.

Lord Jackson and Miss Parsons paired off and Lord Thadford and Lady Jayne did the same. The six of them walked together at first and then gradually one couple moved slightly ahead of them and the other fell a bit behind.

Reed chuckled. "It seems everyone wants a bit of private conversation. I suppose Her Grace is still hoping that more than one match might be made at this house party."

"I think Lord Thadford is most interested in Lady Jayne," Vanessa said. "I saw a few of the heated looks he was giving her last night and she couldn't seem to take her eyes off him at breakfast this morning."

"Thadford is a good man. Lady Jayne is a handful but I think he could manage taking her on."

"The viscount mentioned you sowed your wild oats together."

He snorted. "He would have. Yes, we knew one another

from school and did a bit of running around together. I was hoping you wouldn't be taken with him but if you were, I would have stepped aside. That is how much I like him and how much I think of him."

"Do you think Lady Jayne was holding out for a duke?" Vanessa asked. "After all, her father is one."

"I couldn't say. I don't really know much about her."

"She's been quite nice to me. If she was disappointed that the Duke of Woodmont already had a bride, she hasn't behaved that way." She paused. "Are you certain you want to wed me, Reed? I have absolutely no social connections and no dowry."

He placed a hand over the one tucked into the crook of his arm. "I want you for *you,* my sweet love. Not what you could do for me or bring to me." He grinned wickedly. "Besides, anyone who can heat my blood with just a kiss the way you do? I have found my perfect match."

Her face flamed at his words. "Hush, someone will hear you."

"Who cares if they do?" He smiled. "I am in love with the most wonderful woman in England. Of course, I enjoy kissing her." He paused, growing serious. "I would like to look into your financial situation, however. With your permission, of course. Not that I need or want anything material from you, but I think something is afoot."

"I don't understand."

"I have never heard of a widow being left as destitute as you, Vanessa. The marriage settlements drawn up should have seen to your support in the event your husband predeceased you. With Hockley being so much older than you, that would have been quite important."

"Remember who negotiated those contracts, Reed. It was my brother, who was backed into a corner, thanks to his gambling debts. He owed Horace the Horrible and practically everyone else in town. I doubt he gave any thought to my welfare if and when I became a widow. He was trying to save his own hide."

"True," Reed agreed, "but I still think something would have been written into the contracts. Might I pursue this once we are wed?"

"Feel free to do so. Just don't be disappointed when you find nothing was provided for me."

Viscount Thadford and Lady Jayne caught up to them just as Blackburn came into view. Lord Jackson and Miss Parsons slowed their pace and the six of them entered the village together. The group did one sweep through the village and then the ladies decided to do a bit of shopping since Louisa had recommend the milliner. The men planned to go to the tobacco shop and Lord Jackson wanted to stop at a small bookshop they passed. They decided to meet in front of the inn where they would ask for a private room and enjoy some refreshments.

"I will call at the inn now and make those arrangements," Reed said. "I will head straight for the tobacco shop when I am done."

"I also want to look for gloves," Lady Jayne said. "If the milliner has none, we must find somewhere that does."

Those who traveled by carriage had now arrived and joined them. Lord Thadford suggested a time for them to rendezvous and they all went their separate ways.

The ladies went to the milliner's and Vanessa decided she would purchase a new hat for her wedding, using the funds her stepson had provided. She still hated going to Reed with practically nothing but she knew he didn't really care about material possessions.

Since the milliner had nothing but hats, she recommended that they stop next door at the local dressmaker's shop. Lady Jayne found three pairs of gloves for herself and then before they left, handed one pair to Vanessa.

"For your wedding," she said. "The something new. We can work on the something, borrowed, and blue."

"How about a blue garter?" suggested Miss Maxwell.

"Oh, and I have a locket you are welcomed to borrow," Lady Rosalie said. "That only leaves something old."

"It will be my gown," Vanessa confided. "I haven't had any new ones made up since my marriage several years ago. I met with Lady Danbury's housekeeper and she was going to put some new trim on the gown I plan to wear."

"Oh!" Miss Parsons said. "I am sorry to hear that."

"I don't mind marrying Lord Boxling in a gown that may have seen a more fashionable day," she said. "The fact I am marrying at all—especially a man I love—is more than enough."

Lady Jayne said, "Why don't the rest of you head to the inn? I have one more stop I need to make and I could use Lady Hockley's opinion on my purchase."

The others agreed and set off and Vanessa asked, "What purchase?"

"I had nothing in mind," Lady Jayne admitted. "I merely wanted to get you alone and ask your opinion of Lord Thadford."

"You are interested in him."

"Very much so," Lady Jayne said. "I believe he was eyeing you before me, though, and thought you might be able to give me insight into him."

"He is a lovely man and seems very ready to wed," Vanessa shared. "He is also a longtime friend of Lord Boxling. My fiancé thinks quite highly of the viscount."

"I find him intelligent and amusing. I have put off marrying, not wanting to go straight from the schoolroom into a marriage. Papa is ready for me to do so, however. Most of the men of the *ton* have bored me to tears. Lord Thadford constantly has something new to say or a topic to discuss I had not even thought of."

"Then I would spend as much time as you can with him during these next few days," Vanessa advised. "I think your heart will speak to you and lead you to a decision."

"Very well. Thank you, Lady Hockley. I value your opinion." Lady Jayne slipped her arm through Vanessa's. "Shall we head to the inn?"

She still found it hard to believe anyone valued her after all the ugly things Horace the Horrible had said to her over the years. He rarely spoke to her and when he did, it was only to tear her down. To now have a fiancé and several good friends astounded her. And this daughter of a duke was also being so friendly and kind to her.

They approached the inn, not seeing any of the others in sight. Vanessa supposed everyone must have already arrived and gone inside.

Just before they reached the inn, the door opened. Her heart nearly stopped. Out walked the new Lord Hockley.

And when he saw her, his face soured.

CHAPTER SIXTEEN

V ANESSA HALTED IN her tracks.

"You," Lord Hockley sneered. "I thought you were gone from here."

She would not cower again in the presence of anyone named Lord Hockley.

"I did vacate the dower house after being instructed to do so," she said calmly, even as her belly churned.

"You were supposed to be gone," the new earl insisted with disdain. "Away from here. Serving as some companion or governess."

Biting her tongue to keep from saying anything more to him, Vanessa was startled when Lady Jayne spoke up. "I know you. Or *of* you," she said, clearly revealing her opinion of the earl. "You are Lord Hockley. Why are you being so incredibly rude? And to a lady, no less."

The earl turned his attention from Vanessa. "Are you the one who helped her? It is Lady Jayne, isn't it? I sent this woman away. She was to go to London to find work."

"*She* has a name, my lord. One you should be familiar with. *Lady Hockley* is my friend and has no need to find employment. She is to be wed to Lord Boxling on Saturday."

"Boxling?" her stepson asked, bewildered by this announcement. "What on earth are you talking about?"

"Nothing which concerns you, my lord," Vanessa said, tugging on her friend. She didn't like Lord Hockley knowing she was in the area, much less that she was to wed.

"How the blazes did you manage that? You are an absolute no one," he said spitefully. "Oh, this is rich. Your brother will most definitely chase you down now."

"My brother?" Vanessa asked, clearly puzzled by the reference to Stillwell.

"Yes. Your brother. Lord Stillwell came to see you only yesterday. I told him you were gone and good riddance to you. That you had embarrassed my family by marrying my father and made laughingstocks of my sister and me. That old goat never should have wed you. He only did so because of Stillwell's gambling debt. It was the only way to get any money owed to him at all."

Humiliation filled her, having Lady Jayne hear all of this. But her new friend squeezed her arm reassuringly.

"Lady Hockley has been treated abominably by you and your family, my lord. Be glad that Lord Boxling doesn't come and tear you limb for limb just for the sport of it. Lord Stillwell, as well."

The earl snorted. "Stillwell is in dire straits. He had to be by coming to look for you. He told me he needed money desperately and thought he would get at least some of it from you."

"How could he? Nothing was left to me," she retorted and then added, "unless you kept what was owed from me."

The earl flushed a brick red at her implied accusation. "I should never have stopped and wasted my time with you."

He brushed past them.

Quietly, Lady Jayne said, "Is it true you were left penniless?"

"Yes," she said, mortified.

"I will have my father look into this matter," Lady Jayne called out, causing Lord Hockley to stop and turn. "I am certain you know of my father, my lord. As a duke, he is a most powerful man. If you deliberately kept monies owed to my friend after she lost her husband, you will be in more trouble than you ever imagined, Lord Hockley." She paused and with arched brows added, "Perhaps even more trouble than Lord Stillwell finds himself in."

The earl marched back toward them. "See here, Lady Jayne," he said, pointing his finger at her.

"I will not have you sticking your finger in my face!" she huffed. "Step back, my lord."

Lord Hockley did as told. Looking contrite, he said, "I am sorry you have received such an unfavorable impression of me, my lady. Poisoned by this one's words, of course."

Layne Jayne sniffed. "Lady Hockley has never even mentioned you to me, my lord. You are nothing to her. My advice is to stay far away from her and Lord Boxling. You do not want the viscount—or my father—as your sworn enemy."

He bobbed his head several times, speechless, and then turned and strode away.

"What a vile little man." Lady Jayne shook her head. "I did not know his father—your husband—but if he was anything like the current Hockley, I must give you my sympathies."

Tears welled in Vanessa's eyes. "I am sorry you had to bear witness to that confrontation. Much less learn of the circumstances of my first marriage. My brother did owe the earl a vast sum of money and my dowry—and me—were handed over."

"I cannot begin to imagine. I am so sorry, Lady Hockley. And then to have that bloody little bastard toss you out? It is wrong on every level imaginable." She squeezed Vanessa's hand. "I am certain it makes marrying Lord Boxling all the more sweet. He is a remarkable man and will love and protect you with a fierceness few women know."

She blinked back the tears. "Yes, he does love me and I love him. I would wed Horace the Horrible a thousand times over if Lord Boxling were waiting for me on the other side."

"Horace the Horrible?" Lady Jayne asked—and then burst into laughter.

Soon, Vanessa joined her. This time, tears of laughter spilled down her cheeks.

"Yes. It was my name for him," she admitted.

"It sounds like something from a novel," Lady Jayne said. "Oh, what if we decided to write one together? We could have Horace the Horrible and . . . what is the new earl's Christian name?"

"Milton. And his sister is Mathilda," Vanessa provided.

"Hmm." Lady Jayne thought a moment. "Milton the Mad, I think, for he was hopping mad as he left *and* most likely touched in the head for being so cruel to one so loving and kind. Or perhaps Milton the Muddleheaded. As for Mathilda? I don't even know her but I would say Mealy-Mouthed Mathilda. Or Mirthless Mathilda."

Vanessa laughed again. "Oh, they would despise those monikers."

Lady Jayne grew serious. "I meant what I said. There is something sly about that man. If he turned you out without a pound to your name, I fear he is keeping what is yours from you."

"Lord Boxling believes the same and wishes to look into the matter once we are wed."

"I should have known he would take care of you," her friend said. "Still, if he needs any help at all—if Lord Hockley tries to block him from finding out the details of the marriage settlements—then you are to let me know. Papa will become involved if I ask him to do so. At the very least, you should have been given a copy of the marriage contracts."

"That was never an option. My brother negotiated them and was so deeply into debt to Lord Hockley and many others, I doubt he had my best interests at heart."

Lady Jayne patted Vanessa's hand. "Let's get you wed and then Lord Boxling can see if he can discover the details. We should go in and join the others."

"Thank you," she said simply. "For not judging me based upon what Lord Hockley said."

"I liked you from the moment I met you. I am a woman who knows my own mind and, frankly, I would never take a man's word over another female's. You have my support, Lady Hockley, and my friendship."

They moved to the door and went inside. The innkeeper greeted them and asked if they were with the party from Danfield. When they confirmed they were, he led them upstairs to a private dining room, where they found the other eight guests.

"There you are," said Miss Parsons. "We were starting to get a bit worried. Lord Boxling was ready to go out to look for you."

"We are here now," Lady Jayne said. "Have refreshments been ordered?"

"They should arrive any minute," Lord Thadford confirmed. "Please, come and join us. I saved a seat next to me for you, Lady Jayne."

Vanessa went straight to Reed, who seated her beside him. "Is there something you are not telling me?" he asked quietly.

"I am just a bit nervous, knowing I will meet your family soon," she said, not wanting to explain her encounter with Milton the Muddleheaded. That is how she would think of her stepson from now on. "I am grateful I had Lady Jayne for company. She is a very understanding woman."

"She seems to be hitting it off with Thadford as you believed," Reed said, glancing at the couple.

"I hope they become the second betrothed couple of the house party," Vanessa declared. "Lord Thadford could not do better than Lady Jayne."

Reed leaned close, his lips grazing her ear. "Well, he *tried* to do better but failed. And I am glad he did."

A tingle feathered along her spine.

"But," he amended, "Thadford would do almost as well as I have if he could land Lady Jayne."

The food and drink arrived then and they were a merry group. She noticed Lord Thadford holding a sample of something to Lady Jayne's lips and heard her low laugh as she took it. Hope filled her that those two would find what she and Reed had discovered with one another.

They finished eating and left the inn, finding two carriages waiting for their party.

"Let Lady Hockley and Lord Boxling ride in the first one," Lady Jayne said. "With his family arriving this afternoon, they should be the first back so they can ready themselves."

The carriage ride back to Danfield was a short one and once they entered the foyer, Reed asked the butler for hot water for baths to be sent up for both of them.

He escorted her to her bedchamber and said, "I will meet you in Lady Danfield's parlor once I am dressed." He captured her hand and kissed it tenderly.

She entered her room, happiness filling her. Then she came to an abrupt halt.

On her bed was the most beautiful gown she had ever seen.

Vanessa went to it, fingering the delicate silk.

A knock sounded at her door and she answered it, finding the Three Cousins before her.

"May we come in?" asked Tessa.

"Of course," she replied. "I think I know now what the surprise is."

"I am the closest to your size," Adalyn began. "Or at least I was before this," she declared, rubbing her enormous belly. "We are identical in height. Ev and I live only a stone's throw from Danfield so I sent Louisa over to Cliffside in search of what I thought would be the perfect gown for your wedding. Mind you, it might need a nip or tuck here and there. I hope you might wish to wear it."

Vanessa lifted the gown and held it up to her. "It is beautiful," she said, admiring the shade and how the skirts draped elegantly.

"Oh, I do think it will suit you well," Louisa said. "I sent for my lady's maid. She is a wonder with a needle and thread."

The maid arrived and had Vanessa try on the gown. The length was perfect, as was the fit everywhere except her breasts. Adalyn was slightly more endowed in that area and the maid said she could take it up slightly. She left with the gown in hand as the hot water arrived for Vanessa's bath. Her friends helped her to bathe and dress and Tessa even arranged Vanessa's hair for her.

"You are ready to meet Lord Boxling's family," Adalyn declared. "They are going to fall in love with you as he did."

"I hope so," she said, nerves flitting through her. "He thinks so much of his sister and has great respect for his stepmother, who is only a few years his senior." Sighing, she added, "I feel I must win their approval and worry that they will find me lacking."

"Nonsense," Tessa proclaimed. "Lord Boxling values their opinions but nothing would stop him from wedding you, Vanessa. He has gone to the trouble to purchase a special license for the two of you. And I see the way he looks at you." Her friend smiled. "It is with such love and devotion. All women should be so lucky as to have their husbands hold them in such regard."

Yet she couldn't help but feel differently, despite what her friends said. Lurking in the back of her mind were all the disparaging comments Horace the Horrible had made to her throughout their marriage.

"Come," Louisa said. "You look lovely. Lord Boxling's relatives will soon arrive and you should greet them."

"He asked me to meet him in your parlor," Vanessa said.

"Then go to him," Louisa told her. "I will have our butler come straightaway to find you when the carriages arrive." She squeezed Vanessa's hand. "Owen and I will also be by your side to welcome them to Danfield."

They left the bedchamber and she parted from her friends, making her way to meet Reed. She found him waiting for her and he rose, coming to her and taking her hands in his.

"You are a picture of loveliness," he complimented. "I wish we were marrying today." With a wicked grin, he added, "I would like nothing more than to kiss you until my family arrives but will refrain from doing so else they'd know what we had been up to."

He led her to the settee and they sat together, their fingers entwined, as she asked him to tell her about Boxwell Hall. Reed described the land first, making her realize the pride he took in the estate and his tenants. Then he spoke of the house itself.

"If there are any changes you wish to make in its décor, feel free to do so."

"I am sure it is fine."

"No," he said firmly. "I want you to put your stamp on the house. Make it your own. The place where we will be comfortable and raise our family."

The thought of a child—and how it was made—made her grow queasy. He picked up on her unease.

"You have nothing to worry about. You may make any changes you wish. I do not wish to boast, but I am quite wealthy."

Vanessa was glad he had misread her mood and said teasingly, "It is good to know I will not have to worry about keeping a roof over my head."

He looked very serious and said, "I have sent for my solicitor. He should arrive tomorrow morning. I asked that Lord Danbury and His Grace act on your behalf and arrange for a solicitor, as well."

Surprise filled her. "What?"

"If indeed your brother neglected to look out for your interests in your first marriage, then I do not want the same mistake to be made again for the second one. Your last one. I want it clearly spelled out what you would have when I am gone."

She shook her head. "I . . . don't know what to say."

He kissed her lightly. "Thank you will do."

She gazed up at him. "Thank you," she said solemnly. "For looking out for me. For wanting to always do the right thing."

He cradled her cheek. "I will always protect you, my love. I have also spoken to His Grace regarding how destitute you were left after Horace the Horrible's death."

Vanessa couldn't help but smile at his use of her nickname for her husband.

"I still believe some chicanery was involved, either on Still-well's or Hockley's part. Or both Hockleys. Don't worry. We will get to the bottom of it. And if it is true you were left with nothing?" He smiled, his thumb caressing her cheek. "At least you have me."

He kissed her again and they broke apart at the knock that sounded at the door. The butler entered.

"My lord, my lady, carriages have been spotted. Lord and Lady Danbury request that you join them outside to greet their new guests."

"Thank you," Reed said and he turned to her. Smiling, he said, "I hope you will like them."

Vanessa chuckled. "I hope they will like *me.*"

With that, her fiancé accompanied her to the front door, where they joined their hosts. She saw two carriages almost at the house and another two in the distance. Steeling herself, she hoped she would make a favorable impression on the new arrivals.

Chapter Seventeen

T HE FIRST TWO carriages rolled to a stop and Vanessa watched as a flurry of activity occurred. Trunks began being handed down. Servants spilled from the second carriage. A footman placed stairs down and opened the door of the first carriage. She waited, her heart in her throat, as the first person appeared.

Reed slipped an arm about her shoulders and gave them a reassuring squeeze.

"It is my sister's family," he said quietly. "That is Viscount Rivers. He is Pamela's age, three years my senior."

Lord Rivers turned and waved and then reached out a hand to assist his wife from the carriage. The couple began making their way toward them when a cry sounded.

"Uncle Reed!"

Vanessa saw a young girl scrambling away from what had to be her nursery governess, making straight for Reed. A young boy struggled in the woman's arms and she set him on his feet, where he began following his sister.

"Eve!" cried Reed, scooping up the little girl and kissing her cheek. He bent and lifted the toddler in his other arm. The boy gave Reed a sloppy kiss, which he didn't seem to mind at all. If Vanessa had ever harbored any doubts about the man she was scheduled to wed, they would have been dispelled in this moment.

Eve began to tell him some story, which Reed listened to with wide eyes. Vanessa glanced and saw Lord and Lady Rivers had now reached Louisa and Lord Danbury.

"I will introduce us since my brother has his hands literally full at the moment," the woman said, a dark-haired beauty who resembled Reed. "Lord and Lady Rivers."

The Danburys greeted them and Lord Danbury turned to Vanessa. "I am happy to introduce you to Lady Hockley," he said.

Lord Rivers took her hand and bowed over it briefly. Lady Rivers smiled widely and unexpectantly threw her arms about Vanessa, giving her a tight embrace.

The viscountess pulled away and gazed deeply into Vanessa's eyes. "I am sorry for my unladylike greeting. I am simply thrilled that my brother has found the woman he wishes to wed." She paused. "Is it a love match? Oh, I am not normally so nosy."

"Yes, you are, my dear," Lord Rivers said, a twinkle in his eyes.

"Oh, perhaps I am," Lady Rivers admitted. "But I so want Reed to be happy."

Vanessa nodded. "It is a love match, my lady. I did not seek one but I find I am very happy in finding love come to me. To us."

Lady Rivers grabbed hold of Vanessa again, hugging her tightly. When she stepped back again, Vanessa saw tears in the woman's eyes.

"Oh, this is marvelous," she proclaimed. "And you must call me Pamela. I won't stand upon ceremony. You are family."

Now tears flooded her eyes. "I am Vanessa."

"What a lovely name," Lady Rivers said.

Reed walked to them, balancing a child in each arm. "This is Eve and Pip."

"Pip!" the little boy echoed.

"Are you the lady Uncle Reed gets to marry?" Eve asked.

"I am," she confirmed.

"This is your Aunt Vanessa, my sweet," Pamela said.

Eve studied her a moment. "Vah-nes-sa," she said. "That's pretty. Aunt Vanessa. You're pretty."

"Why, thank you, Eve. You are very pretty, too."

"I look like Mama. Pip looks like Papa," the little girl said.

The first two carriages had pulled away, making room for the new ones. Pamela motioned for the nursery governess and the servant hurried over.

"These two need their naps," she said.

"I will have our butler show you the nursery," Louisa said. "It is quite crowded. Our Margaret is there, along with the Duke of Camden's boy and Lord Middlefield's son and daughter."

"All these children at a house party?" Lord Rivers asked and then smiled. "I rather like it. I will go up with the children and make certain they settle in and make new friends. Hand the little monsters over."

The viscount took his children from Reed and departed as the occupants of the second carriage now spilled out. The woman, Reed's stepmother, was the first from the carriage. She was a tall, willowy blond. One of the girls that followed closely resembled her mother in height and coloring. The other, looking slightly younger, was shorter and dark-haired and must have taken after Reed's father.

"My dear Boxling," the dowager viscountess said.

"Hello, Constance. Come meet our hosts. You, too, girls," Reed said.

He made the introductions and then turned to her. "And this is Lady Hockley. My stepmother, Lady Boxling, and Camilla and Nicola, my half-sisters."

They exchanged greetings and Vanessa saw Lady Boxling sizing her up. Turning to Pamela, she said, "I am certain you are as happy as I am that Boxling has decided to wed."

"Oh, very much so," Pamela agreed. "And it is a love match," she shared.

Vanessa felt the color rise in her cheeks as the two girls giggled.

Nicola said, "I knew you would find a bride at this house party, Reed. Camilla didn't think so."

"I didn't say that," her sister disagreed. "I said he might find one. You were the one who insisted he would."

"Well, I have found the best bride possible," Reed told them. "I am happy that all of you could drop what you were doing and make time to attend our wedding."

"Did you get a special license?" Nicola asked. "Is that why no banns have to be read?"

"How do you know about that?" her mother asked, disapproval in her voice. "Young ladies ought not to be discussing things such as that."

"Camilla is the one who told me about it," retorted Nicola. "I didn't know what one was until she informed me."

"Well, Nicola doesn't want—"

"Enough," Reed said. "There will be no arguing. Yes, I purchased a special license because I am madly in love with Lady Hockley and cannot wait to wed her." He looked at her lovingly. "Even waiting three weeks was too long, in my opinion."

"That is so romantic," Nicola said.

"I quite agree," Pamela said.

"Why don't we go inside?" Louisa suggested. "I have arranged for you to have tea in the library, separate from our house party guests. I thought it would be nice for you to have a more intimate setting so you can get to know one another better."

"That was a lovely idea, Lady Danbury," Lady Boxling said. "Come along, girls. We shall get settled in our rooms and then come down to tea."

Louisa led the group inside and told them a servant would bring them to the library in half an hour. She then led the newcomers upstairs.

Lord Danbury fell into step with Vanessa and Reed. "If you will act as hostess, Lady Hockley, Louisa and I will have tea with our other guests. Lord Boxling, if you could spare a moment, His Grace and I would like to speak with you in my study regarding the contracts."

"Of course," Reed said. He looked to her. "I will be there shortly. Go ahead and begin with tea once the others arrive."

"All right."

Vanessa went to the library and stood by the window, looking out across the lawn. Though she dearly wished she could pace the room, she did not want to appear out of breath or nervous when the others arrived. So far, she liked Pamela quite a bit, probably because Reed's sister had been so openly affectionate with her. Lady Boxling was quite pretty but hadn't said much. His half-sisters seemed a bit argumentative with one another but having never had a sister, Vanessa did not know if that was unusual or not.

As for young Eve and Pip, the pair already held her heart. They seemed to worship Reed and he was quite taken with them. She couldn't wait for them to have children of their own because he would be the most marvelous father.

The door to the library opened and two teacarts were wheeled in by maids. The Danfield butler asked her if she might need anything else and she said no, knowing Louisa would have checked the carts to make sure they had everything they needed. She gave thanks for such a wonderful friend. It still amazed her how their chance encounter in a graveyard had led to an invitation to this house party.

And a marriage proposal.

Pamela breezed into the room, all smiles, and kissed Vanessa's cheek. "Drake may or may not join us. I left him in the nursery, children crawling all over him."

"It would take a good father to allow his own children to do so. It takes an even better man to allow other people's children to do that."

Pamela smiled. "That's my Drake. My rock. We wed when we were both twenty-one. He was fresh out of university and I had waited to have a Season until Reed went away to university himself."

"He told me you were like a mother to him."

"Yes, I have always had that bit of nurturing about me." She sighed. "Drake and I wanted children and thought they would come along quickly. When they didn't, I feared they might never appear. I was twenty-nine when I had Eve and then Pip arrived two years later. We have no idea what took so long because we were trying *very* hard."

Vanessa blushed at the words.

"We are still trying," Pamela said cheerfully. "My courses are due to come early next week. I hope I do not see them."

She frowned, uncertain of what Pamela meant. Her governess had told Vanessa all about her courses when they first appeared and how she would continue to bleed each month until she was old. For them not to appear made no sense to her.

"Is something wrong, Vanessa? Oh, Reed told me you had been wed before. Were you unable to have children? Oh, I have gone and put my foot in my mouth. I am very sorry."

"No, it is not that," she said carefully.

Before she could say anything further, Lady Boxling and her daughters entered the room and joined them.

"Please, won't you all have a seat?" Vanessa asked, taking her role as hostess seriously.

They all settled into a grouping of seats and she told them that Reed would be joining them shortly.

"Good," Camilla proclaimed. "We can talk about him and ask you all sorts of questions."

Lady Boxling frowned. "Camilla, remember your manners."

"But Mama, I want to hear how Reed and Lady Hockley fell in love." Camilla glanced back at Vanessa. "It had to be very fast. Was it love at first sight?"

"Quit with the personal questions," Lady Boxling warned. "Else you will be sent back to our room."

"Yes, Mama," Camilla said meekly, causing Vanessa to feel sorry for the girl.

"We are to be family, Lady Boxling. I do not mind answering

your daughter's questions. I think your half-brother and I found very quickly we had several things in common. It is hard to say how or why, but love seemed to blossom quickly between us."

"It sounds like a novel," Nicola sighed. "Mama says you are marrying on Saturday. That is Reed's birthday. Are you getting him a present for it or just one for your wedding?"

She was taken aback. "Oh, I did not know about his birthday." She also hadn't thought about a gift for the wedding, not knowing if that was the practice between engaged couples. She felt ignorant in so many ways of social customs. She would have to draw Louisa aside and see what she needed to know about the upcoming wedding.

And the wedding night.

"I would make certain you had cake at the wedding breakfast," Nicola recommended. "Reed adores cake."

"We are having cake," she confirmed. "I have noticed that during tea, Lord Boxling is drawn to both lemon and strawberry. I have asked Lady Danbury's cook to make a lemon cake and strawberry pie for the wedding breakfast."

"Reed is going to be so old," Camilla said. "Thirty. That is ancient. Twice my age. How old are you, Lady Hockley?"

"Camilla," Lady Boxling said, exasperation evident in her voice and face. "That is much too personal."

The girl's pout was a pretty one. "I just want to *know* about her, Mama. After all, she is going to be family."

"Then I shall pour out and tell you about myself," Vanessa said calmly, knowing if these girls continued to pepper her with questions, she might break apart. If, though, she controlled the conversation, she could tell them only what she wished them to hear.

"An excellent idea," Pamela said. "I will help you."

As Vanessa poured out, Pamela made certain everyone had a plate and they began filling them with the delectable items the Danbury cook had provided.

Once everyone had tea, she said, "I grew up as an only child, so I was not fortunate to have a sister as the two of you do. I always wanted a sibling, a sister, in particular."

"Then you need to have lots of babies," Nicola suggested.

She blushed. "I hope we do." Continuing, she said, "I remained in the country with my governess when my parents went to London for the Season each spring."

"We stay in town most always," Camilla offered. "Mama hates the country. She says it bores her. Have you been to London, Lady Hockley? I may call you that if you'd like. I know you are truly going to be our sister-in-law but I don't know what I should call my half-brother's wife."

She thrilled at being asked that question. "I think that is a lovely question, Camilla. Please, since we are to be family, call me Vanessa. I have only been to London for a short period of time and did not see much while I was there. You see, I married and then came to stay in the country for the duration of my marriage."

"How old were you when you wed?" Nicola asked, interested. "You don't seem very old to me."

"I was nineteen when I wed. My come-out was delayed a year because both my parents fell ill near the same time and passed away. I spent that year in mourning and then went to town the next Season and stayed with my brother until my marriage."

She wasn't telling any untruths but she certainly was glossing over the facts. She thought it better to do so, however.

"After I wed, I moved to the country with my husband." Anticipating the next round of questions, she added, "He was quite a bit older than I was and he passed away last May when I was five and twenty. My stepson, who is actually older than I am, became the new Lord Hockley. I moved to the dower house. It was much smaller but I actually preferred living there."

"Why?" Nicola asked. "I would be so lonely."

"There is a difference in being lonely and being alone. I found I enjoyed the solitude. I played the piano and even taught myself how to play the flute."

"The flute?" Pamela asked. "How delightful. You must play for us soon."

"Tonight!" Camilla suggested. "If Mama will allow us to eat with the adults, we can go to the drawing room afterward and hear Vanessa play."

They asked her a few other questions about the house party and she was able to answer those since they mostly involved the activities Louisa and Adalyn had planned.

"Are there any other couples who have become betrothed?" Nicola asked. "Reed said that's what happened at house parties. I think he really wanted to wed. Why didn't he find someone during the Season? I thought that was where people found their spouses. If you can find someone at a house party so easily, then why have the Season at all?"

"So many questions!" Lady Boxling said. "Drink your tea, Nicola." She sighed, looking weary as she did so. "Girls are wonderful—until they are about ten or twelve. Then they become needy and irritable and forget all manners taught them when they were young."

"I actually have the same questions as you do, Nicola," Vanessa confided. "This is the first house party I have ever attended. While my friend, Lady Danbury, told me engagements were a common occurrence during them, I was a widow coming off my year of mourning and hadn't anticipated any offer of marriage. So, I am a bit surprised myself. I will tell you this—I believe people have longer and more meaningful conversations at a house party. The Season is filled with so many events and you go from one to another and see a sea of faces, sometimes a blur. This house party, I have made good friends I believe I will be close to for life, as well as found the man I love."

She smiled at the two, on the cusp of womanhood and probably curious about everything. "Go into your Season hoping for the best but do not expect to find a husband to your liking right away. Some ladies have more than one Season before they make up their minds and find the right spouse for them. Then there will always be house parties you might attend and who knows? You might even find you receive an offer of marriage while there."

Camilla frowned in thought. "Mama says—"

"I think you have spoken quite enough, Camilla," Lady Boxling warned, glancing from Camilla to her sister. "You, too, Nicola. You may be excused. Return to your room. I will talk with you later."

Both girls set their saucers down and rose reluctantly. Nicola pleaded, "Will we be able to attend dinner tonight, Mama?"

"No, I think not," her mother said, disappointing Vanessa

She decided Reed's stepmother was being too hard on her daughters. "Perhaps the girls might join us in the drawing room after dinner, Lady Boxling. After all, they wished to hear me play my flute."

"Oh, may we, Mama?" Camilla asked, her eyes lighting with excitement. "Please?"

Lady Boxling considered it. "Very well," she said succinctly.

Vanessa knew the woman wanted to berate her for overriding her but she didn't care. She had decided she did not like Lady Boxling very much but did enjoy the enthusiasm of her daughters. It was a good thing Lady Boxling spent most of her year in London. Vanessa would have hated to be around her very often.

After the girls left, Pamela said, "That was a lovely compromise, Vanessa, having the girls come to the drawing room after dinner concludes. I have always thought young ladies of good breeding needed experience in social situations. This will give them a chance to mingle briefly."

She could have hugged Pamela for saying as much. Vanessa saw resentment in Lady Boxling's eyes but she kept quiet, most likely because she viewed Pamela as her equal.

Reed joined them soon after. "Did I miss seeing the girls? They are already gone?"

"They needed to rest after our journey," Lady Boxling told him. "You will see them after dinner tonight."

"Yes, Vanessa has agreed to play her flute for us."

He smiled warmly, taking her hand. "Then you are in for a treat. I have heard her play once and hope she will play for me every night." Then he kissed her fingers, his eyes darkening.

Pamela sighed. Lady Boxling gasped.

Vanessa grinned. "I will play for you as much as you like, Reed," she said, deliberately using his Christian name, simply to irritate Lady Boxling.

As expected, Lady Boxling rose. "I think I will also rest a bit before dinner." She excused herself.

The moment the door closed, Pamela said, "I have never liked her, Reed. I know you get along with her well but I find her haughty. She is so hard on her girls, too. I don't see her as very nurturing and Camilla and Nicola are at an age where they need that. Especially having lost their father. She also wanted to be rude to Vanessa but—"

"What?" he asked, his features hardening.

"It was nothing, Reed," she said, hoping to calm him. "I like the girls very much. And we won't see much of Lady Boxling since she remains in town most of the year."

"Remember, she is headed to her own house party in Bath after our wedding. The girls will stay behind at Boxwell Hall. I hope that is agreeable with you."

"It is," Vanessa reassured him. "I will be happy to spend time in their company."

Pamela snorted. "They will probably want to stay with you and allow their mother to return to London without them."

Reed's brows knit together. He looked at Vanessa. "Would that bother you if it happened?"

"You mean if the girls remained at Boxwell Hall most of the year?" she asked. "I would welcome them. They are sweet-natured. I wouldn't mind taking them under my wing and teaching them how to run a household."

He sighed. "We will cross that bridge when it comes."

Pamela gazed at her brother levelly. "Oh, it will come, Reed. I guarantee you of that."

Chapter Eighteen

R EED ESCORTED VANESSA to her bedchamber and decided to
seek out Constance. He found the Danfield housekeeper and
asked what room his stepmother had been placed in and went
there straightaway. Although more than anything, he wished to
confront Constance about her rude behavior toward Vanessa, he
knew just how prickly his stepmother could be. Knowing she
would be gone soon for a good chunk of time, he decided to keep
the peace and merely get the jewelry he had requested her to
bring.

He had noticed from the beginning that Vanessa wore no
jewels of any kind and doubted Hockley had ever gifted her with
any. Even if he had, the new earl would have confiscated them
from her. When he had written to Constance to announce his
engagement and upcoming marriage, he had requested that she
bring his mother's pearl earrings and necklace to Danfield. He
had never seen Constance wear the pair, most likely because they
were not glittering enough for her. She was used to the emeralds,
diamonds, and sapphires of the Davenport family. Most of them
would be in London since she spent a majority of her time there
and he foresaw an ugly scene getting them back from her.
Perhaps he would allow her to keep and wear a few pieces instead
of stripping the entire collection from her. He didn't think
Vanessa would mind if Constance kept a bauble or two and it

might keep things calm in the family.

Reed wondered if Constance would ever remarry. She had seemed so in love with his father but she was still a beautiful woman and only in her mid-thirties. He wondered what might happen to his relationship with Camilla and Nicola if she did—or if she would be willing to place her daughters in his care since they were, after all, Davenports and he was their official guardian.

Something told him she might be amenable to this proposal.

He counted the doors and reached the bedchamber which had been assigned to her. Rapping lightly on the door, he did not know if she truly was resting or not. The trip from Boxwell Hall to Danfield was only a couple of hours.

The door opened and Constance looked up at him. "Oh, it's you."

"Yes, may I come in for a few minutes?"

She shrugged and turned away, leaving him to enter behind her. For propriety's sake, he left the door open, not that anything untoward would occur between them. Though similar in age, he had never looked at her in a light other than friendship. Attraction never played a part in their relationship.

"I suppose you've come because she complained to you," Constance said.

Reed knew exactly who she meant but feigned ignorance. "No, I have not seen either Camilla or Nicola yet so no one has complained to me. Why? Is something wrong with one of them? Are you quarreling with them again?"

Relief seemed to cross her face and he decided to let sleeping dogs lie as she said, "Oh, you know I am always at odds with one or both of them. Frankly, they are becoming too much for me to handle. The things they say to me, Reed! If your father were still alive, they would not behave in such an unladylike manner."

"Then perhaps all you need is time away from them. Your girls do love you, Constance, but I have heard there is always some friction between mothers and daughters. I want you to go and enjoy your house party in Bath and as I suggested, you are welcome to leave the girls in my care for as long as you wish."

He paused a long moment and then added, "I do not mind having them remain at Boxwell Hall until next Season and could bring them to town with me then. Would that be agreeable to you? Of course, you would come home for Christmas and spend time with them then."

Her eyes flared with intrigue. "That might be a solution to some of the harmony which has been lost between us. You are right. Mothers and their daughters have a tendency not to get along once the girls reach a certain age. If you promise me you will keep a firm hand with them, I will agree to leave them in your care until next spring. It sounds as if you will be coming to town for the Season. With your new wife." A look of distaste crossed her face. "Although I thought once you found a wife, you would not bother with the Season."

"On the contrary, I plan to attend it every year. This first one to show off Vanessa. Both she and I have made good friends, especially at this house party, and I know we will want to socialize with them both during the Season and beyond."

He cleared his throat and then asked, "Did you bring Mama's pearls as I requested?"

"Yes, I did." Constance crossed the room to a trunk on the far side of the room, withdrawing a velvet box and bringing it to him.

"I never wear these," she informed him. "They were favorites of your mother and, frankly, I did not want to remind Boxling of his connection with his first wife. Yes, I know he loved your mother, but he also loved me."

He saw hesitation on her part and said, "Constance, you will most likely always love Father. But that does not mean you cannot go on living yourself. You did your time of mourning and have rejoined Polite Society. You are still an attractive woman in your prime. If you wish to wed again in the future, I would have no problem with that. In fact, I know Father wouldn't either. He would not want to see you grieve for decades. If you find someone you wish to spend the rest of your life with, then accept his offer of marriage." He paused and then taking a chance, said, "Of course, Camilla and Nicola will always be Davenports and I am the one who would look out for their interests. If you believe your marriage would have a better chance of thriving without the girls constantly in your presence, then they are free to remain with me at Boxwell Hall until the time they make their come-outs."

Reed had several times mentioned only himself as having custody, not wanting to remind Constance of Vanessa's presence in the girls' lives. He felt she would be a wonderful influence on them but thought Constance would be of a different opinion. Much to his surprise, tears flooded her eyes.

"You do not think I would be disloyal by wedding again?" she asked.

"Of course not. You have many years left and Father would want you to be happy in them. There is no need to be miserable, Constance. Father is gone but you are here and alive. Live for yourself and find happiness."

She stepped toward him and embraced him. "Oh, thank you, Reed. I have been so lonely since Boxling passed. I thought the girls would bring comfort to me but all we have done is argue."

She stepped back and then said, "I am going to admit something to you which I am a bit ashamed of."

"What is it, Constance? You know you can confide in me."

"I loved your father so very much and never really wanted to have children. I was disappointed when I found myself with child. He already had you as his heir and I knew I would not have to provide one to him. Then Camilla was born and I was sorely disappointed she was a girl. It would have been nice to have at least provided a spare to him. We were quite careful after that but I found myself with child again. Reed, it is awful. A woman is sick for so many months and this tiny, squirming, crying creature emerges. Nicola, being another female, disappointed me even more. I never really bonded with either girl and have not enjoyed the time I have spent with them. I leave them in the care of others, especially now that they are becoming so unruly and rude to me. I do not blame their governess. I blame myself. I have no maternal instincts and . . ." Her voice trailed off.

Reed knew he was about to make a decision that would affect both Vanessa and him but he could not leave those precious girls in their mother's care any longer.

"Then I will assume control full-time, Constance. I know you mentioned you had given their governess a two-week holiday for the time you had come to Boxwell Hall. When she returns, I will inform her that she is to remain with them in the country. If she or the girls have left anything at the London townhouse, I will send for it. I don't want you to worry about Nicola and Camilla. They will be in good hands. They will also see you, not only at Christmas, but when we come to town next spring for the Season. They will make their come-outs before we know it and you are welcome to be as active in that process as you wish."

She took his hand. "Thank you, Reed. It was quite hard to admit to you how I feel about them. I know they are good girls for the most part but I have a tendency to be short with them and even sometimes spiteful. I know they will be happier to remain with you."

"I hope you enjoy your house party, Constance, and that you do find someone who will make you as happy as Father did."

"And I hope that you will be happy in your marriage, as well, Reed. I know the new Lady Boxling will need access to all of the Davenport jewels."

"You don't have to hand over the entire lot right away, Constance. Eventually, yes, I would like to see Vanessa wearing them. In fact, you may choose a few pieces to keep as your own."

"Thank you, Reed. You are as good and kind as your father was. I may do as you suggest. If—or when—I do wed again, though, I would return them to you. I would not want my new husband to be reminded of the generosity of my old one."

"When would you like to tell the girls about our plans?" he

asked.

"We don't want to overshadow your wedding," Constance said. "I know after the wedding breakfast tomorrow, we all plan to return together to Boxwell Hall. We may talk about it in the carriage then if you wish. I think it will be better coming from both of us." She paused and then said, "It will be better, actually, coming from you."

"You want them to think this is my idea and not yours?"

"Yes, I do. There is already animosity between us. If Camilla and Nicola think I am dumping them on you, they may become resentful. Could you possibly let them believe this is your idea?"

"I can do so. But," he said sternly, "Vanessa is going to be a large part of their lives if they are living with us at Boxwell Hall. I know she will never say a negative word about you to them and I wish for you to reciprocate. They will need more than their governess. They will need a woman to nurture them. I intend for Vanessa to be that woman. Hopefully, we will have children soon and the girls will be able to enjoy time with their young cousins."

He saw she warred within herself and waited to come to a final decision.

"All right, Reed. I will make certain that I always behave pleasantly toward your viscountess and speak well of her in my girls' presence. I hope that will satisfy you."

"I think it will be satisfactory to all parties, Constance. Thank you. I will see you at dinner this evening."

Reed left his stepmother's bedchamber, his heart a little lighter. He had not known how Constance viewed her children and her admission made more sense now. Just as he supposed not every man felt paternal toward his children, especially females who did not inherit in this male-dominated English society, but he had never thought about females being the same way. He was relieved that Constance had given the girls over to him. Already, he was their legal guardian and now he would have plenty of time to spend with them being at Boxwell Hall year-round. He also thought Vanessa would be pleased. It would be interesting, going into a marriage, with two daughters of the house to be responsible for. He looked forward to that challenge and knew Vanessa would, too.

CHAPTER NINETEEN

VANESSA AWOKE EARLY, excitement filling her.
It was her wedding day.

It still boggled her mind that today she would become Reed's wife, as well as an instant mother figure. After she had played her flute for the entire group, Reed had taken her aside and shared with her the conversation he'd had with Lady Boxling. Vanessa hid her shock at the woman's lack of maternal feelings toward her two lovely daughters. Reed explained that he had wanted to remove them from their mother's care and thought if he didn't act in the moment, the opportunity might be lost.

She had agreed with him that he had acted correctly, assuring him that she didn't mind in the least that he had made the decision to keep Camilla and Nicola at Boxwell Hall permanently without her. He told her he would never behave so rashly again and make certain she was always a part of every decision that would affect their life together.

For her part, she looked forward to discovering more about the girls. They would become a precious part of her new life. She would be filled with pride each time they referred to her as Vanessa. It had been hard to remain silent when she wanted to share with them how they would soon be together at Boxwell Hall. She agreed, though, that telling them in the carriage on the way home was for the best. Making it sound as if it were Reed's idea that they stay made perfect sense. It would not do to cast their mother in an unflattering light. After all, she would still want to maintain a relationship with her daughters, albeit in a different way in the future. Especially if she did remarry, as Reed believed she would, Lady Boxling would have to balance her new life with a different husband along with the daughters from her first marriage.

Vanessa went to the dressing table and opened the square, velvet box containing a set of pearl earrings and necklace. Reed had given them to her, telling her they were his mother's favorites and that he hoped she might wish to wear them for their wedding, saying it would be as if his mother were a part of their ceremony.

Tearfully, Vanessa had told him how her own mother had given her a pair of pearl earrings for her sixteenth birthday and how Stillwell had refused to let her keep them.

"This will be as if Mama were also with me as I wear them," she had told him, thinking her mother's earrings had been sold long ago to pay off more of her brother's gambling debts.

A knock sounded at the door and a maid appeared with a breakfast tray.

"Lady Danbury said you were to eat in your room, my lady. You aren't to see Lord Boxling until you walk down the aisle."

Vanessa did not know if that was custom or superstition. Her own first wedding had been so very different. She thanked the servant for the tray and found she was hungry. She ate everything on it and then started to ring for someone to help her dress when she heard another knock at the door.

She answered it and found the Three Cousins there. They were already dressed and looking lovely.

"We have come to prepare you ourselves for your wedding," Adalyn told her as the three women entered the bedchamber.

"Thank you so much for everything."

Vanessa took Louisa's hands. "I think back to our chance meeting in the graveyard and how much my life has changed because of it. I was a stranger to you, Louisa, yet you opened your home and heart to me."

She looked from Tessa to Adalyn and added, "And I was given a sweet friendship with the two of you, as well. I cannot thank you enough for the difference the three of you have made in my life. If I had not gone to rail at Horace the Horrible. If Margaret had not been ill with a fever and caused Louisa's meeting at the church to be postponed. So many things happened for the stars to align and fate to take control of my destiny. Now, I am to be wed to a dear, marvelous man, one I have come to love in such a short period of time. One who loves me in return."

Tessa took Vanessa's hand and squeezed it. "I will tell you from experience that love between you will only grow over time. As much as I loved Spencer on our wedding day, it is but a fraction of the love I hold for him now. I find every day that I fall a bit more in love with him. There will be events that will bring you closer together. Oh, I am not saying that every day is a perfect one. Far from it. Adalyn and Louisa will attest to that. Couples do argue, especially those who feel so passionately about one another. But the bond of your love will be there to help you over any hurdle."

"And when you have children together?" Tessa's eyes lit up. "Then the love you have will grow exponentially and your heart will almost burst from the love you have for that child and those to come. Love holds no limits, Vanessa. There is always room in your heart to love your husband more and each child that comes. We are so happy for you that you have found your soulmate in Lord Boxling."

"This friendship is not one that merely happened at a house party," Adalyn said. "Our friendships are ones for life. I have talked to Ev and Lord Boxling has become quite close with the Second Sons. I feel that we will be seeing much of each other, whether it is during the Season or away from London."

Vanessa blinked away her tears as Louisa said, "We are just so happy for you. I look forward to introducing you to the other wives of the Second Sons. I know they will love you and we will always be a tight circle of friends."

"May I ask something? Today is Reed's birthday. Camilla and Nicola told me about it. Should I have gotten a gift for him? Or for our wedding?"

Adalyn shook her head. "I have never heard of a bride giving a gift to her groom. Sometimes, a groom will present a gift to his bride. Remember, though, that we are in the country. Because of that, Reed may not have been able to get something for you. He may talk it over with you and see what you might want and give it to you later. As far as his birthday is concerned, *you* will be that special gift for him, the best he has ever received."

Her cheeks heated as she said, "With the three of you here, knowing you are deeply in love with your husbands, I do have a question in regard to . . . our wedding night." Vanessa swallowed. "I want . . . to please Reed." Embarrassment flooded her and she focused on her feet.

"How were your relations with Horace the Horrible?" Louisa gently asked.

She teared up. "We only were together the one time and . . . he . . . found me lacking." Looking up, she said, "I am afraid Reed will be the same."

Louisa took Vanessa by her elbows. "Horace the Horrible was an old fool who thought himself saddled with you so your brother could honor his gambling debt. It had nothing to do with you. Horace the Horrible was angry at your brother and took out that anger on you. He was a disgruntled grump."

Louisa stepped back and Tessa asked, "What is it like when Reed kisses you?"

"Fantastic. Everything melts away and I am filled with such a rush of powerful feelings."

Tessa smiled. "Things will have a way of working out. You will learn how to please each other. I guarantee it."

"How do you . . . oh, this is awkward. How do you . . . get over . . . the hurt?" she asked, her voice small.

"It only hurts the first time and never again. Since you coupled with Horace the Horrible once, it won't hurt any at all, Vanessa," Adalyn assured her, though Vanessa still couldn't understand how it wouldn't hurt again if Reed did the things Horace the Horrible had done.

"What about your courses ceasing?" she ventured, curious about what Pamela had mentioned.

"Oh, that," Louisa said brightly. "They do stop for a bit when you are with child but they come back again as regular as ever shortly after you give birth. Did your mother not speak to you of these things?"

"No," Vanessa admitted.

Louisa hugged her. "I promise everything will be fine. Lord Boxling will take wonderful care of you. You will be so good together."

She hoped that to be the case.

"For now, we need to see you are ready to meet your groom," Adalyn said. "You don't want to keep him waiting."

Her friends fussed over her for the next hour, with Tessa working magic on Vanessa's hair, piling it high and letting small wisps frame her face. Louisa fastened the pearl necklace and Vanessa placed the earrings on her lobes. She stood, glancing in the mirror, feeling good about her appearance.

Turning, she smiled at these three women, friends for life. "What do you think?"

Adalyn began weeping, apologizing. "Everything moves me when I am carrying a babe," she said, wiping away her tears. "You are so very lovely, Vanessa. Boxling is a fortunate man to land a bride who is as beautiful on the outside as she is on the inside."

But she knew she was the lucky one for having such an amazing, generous, loving man want her as his wife. A flicker of doubt rippled through her.

Would he want her after tonight? Or would he reject her as Horace the Horrible had?

No, Reed loved her. Any flaws she had, any inexperience she possessed, they could work through. She would learn to do whatever pleased him, whether it hurt or not.

"I have a carriage waiting for you downstairs," Louisa said. "Coachmen have been ferrying the houseguests to the village for the last hour or so. We are most likely the last ones at Danfield."

Vanessa accompanied her friends downstairs and found the place deserted of guests. The butler opened the door and escorted them to the waiting coach and the four of them rode the short way to Blackburn, passing the church's graveyard. She would never visit Horace the Horrible's grave again and hoped she would never give her first husband another thought for the rest of her life.

She did worry for a moment, though, that Stillwell had come to seek her out, wanting money. He would soon learn of her marriage to Reed because Pamela had insisted they send word to place an announcement in the London newspapers. Even if Vanessa had squelched that idea, her brother would eventually learn she had married a wealthy viscount. She hoped Stillwell would stay away and decided she would have to share with Reed that her brother would most likely approach them for money.

But not now. Not today. Not when she was ready to walk down the aisle toward her groom. She would wait until they reached Boxwell Hall and settled in before she brought up any conversations regarding her profligate brother.

The carriage door opened and her friends descended from the vehicle, leaving her alone for a moment. Vanessa closed her eyes and savored her last moment as a widow.

And stepped from the coach ready to become Viscountess Boxling.

They approached the doors to the church where the Duke of Camden waited anxiously.

"There you are, Addie," he said, his worry melting as he looked adoringly at his wife. "Come and sit. You look tired." He glanced to Vanessa. "But you look the picture of beauty and grace, my lady."

"Thank you," she said, smiling at his compliment.

Lord Danbury stepped outside as the others moved through the doors.

"We did not speak of this, my lady, but if you would prefer an escort down the aisle to your groom, I am happy to offer one to you."

"I would appreciate that, my lord."

"Call me Owen," he suggested. "You are most certainly a member of the Second Sons' wives circle now. We are all informal when around one another. I understand Lord Boxling is himself a second son. I believe we will adopt him into our group."

"That is very kind of you, Owen. I know Reed would treasure your friendship."

"You are marrying a good man. I am glad things have worked out so well for you. Shall we?"

He offered her his arm and she placed her fingers upon his sleeve. Moving through the doors, they entered the church.

It was exactly how she had pictured it.

The gardener and his wife had assembled the flowers they had discussed, along with greenery entwined among them. The entire church smelled and looked divine. As Owen guided her down the aisle, Vanessa was aware others were present.

But she only had eyes for Reed. Her love. Her husband-to-be.

They approached the altar and her smile widened, seeing how very handsome he was in his elegant suit. His dark, wavy hair still looked a bit untamed and was exactly as she liked it. She saw the sparkle in his eyes, the love she felt for him reflecting back to her. A peace washed over her, a tranquility of calm and deep love. She would now spend every day of the rest of her life with Reed Davenport, Viscount Boxling.

Vanessa doubted Heaven could be any better than what she now experienced on Earth.

He took her hand, their fingers entwining, and he leaned down to her ear. "You look ravishing," he said huskily. "I am so proud that you wish to be my wife. I love you, Vanessa. Before all this begins and we proclaim that love publicly, know that in this moment, it was simply the two of us, swathed in love."

Reed brushed his lips against her temple and she heard a few sighs come from the females sitting in the pews. Then he turned to Reverend Smythe, who began the ceremony.

"Dearly beloved, we are gathered together here in the sight of God, and in the face of this congregation, to join together this man and this woman in Holy Matrimony."

As she pledged to love, honor, and keep herself only to Reed, Vanessa threw off the shackles of the past and experienced a beautiful moment of true freedom, knowing she bound herself to this man openly and willingly, unlike how she had been forced to wed Horace the Horrible in the past.

It was the most liberating moment of her life.

Surprise filled her that Reed had a ring to give her. He must have seen it because he whispered to her, "I bought it in London when I purchased the special license. If you don't like it, I can replace it with another."

"No," she said softly. "It is perfect. Just as you are."

Reverend Smythe cleared his throat, seeming aggravated at them, and they kept quiet the rest of the ceremony, only speaking when asked to do so. But after all the prayers were said and the clergyman pronounced them man and wife, it was Reed's kiss which spoke volumes. He took her in his arms for a long, deep, satisfying kiss, showing the world just how much he loved his new viscountess.

Then it was back up the aisle in a rush as he hurried her to the waiting carriage which would take them back to Danfield. Alone now, he pulled her onto his lap and kissed her the entire way there.

Vanessa felt truly married.

And loved.

CHAPTER TWENTY

T HE NEXT TWO hours flew by. Vanessa had requested that the wedding breakfast be held on the terrace if the weather was good. The day was a bit overcast but it did not look like rain and so they did eat outside. The newlyweds were given their own special table for two but between courses they circulated about the other tables, visiting with everyone present.

At Pamela's table, her new sister-in-law hugged her warmly. "You are absolutely the most beautiful bride I have ever seen," she declared.

"I beg to differ," Lord Rivers disagreed. "I remember our wedding day at how you floated down the aisle at St. George's. You were a picture of loveliness, my dear. You always will be." He took her hand and gazed at his wife with love.

Good feelings filled her, knowing how happy Pamela and her earl were. She also thought Eve and little Pip a delight and told Pamela to come often to Boxwell Hall so that she might see them more often.

"We are happy to visit you and hope you will come to see us, as well." Pamela looked across the terrace and Vanessa saw she focused on Lady Boxling. The other Lady Boxling. "Reed confided in me that Camilla and Nicola will be living with you permanently."

"Yes, he and their mother decided that would be best for

them at the present."

"I think without the burden of motherhood upon her, the dowager viscountess might actually become more pleasant," Pamela said. "Some women are not meant to be mothers. She is one of them." She took Vanessa's hand. "You will be a good sister-in-law to them and see they receive the attention they deserve and the love they seek. It may be tricky, taking on girls of that age, but I believe you are up for the task."

"I believe, together, that Reed and I will make Nicola and Camilla feel loved and wanted," she replied.

Vanessa moved back to her table and again ventured out after the next course, visiting with Lady Rosalie and Miss Parsons and then the next round with Lady Jayne and Miss Maxwell.

Before the next course came out, Lady Jayne said, "Might I walk you back to your table, Lady Boxling?"

Vanessa agreed and as they strolled toward it, Lady Jayne confided, "Lord Thadford has offered for me. He did so two nights ago."

"Why have you said nothing? This is wonderful news."

"I did not want to steal a moment of attention from your happiness but I did want you to know before you departed for Boxwell Hall that I have accepted him. We plan to wed in October. He will accompany me home and meet my father. Oh, I do hope you and Lord Boxling might attend our wedding."

"I will make certain that we are there," she promised, embracing her friend. "I am very happy for you. Viscount Thadford will make for a good husband."

"He and Lord Boxling are good friends so I hope that you and I will see each other often," Lady Jayne said.

"Plan on it," Vanessa told her, taking her seat again and sharing the good news with Reed.

The breakfast came to an end, with a round of toasts that began sweet and then turned a bit bawdy. She found herself blushing as Louisa came over and told her it was time to go upstairs and change into her traveling clothes.

She accompanied her friend upstairs. Soon, they were joined by Adalyn and Tessa and the four women said their private goodbyes, promising to stay in touch.

"Send word as soon as the baby—or babies—come," Vanessa said. "I am already of a mind to steal little Edwin from you because he is so precious. Perhaps I will abscond with one of your newborns."

Adalyn chuckled. "I don't know if I will make it all the way to November or not. Already, I am finding it difficult to get around. Ev says that once we return to Cliffside at the house party's conclusion that he is ordering me to bed."

"I think that wise, Adalyn," she said. "You want to do what you can to keep them inside you as long as possible, in order to give them time to grow and be able to thrive outside your womb."

They returned downstairs and the butler informed her that her trunks and Lord Boxling's had been placed in the carriage, as had the dowager viscountess and her daughters. She thanked him and then found Reed, who was saying his goodbyes to the Second Sons.

"You are one of us now, Boxling," Owen told him. "No shaking us off. You'll have to meet the other two of us soon."

"I look forward to that," Reed said.

Everyone accompanied them outside and Vanessa noticed how Lady Rosalie and Viscount Darton stood especially close, as did Lord Wakeford and Miss Maxwell.

"Write to me and tell me if there are any other engagements which come from your house party," she whispered to Louisa before Reed handed her into his carriage.

Next came Lady Boxling, followed by Nicola and Camilla, and the three of them sat opposite her and Reed. They all waved goodbye as the carriage began to move and then she settled against the cushions. Reed took her hand, threading his fingers through hers. She saw that both girls had noticed and winked at them, sending Nicola into a fit of giggles.

The adults were quiet for half an hour as Camilla and Nicola chattered away, talking about the various house guests and how much they enjoyed getting to come to Danfield.

"I liked playing with the children in the nursery," Camilla declared.

"I didn't know children came to house parties but I am glad they did," Nicola said.

"Children usually don't," their mother said. "It seems the crowd the Danburys run in are an exception." She looked pointedly at Reed and Vanessa knew it was time to discuss the upcoming living arrangements for the girls.

"When will you be leaving for your house party, my lady?" Vanessa asked, getting the ball rolling.

"If it is agreeable with Reed, I will leave first thing in the morning for Bath."

"How long will you be there?" Reed asked.

"The party runs for ten days but my hostess has asked me to stay on a bit. I will only do so if you do not mind the girls staying with you a bit longer."

That gave her new husband the path he needed to follow. "Do you mind if I broach something with you, Constance? It is regarding the girls."

Both Camilla and Nicola sat up expectantly, their eyes darting from Reed to their mother and back.

"What if you returned to town this autumn and allowed them to stay at Boxwell Hall with Vanessa and me? I enjoy their company so much and I know my wife would like to get to know them better. I know how busy your social schedule can be when you are in town. I, too, have many obligations on the estate. I think Camilla and Nicola would be good company for Vanessa and help her to settle into Boxwell Hall nicely. It would give you some time to yourself without having to worry about the girls and help me out."

Vanessa watched Lady Boxling pretend to consider what had already been decided and thought she could go on the stage if she ever sought a career.

She turned to her daughters. "I don't want you to think I am abandoning my duties to you, my sweets. Would this be something you might be interested in? We could have your governess also come to stay and continue with your lessons."

Nicola spoke up first. "I would prefer to stay at Boxwell Hall, Mama. I get so bored in town."

"I do, too," Camilla piped up. "At Boxwell Hall, we can learn to ride."

"You do not ride?" asked Vanessa, surprised.

"Mama isn't fond of riding," Camilla said. "If we lived in the country, though, lots of people get around by riding. Would you teach us to ride, Reed?"

"I think Vanessa should do so," he said. "She rides daily and is quite skilled on a horse. I believe she would also have far more patience in teaching you. Once you learn to do so, however, I will be happy to take you out whenever you desire."

He looked back to his stepmother, continuing the charade. "I am happy, as the head of the household, to have the girls stay permanently, Constance. Vanessa and I can bring them to town each spring with us when the Season begins. You can come to us at Christmas—really, anytime you choose. I think, as the girls' guardian, this would be best. Vanessa is quite capable of running a large household and I am sure she would like to teach the girls to do the same, as well as give them riding lessons. What do you say? May Camilla and Nicola remain with us and see you whenever they choose?"

Lady Boxling cocked her head as if considering his proposition. "Yes, Reed, I believe it would be an ideal arrangement. As long as my girls are content, so I am."

"We will be, Mama," Camilla said. "We will do well in our lessons with our governess and with Vanessa."

"And you can come whenever you wish, Mama," Nicola added. "We will be with you every Season. It is the best of both worlds," she said, her excitement obvious.

"I am glad that is settled," Reed said. "I was hoping you would be amenable to my idea."

Vanessa saw gratitude flash in Lady Boxling's eyes. As her daughters began talking animatedly, she mouthed, "Thank you."

Nicola asked about having their clothes sent down from London and Vanessa decided as Lady Boxling, she would take charge of this situation.

"You should have brought enough things from town to wear for now. When your governess' holiday ends and she reports to Boxwell Hall, we will tell her of the new arrangements. I can either send for your things and hers or perhaps Reed will take us to town for a day or two so I may supervise the packing. I have not been there in many years. Perhaps you would have a few places you might wish to show me."

"We do," Camilla said. "There's the dressmaker and the milliner's and a wonderful bookshop."

"And Gunter's," Nicola reminded. "Don't forget Gunter's."

"We can look in the stables and see what horses might suit you," Reed added. "If none do, then I can go to Tattersall's while we are in town and purchase new ones for you."

Nicola bounced like a small child on the seat. "Oh, this is going to be ever so much fun." Then she looked guiltily at her mother. "You will also be having fun, Mama. At your house party and in town."

Lady Boxling smiled at her daughter. "You are exactly right, my sweet. It will be good for all of us." She glanced to Vanessa and extended an olive branch, saying, "You must promise me to be good to Vanessa. And good for her. She will take over many things which I have done for you."

"Do not worry about us, Mama," Camilla said. "I am the oldest. I will make certain Nicola behaves."

Her sister stuck out her tongue. "Who will make *you* behave?"

"We will," Reed said, his voice deep and firm. "There is always time for fun and games but neither Vanessa nor I will tolerate disrespect or nonsense from either of you."

"Yes, Reed," they said in unison.

After several minutes of silence, Nicola said excitedly, "There it is! Boxwell Hall!"

The carriage turned from the main road and rolled up a lane lined with trees in full bloom. Vanessa looked out the window, seeing the beautiful green of the earth and watching as they passed fertile fields.

This would be her new home.

They arrived at the house, one quite larger than she had expected. The carriage slowed and then stopped and she could see a bevy of servants in two lines. She turned to Reed.

"I asked Brady, my butler, to have everyone assembled upon our arrival so that you might meet your staff."

She squeezed his fingers. "That was most thoughtful of you, my lord."

"I am always thinking of you," he said in her ear, causing a shiver to run along her spine.

Reed got out first and helped the others out so that she would be the last exiting the carriage, commanding the most attention because of the servants' anticipation. When she stepped out, she noticed every eye on her and did her best to move gracefully and stand tall. Mama had always said beautiful posture would impress others and Vanessa desperately wanted to impress the servants that would work for her. She wanted them to be proud of their mistress.

Lady Boxwell ushered her daughters inside as Reed took Vanessa to a couple who looked to be in their early forties.

"Lady Boxwell, I would have you meet the Bradys. They serve as my butler and housekeeper.

The butler bowed to her and the housekeeper bobbed a curtsey.

"It is my pleasure to meet you," she said warmly. "I look forward to working with you as we manage Boxwell Hall together."

"Thank you, my lady," Brady said. "We are delighted to have you here. Please come and meet your servants."

The butler took her through both lines, telling her the names of each servant and what they did at the house or on the estate. She greeted each person individually, repeating their names and committing as many as she could to memory.

Once they had been through the lines, Mrs. Brady offered to take her to her rooms.

"I'll have hot water sent up for you to wash, my lady, unless you would prefer a full bath."

When she hesitated, Reed said, "Yes, a bath will be perfect, Mrs. Brady. It was a full morning with the ceremony and wedding breakfast and now the journey back to Sussex."

"Very good, my lord," the housekeeper said. "I can also have a light supper sent up for you to share. Would you care for that to be set out in your rooms? And what of a bath for you?"

"Hot water is fine for me, Mrs. Brady. And do send up something for us to eat and some champagne if you would."

"Yes, my lord. One moment, my lady. Let me tell Brady what is needed and then I'll take you upstairs."

The housekeeper went to speak to her husband and Reed said, "I thought a hot bath would relax and refresh you."

"That was thoughtful of you."

"Do not hesitate to ask for what you want or need, Vanessa. This is your staff now as much as it is mine."

She bit her lip. "I am afraid I am not used to having a bevy of servants waiting upon me, Reed. The last year I spent in the dower house was with a lone scullery maid. She did cook for me but I had to haul my own bath water and wash my own clothes."

His palm went to her cheek. "Oh, I will enjoy spoiling you, my love." He brushed his lips quickly against hers. "Besides, you are a clever woman. You will take to running a household with ease."

Mrs. Brady returned and took Vanessa upstairs to a huge suite. It included a sitting room, a bedroom, and a dressing room that contained a large bathtub.

The housekeeper pointed. "Through that door is his lord-ship's dressing room and then his bedchamber and study." She smiled. "In case you wish to see him at night."

She felt her face flame at the suggestion and the housekeeper chuckled. "Nothing wrong with that, my lady. You are quite beautiful and Lord Boxling is a handsome man. I'm sure before long we'll have little ones running through the halls of Boxwell Hall."

"I hope so, too, Mrs. Brady."

Her trunks arrived and the housekeeper began instructing two maids on how to handle everything.

"You didn't bring your lady's maid with you?" Mrs. Brady asked.

"No, I did not," she said, closing that door because she did not want to share that she had never had one during her marriage or year of widowhood. "But I would appreciate your recommenda-tion regarding one. Is someone on the staff now a good candidate for the position?"

"I can have a maid help you to dress but no, none of them would suit as a lady's maid. Brady will have to send to London for one."

"I wouldn't want him to go to any trouble."

"Not a bit of trouble at all. We cannot have our own lady without the proper staff. You need a maid from London, you do. One who can dress your hair and sew and knows all about fashion and how to put accessories together. We'll get you fixed up in no time. For now, I can help you bathe and I will have a maid help you to dress and undress each morning and night."

"Thank you, Mrs. Brady."

The housekeeper's eyes grew misty. "No, thank you, my lady. His lordship has a spring in his step that has been missing since his father's death. I would venture to say you are the one who has put it there and that the two of you are a love match."

She nodded shyly. "We are."

After her bath, Mrs. Brady assisted Vanessa in dressing in a new night rail, a gift from Louisa. It was made of silk and filmy, leaving little to the imagination. She could sense the blush spreading from her face to her neck and roots and quickly shrugged into her dressing gown, belting it tightly.

"I will see you in the morning, my lady."

"Thank you for your help, Mrs. Brady."

The housekeeper left and Vanessa stood, taking deep breaths.

"You love Reed," she told herself, wrapping her arms protectively about her. "He loves you. Everything will be fine," she told herself. "Even if he hurts you, it will all go toward making a babe."

"Vanessa?"

She turned quickly and saw Reed had entered through the door leading to her dressing room. Her mouth grew dry at the sight of him, his dark, silk banyan showing off his physique.

"Are you ready to come to supper?" he asked.

She nodded. "Yes, of course."

"Come through here," he said. "Our rooms connect together." Reed took her hand in his and pulled her through the first door.

As her new husband led her from her rooms to his, fear pooled in Vanessa's belly.

CHAPTER TWENTY-ONE

R EED PACED HIS bedchamber, eager to bring his new wife to it but knowing he did not want to rush her. Though she had responded with enthusiasm to his kisses, he believed she had little experience in the marriage bed. Old goats such as Horace the Horrible only worried about pleasing themselves and never their young wives. Reed also suspected Vanessa's first husband had been physically rough with her. As a young, inexperienced virgin—one who had lost her mother and probably knew nothing of what happened between a man and a woman—she probably had been frightened of what occurred.

He would make certain he assuaged all of her fears. After all, they loved one another.

Finally, he cut through the rooms connecting his suite to hers. He thought about knocking and decided to quietly slip into her bedchamber. A few tender kisses should help.

But when he opened the door, he saw her standing in the center of the room, her back to him, her arms tightly wound about her as if she wished to ward off the world.

"You love Reed," she said. "He loves you. Everything will be fine." She paused. "Even if he hurts you, it will all go toward making a babe."

In that moment, he realized how deeply wounded the woman he had married truly was. Physically and emotionally.

What in the bloody hell had Hockley done to her?

At that moment, he didn't know if he should make love to her tonight. He would have to improvise and take his cues from her.

"Vanessa?" he said softly.

She wheeled about, her eyes wide and wild. She was like a fox surrounded by hounds, frightened beyond words.

"Are you ready to come to supper?" he asked, keeping his voice even and gentle.

Her head bobbed up and down. "Yes, of course."

"Come through here. Our rooms connect together."

Taking her hand, Reed led her through the dressing room door. He sensed the tension running through her body as they crossed all the way to his bedchamber. He didn't stop there but continued on to his study, where Brady had set up a light supper and the champagne that had been requested.

They arrived at his bedchamber and passed it to reach the study.

"I thought you might need a little something since the wedding breakfast was several hours ago."

He led her to a chair and seated her and took the one next to her. The champagne was still in a bucket and he removed the bottle and opened it, pouring each of them a flute. Handing the champagne to her, he saw her hand tremble as she accepted it.

"To us," he toasted. "To you. I feel I am the most fortunate man in all of England to have found such a compassionate, caring woman. May we share many years together, lived in love and happiness, and may we be blessed with many children."

He touched his flute to hers and took a long pull from it, noticing she took a small sip and set it down. Her hand shook so badly, however, that the flute tipped over, spilling its contents across the table.

Immediately, Vanessa leaped to her feet and cried, "Oh! I must find something to clean this up." She gazed around, biting her lip.

He rose and took her wrist, rubbing his thumb against the tender underside, seeking to calm her.

"It's all right, love. Nothing has been damaged. Are you hungry?"

Her gaze dropped and she said, "No, not really."

He set his own flute down and, still holding her wrist, led her to a large, comfortable chair. He swept her into his arms and took a seat in it, holding her close. She wriggled but he told her no softly and used his hand to bring her head to his chest. Reed simply held her, feeling the tremors through her body.

"You know we can talk about anything, don't you? We are two who have now become one through our love and through the laws of God and man. I sense how upset you are and I want to help you—but I need to know what is wrong before I can fix things."

She began to weep and he fell silent, stroking her back and hair in slow, gentle movements so as not to frighten her. She reminded him of the first doe he had shot and killed when he was a young boy. He and his father had waited several hours when a doe wandered into sight. For a moment, the animal's gaze had connected with his and it was as if the deer had frozen in place. Reed could even see the movement in its chest, its heart beating so wildly. Yet it was so scared, it couldn't seem to move. His father had whispered to shoot and so Reed did, having regretted that kill both in the moment and to this day. Vanessa reminded him of that deer.

Her sobs subsided and she whispered, "I am so frightened, Reed."

"Tell me what is upsetting you and I will make it better, Vanessa. We are a couple now, stronger together than individually, and anything that troubles one of us troubles the both of us. I always want us to talk through any problem we might have because our love is strong enough to solve anything."

"I am . . . I am afraid I will not please you."

He continued gliding his hand slowly up and down her back.

"You please me in every way, Wife," he told her. "Why would you think otherwise? Be honest."

"B-b-because he found me lacking. And he hurt me. He . . ."

"Your husband?"

Vanessa nodded. "Louisa told me it wasn't about me. That he was angry at my brother and took out his anger on me. Oh, Reed, he said and did such awful things to me." Her eyes welled with tears. "Things . . . I don't . . . I don't wish you to see."

"He hurt you physically and through his words," he stated. "But Hockley is dead and gone, Vanessa. I am the one here with you now. I am the man who loves you and always will. We will work through this together. If you don't wish to make love with me now, we don't have to. We can wait as long as necessary. But I will say this—I think once we do couple, you will see our marriage will be different in every way than your first one."

He took her chin in hand and raised it until their gazes met. "Do you trust me?" he asked, seeing the tears welling in her eyes.

"You know I do."

"Then we shall start anew tonight. Everything you knew—or thought you knew—is in the past. Close the door to those experiences and the foul words and deeds that came from Horace the Horrible. We will never speak of him again. Agreed?"

She nodded, doubt still clouding her eyes. He needed to re-move that doubt and show this woman she was utterly loved.

"I value you in so many ways and I want to show you tonight if you will let me. Will you?"

Again, she nodded. "I do love you so very much, Reed," she told him softly.

"And I love you with a depth and breadth I never knew pos-sible. Our lovemaking will only enhance what we feel for one another. It is a beautiful way to express our feelings for each other. There are many ways to do it. Kissing is key and I know you have enjoyed our previous kisses."

She nodded shyly but he saw the corners of her mouth turn slightly upward.

"May I kiss you, Vanessa? Everywhere?"

Her brows knit together. "What do you mean by everywhere?"

Reed gave her a devilish grin. "Oh, my dearest love, you will soon see."

With that, he lowered his lips to hers. He knew he would have to take things very slowly so as not to trigger any negative memories she possessed. It might take months—even years—to erase what had been done to her and what she had suffered but he had all the time in the world now. He would use it to show his wife how much he truly did love her.

Vanessa warmed to Reed's kiss, her body heating as it always did whenever he touched her. She tried to push away all the terrible memories and let go of the past. She vowed to live in the present tonight, with this man, who meant the world to her. The fact that he valued her said volumes and let her know he was nothing like her first husband.

They kissed slowly for a long time, with Reed finally easing her mouth open and sweeping his tongue inside. The kisses were deep, long, and drugging, causing her bones to melt. She entwined her arms about his neck and pressed closer to him, wanting more of him, knowing he would give her everything she desired, whether she knew what that was or not.

He broke the kiss and his lips glided across her cheek, kissing it and then moving to her nose. He kissed the tip of it and moved his way up to her brow, pressing slow, hot kisses to it. One of his hands pushed into her hair and she began to feel the pins spill from it. His fingers glided through her tresses until no pins remained and they kneaded her scalp, causing delicious tingles to ripple through her. His lips trailed to her ear and his teeth found her lobe, biting softly into it, which caused a rush to surge through her. His tongue outlined the shell of her ear, bringing more delicious shivers to her. Vanessa found herself relaxing, eager to see where he might kiss her next.

He returned to her mouth and kissed her long and hard,

heating her blood. She wanted more of him and tamped down the slight fear remaining within her, knowing she could trust him.

His lips ran down her cheek to her throat, where he found her pulse point as it beat wildly. His tongue swirled around it and then he nipped lightly at her throat, causing a sigh to come from her.

Reed lifted his head and their gazes met. She saw the fire in his eyes and knew she had been the one to put it there, which caused her to slowly smile, feeling her feminine power.

"May I take you to our bed?" he asked.

Vanessa liked that he called it their bed instead of his and she nodded.

Reed rose with her secure in his arms and left the study, taking her into the bedchamber, and placing her on the bed. As she perched on the edge, he stepped back and untied the belt of his banyan. He parted the material and slipped out of the robe.

She gasped.

She knew from previously embracing him that he had a hard wall of muscle along his chest and the cut of his clothes allowed her to see his shapely calves and huge biceps. He stood naked before her now. Her heart pounded so quickly as she studied his glorious form. He stood, letting her drink him in leisurely. His shoulders were broader than she had thought and his chest was a thing of beauty. Her fingers itched to touch the muscles and ridges and the flat belly. His chest was dusted lightly in dark hair, which ran down to a thin line and ended where his cock stood at attention.

Vanessa swallowed. It was so large that she began to panic, biting her lip and wrapping her arms about her.

He took it in hand and said, "See this? This is because of you, love. It shows how much I want you. You do this to me. You. No other woman." He paused and then said, "I have had relations with numerous women over the years. Not one time did any of them touch my heart, though. Tonight, when I enter you, I will be making love for the first time and it will be an experience I have never had. You are the woman I love, Vanessa. You have made the difference in my life. Would you care to touch me?"

She found herself nodding and slipped off the bed, coming to her feet. She took two steps toward him and placed her palm against his chest. It was as hard as a stone wall.

"Touch me," he commanded softly. "Run your fingers over my skin. I long for you to do so."

Hesitantly, she brought her other palm to his chest, and began moving them over his bare skin. Just as when he touched her, she experienced a racing heart and those marvelous tingles as she touched him. Soon, she ran her hands up and down, across, and even around to his back.

She had yet to touch his manhood, though.

He must have sensed her reluctance because he took her wrist and guided her fingers to it.

"Grasp me in your hand," he said.

She did so, finding his rod hard and stiff. He dropped his hand and let her move her fingers over it. She found the tip of it to be as soft as silk.

"You are made so differently from me," she said in wonder.

"We are made to fit together. Now, I must ask you, sweetheart, to stop touching me. Because if you don't, I will come."

She frowned. "What do you mean?"

"It means my seed wants to spill out and I would rather it spill inside you so that we hopefully could make a babe this night."

Her body heated at that thought.

"May I touch you now?" he asked. "Only if you want me to do so."

"I do," she said firmly—and meant it. She loved and trusted this man and now knew her fears were baseless. Reed would never hurt her. He would love her and take care of her always.

With a boldness she never knew she possessed, she reached for the tie to her dressing gown and unknotted it, parting the material as he had, and shrugging out of it, letting it fall to the floor. She warily watched his eyes roam over her and saw the pulse in his throat beating, knowing he would soon see her scars from so long ago.

"You are the most beautiful sight I have ever seen," he told her. "A vision of true loveliness."

Vanessa glanced down and saw that nothing was left to his imagination, only covered by the thin layer of material.

"Will you help me remove my night rail?" she asked.

A slow smile spread across his face. "With pleasure, Viscountess Boxling."

He took the hem of her night rail and lifted it slowly. She never knew how sensual removing a garment could be until Reed's fingers skimmed her body. He tossed it aside and gazed at her in wonder. Though her scars were now on full display, he seemed not to notice them.

"You are simply perfection, Vanessa. I will be the envy of every gentleman of the *ton*." His hand moved to her breast and touched it gently. The other one did the same and he cupped her breasts, his thumbs slowly moving back and forth across the nipples. His thumbs then grazed her nipples and she whimpered in need.

"You like that," he said, a glint in his eyes.

"Yes," she whispered.

"We will learn each other's bodies over time and what pleases us. Anytime I do something you like, tell me because I will want to do it to you. Again and again."

The entire time he spoke, his thumbs had moved, swirling around her nipples and across them. He tweaked her nipples lightly and she gasped.

"You like that?"

"Yes. I like that," she confirmed. "So far, I have liked everything." She grinned at him.

"I believe I said I was going to show you about kissing. I shall continue that lesson."

Scooping her up, Reed placed her upon the bed and then joined her. His palm rested on her belly a moment, causing the place between her legs to ache. He left his hand there as he lowered his mouth to her breast and began feasting upon it, kissing, licking, nipping. Something built within her, a deep yearning as he continued. Something she had no name for.

Yet . . .

CHAPTER TWENTY-TWO

R EED HAD THOUGHT disrobing first and allowing Vanessa to
see him in a vulnerable state might actually bolster her. He
encouraged her to touch him and her fingers grazing his muscles
nearly drove him into a frenzy. He maintained control, though,
knowing there would be times in the future when speed would
suffice. For now, slower was better Already, he could see her
relaxing. See her eyes darkening in need.

When she bravely disrobed for him, he could have wept.

Her night rail left nothing to the imagination. Rather, it was
designed to tempt and taunt a lover. She allowed him to remove
it and he took in her body, its beautiful, feminine curves and her
long legs. Her full breasts called out to him and he took her to the
bed and played with them, teasing her and even testing her, as he
worshipped them. He could have continued doing so all night but
he wanted to see if she might be ready to go further in their
explorations.

He moved the hand resting on her belly lower, watching her
eyes widen. She stiffened slightly and he kissed her softly, hoping
she would relax. His fingers found the nest of curls at her apex
and drifted to the seam of her sex, slowly moving up and down it.
Her breath caught and their gazes connected.

"Are you supposed to do that?" she asked, her voice small.

"What we do between us is our concern. No one else's. We

will share many things. Hopefully, you will like this and want more."

He pinned her gaze as he pushed a finger inside her. She drew in a quick breath. "Oh!"

Slowly, Reed stroked her. She swallowed. He moved the finger in and out, tantalizing her. Her eyes began to glaze as he dipped another finger inside her, hearing her gasp. His mouth sought hers and he kissed her deeply, his tongue mimicking the action of his fingers, driving her into a frenzy. She writhed beneath him, whimpering, her nails digging into his shoulders.

"What's happening?" she asked.

"Do you feel something building inside you? As if you are on the edge of a precipice?"

"Yes," she panted. "Oh, Reed."

"Good. I want you to take that leap of faith, Vanessa. Move your body. Call out my name."

Vigorously, she nodded. He kept caressing her, his strokes deep and slow, then speeding up. Her hips now rose, meeting him, her breathing shallow, tiny noises coming from her.

"Open your eyes," he commanded. "I want to see you when your orgasm comes."

"Or . . . gasm?" she questioned, her breath ragged and uneven.

"That is when you climax. You will know when it happens."

"Will it . . . oh . . . I . . . oh . . . Reed!" she cried, tumbling into pleasure.

"Ride the wave, love," he told her. "Don't be afraid."

"I . . ."

Vanessa cried out, her back bowing, her body quivering, as the orgasm overcame her.

"Yes," he encouraged. "Keep going."

She moved with abandon, laughing and crying, and then she stilled. He pulled his fingers from her and held them up, catching her attention, then slowly licking them. Her eyes widened.

"You taste marvelous. Sweet. In fact, I think I need more of you."

He kissed her belly and swirled his tongue around her belly button, dragging it down lower.

"Reed!" she chastised. "What are you doing now?"

He lifted his head. "Seeing if this is something you like. I think you liked that orgasm."

She laughed. "I loved that orgasm."

"The next one will be better."

He continued kissing her until he reached her core. She stiffened.

"You are going to . . . kiss me . . . there?" she squeaked.

Looking up, he said blandly, "I told you I would kiss you everywhere."

Vanessa giggled. It was the most beautiful sound he had ever heard. Reed lowered his head and worked her into a frenzy again, parting her and using his tongue to push her over the edge again. Her fingers pushed into his hair, holding him close to her. She began bucking wildly, sighing and whimpering and then crying out his name.

He loved hearing her like this. Free and open and trusting.

She came again, her juices sweet and flowing. He lapped them up, her taste now embedded on his tongue and his mind. Reed kissed his way back up to her mouth and then plunged his tongue deep within her, allowing her to taste herself.

More than anything, he wanted to push into her. He worried she wasn't ready for that, though. Her body, yes—but her mind? He wasn't sure.

Then it came to him. Give her the control. Allow her to set the pace.

He broke the kiss and fell against the pillow on his side, draping an arm over her.

"Are you ready for more?" he asked.

"There is more?" She thought a moment. "Of course, there is more. You have pleasured me—but I have done nothing for you."

"Oh, sweetheart, you have done plenty for me. When I bring

you pleasure, it comes for me, as well. But there is something we can do together that both of us will like."

Distaste crossed her face. Reed knew he must strike quickly or he would lose her.

He turned and clasped her waist, raising her up over him.

"What are you doing?" she asked, fear in her voice.

"I am giving you the control, my sweet viscountess," he explained. "You will set the pace. You will move as you wish." He paused. "Trust me on this."

She bit her lip, causing lust to travel through him. "I do."

Slowly, he lowered her, positioning her over his shaft. Its tip touched her core.

"Put your hands on my shoulders for now," he instructed.

Vanessa grabbed them, squeezing lightly, and he guided her onto his cock. It slipped in easily because she was so ready for him but heavenly thunder, she was so very tight. He eased her down until she had taken the length of him in.

"You fit," she said, marveling. "You actually fit. I didn't think that possible because you are so large."

"We are well matched, my love." He captured her wrists and eased them from his shoulders. "You may put them back there if you wish but I want you to ride me now. Ride me like you do a horse as you race across the meadow."

"I don't know how," she said, her voice a whisper.

"We will do this together."

Slowly, steadily, he moved and then showed her how to move, too. He talked softly, encouraging her, and they found a sweet rhythm that made his blood sing. Vanessa lost all her inhibitions and moved with passion and grace, filling him with pure pleasure.

And love.

She lowered her hands to his shoulders and then the rest of her body until her breasts pressed against his chest and their dance began anew. His fingers tangled in her hair. His mouth sought hers. They moved together with a freedom he had never known. And when he came, he called out her name.

It would always be her. Forever and ever.

She collapsed against him, her cheek just below his throat. His heart pounded in double time and he could feel hers doing the same as their heated bodies cooled. They stayed together in silence for several minutes and then she stacked her hands and propped her chin atop them.

"That was wonderful. You are incredible, Reed." She paused. "I hope . . . did I . . . were you—"

"It was heavenly," he assured her. "You made everything seem fresh and new and beautiful." He framed her face and kissed her deeply. "I could not be more pleased with you, Vanessa. With our marriage. With our glorious future."

Reed rolled so that they both were on their sides, facing one another. They gazed into each other's eyes and he saw love for him shining in hers.

"I may never want to leave our bed," he told her.

"Well, I will eventually have to return to mine."

"No."

"No?" She looked puzzled.

"This is our bed. Yours and mine."

"You wish for me to sleep with you?"

"Of course."

"But I have a perfectly good bed in my room," she pointed out. "You do remember I have a suite of rooms."

"I do, as a matter of fact. And if you want me to make love to you in that bed, I will. But I want you here, by my side, in my arms each night, love. I want to feel you as I drift off to sleep and awaken with your hair spread across my chest and your scent filling me. Your room is for dressing and storing your things. This room—this bed—is for our pleasure. And sleep."

"I have never heard of this," she admitted. "A couple who shares a bed."

Reed chuckled. "We wouldn't be the first. In fact, you might want to ask your friends about it. I believe the Three Cousins all sleep with their husbands."

Vanessa gasped. "You know this? They do?"

"Your friends have very successful marriages. Ones in which they are deeply in love with their husbands. Sharing a bed is a natural extension of showing that love."

Her fingers played with the hair on his chest, ruffling it. Already, he felt himself stir again and knew he would never get enough of this woman.

Capturing her hand, he brought it to his lips for a long kiss. "I think we have had quite a long day and should get some sleep now. Do you sleep on your side? Your back? I want you to be comfortable."

She smiled. "You are very thoughtful, Viscount. Usually, my side. My right side."

Quickly, he flipped her onto her right side and snuggled against her, his arm going around her waist, drawing her into him, one leg resting on hers. Reed inhaled her hair and kissed her bare shoulder.

"Shouldn't we cover ourselves?"

"I rarely do unless the weather is cold. My nature is hot. I don't believe you will need the bedclothes."

"Mmm. Well, you are rather warm, my lord. I suppose that will keep me warm, as well."

"Saucy little minx," he said, sinking his teeth into her shoulder.

Vanessa moaned. "Do that again and I might have to do something about it," she said coyly.

He tested her, softly nipping at her shoulder again.

She turned in his arms until she faced him. "I warned you that there would be consequences." Her hand reached between them and captured his cock, which sprang to life. "Hmm, what have we here? And what should I do with it?"

Her lips touched his softly. Reed groaned. His hand swept down her back and clasped her arse. It was a very firm, shapely arse.

She teased his mouth open and kissed him, the first time she had initiated contact. He squeezed her buttocks and she sighed into his mouth.

Once more, they made love, leisurely, with hands caressing one another and kisses leaving them breathless. This time, he pushed her onto her back, his hands pinning her wrists to the pillow as his mouth ravished hers. He pushed into her slowly, moving in and out with great deliberation.

"I need you," she said raggedly.

"I need you," he echoed.

"I mean I really need you," she demanded.

Reed smiled. "Then I am at your service, Viscountess."

He began pumping enthusiastically into her, Vanessa's hips rising to meet each thrust. He enjoyed her cries as he did so. He came in a rush, spilling his seed into her as she shouted his name. It was a good thing Constance and the girls had bedchambers in a separate wing.

Hovering over her, he released her wrists, finding her breasts and kneading them. His mouth sought hers for a final kiss and then he moved from her, collapsing. She snuggled against him, her side pressed to him, her arm about his waist, her leg pinned between his two.

"I think I could also sleep like this," she said.

"Good. Because I am exhausted, my lady."

"Close your eyes then, my lord," she suggested. "And I will be here when you awaken."

Reed did just that, drifting off with a smile on his face and his lovely wife in his arms.

CHAPTER TWENTY-THREE

V ANESSA AWOKE, BLANKETED in warmth.
Ten days of utter bliss . . .

She had been Viscountess Boxling for a week and half now and had begun to understand what Tessa meant when she had spoken of loving your husband more each day. It was true. Vanessa had loved Reed on their wedding day. That was before they had made love. His kisses had lit a fire in her but what occurred in the marriage bed had created an unbreakable bond between them. She smiled to herself. Lovemaking didn't always occur in a bed. Reed had taught her that. Since their wedding day, they had made love in their bed. In the stables, lying atop the sweet smelling hay. In the gazebo of the gardens. In the library on a settee. In his study, Vanessa sprawled upon Reed's desk. It amazed her the number of places lovemaking could occur.

And the positions! Her new husband kept showing her new ways to make love. She couldn't decide which she liked best. In the moment, however they were, became her favorite way. She couldn't wait to see what he came up with today.

Miss Grey, the girls' governess, had arrived several days ago after her holiday. Reed and Vanessa had sat down with the woman and explained how it had been decided for Camilla and Nicola to remain at Boxwell Hall most of the year. Miss Grey had been all in favor of more time in the country, having been brought up in the country herself.

"There is nothing like fresh country air," the governess had proclaimed.

The woman had pulled Vanessa aside after two days at Boxwell Hall, saying how happy both girls seemed and how much better they were getting along.

"I am afraid their mother often pitted the two of them against each other. When she paid attention to them." The governess' cheeks had reddened and she quickly apologized for her remark.

"I understand," Vanessa had said. "I believe Nicola and Camilla will thrive under his lordship's care."

"And yours, too, my lady," Miss Grey had insisted. "Why, you already spend more time with them than Lady Boxling ever did. The hours they have spent in the saddle with you have given them both confidence and joy. Not to mention how you are showing them all about running a household."

Vanessa liked having the two girls around. She considered them younger sisters and would delight seeing them mature and make their come-outs. Already, Camilla had spoken to that very topic with Vanessa, saying that she wanted to wait a year so that she and Nicola might debut together. She didn't want her sister to feel left out and lacking in attention. Vanessa had told Camilla nothing had to be decided now but that she appreciated Camilla's thoughtfulness in regard to Nicola.

They would need to go to London soon in order to get the girls' things. Miss Grey's, too. The governess said she didn't have much at the Boxling townhouse in the way of personal possessions but she did want to collect some schoolbooks for future lessons.

Reed began to stir behind her and she smiled as his arm tightened about her. Soon, his lips were caressing her neck and his hands roamed her body. She had found his lovemaking to vary according to his mood. Sometimes, he was sweet and tender with her, making love slowly and leisurely. Other times, he acted with a fierce passion, like a storm rolling through, taking what he wanted with speed and urgency. Vanessa enjoyed whatever he did to her. His every touch caused her to come alive.

She had also learned small ways to please him. Where to kiss him. The pressure to use when she clasped his cock. He had even taught her how to take it in her mouth and pleasure him. It had been a bit awkward at first but once she understood, she became caught up in the excitement and passion.

This morning was a tender time, with her husband kissing her slowly and thoroughly.

Everywhere.

Her climax was a shattering one, leaving her spent and weak. Each time they coupled, she wondered if this was the time they had made a babe. Reed told her not to worry about it. A child would come when he or she was supposed to. In the meantime, they would work on making that child at every possible opportunity.

"You are addictive, did you know that, Viscountess?" Reed asked, lazily running his hand up and down her back.

"I could say the same for you, Viscount," she retorted, glad that she could be so playful with him. All her previous fears had melted away during their wedding night. She knew Reed loved her passionately and would always protect her.

"Have you thought about when we should go to town?" she asked, stroking his face, the stubble a dark shadow.

"How about today?" he asked. "I have caught up with my correspondence. My steward has everything under control. We could go up this morning and stay today and tomorrow, coming back Wednesday. Would that give you enough time to help supervise the packing?"

"That would be more than enough time," she replied. "It would give us extra time, in fact. I would enjoy a ride through Hyde Park and I know the girls have mentioned both Gunter's and visiting their favorite bookshop."

He kissed her soundly. "Then let's go now. Or after breakfast, I suppose."

Reed helped her from the bed and into her dressing gown. Vanessa made her way through the connecting rooms to her own bedchamber and rang for her lady's maid. Brady had sent to London for one and Vanessa was pleased with his choice. Bertha was sweet and unassuming and had already begun making over Vanessa's limited wardrobe. Reed had told her she could have all new gowns and Bertha had said she could make many of them for wear in the country if she had the fabric needed. Vanessa had decided when they went to town that she would allow Bertha to purchase what she needed. The rest of her wardrobe could wait until next spring when they returned for the Season.

As Bertha dressed Vanessa, she explained they would be in London for the next few days. Bertha agreed to pack a few things for her, as well as the girls. Vanessa informed her lady's maid they would leave after they had breakfasted.

She went to the girls, who still ate breakfast in the school-room with their governess.

"Good morning," she said brightly as she entered. "How would you like to go to town for the next few days?"

Both girls responded with enthusiasm and Vanessa explained how they would pack up their London belongings and bring them permanently to Boxwell Hall.

"Reed wishes to leave as soon as breakfast is over. I have Bertha packing for you now, just a few things since you also have the bulk of your gowns in London which you might wear.

"Can we manage a visit to Gunter's?" Nicola asked. "It is my favorite place. Reed usually takes us."

"Then I am certain he would be happy to do so while we are there. I myself have never been to Gunter's and I'm looking forward to trying their ices."

Within the hour, they were on the road to town. Reed told her it would take between two and a half and three hours to arrive.

"We'll stay at our London townhouse, of course. I will want you to familiarize yourself with it and see if you want to make any changes there."

She had been doing that very thing at Boxwell Hall and had decided she wanted to make updates to a few rooms, replacing some carpets, curtains, and furniture. She had shared her ideas with her husband, who agreed enthusiastically and even made a few suggestions himself. Vanessa decided she would look over the London townhouse closely, making notes, and refer to those when they returned to town in the spring. She did not want any work going on in which she would not be able to supervise.

They talked and the time quickly passed. Arriving in Mayfair, they went into the residence, where Reed introduced her to his London butler and housekeeper. He explained they would only be in town for a few days and how the girls would be living with him and his viscountess at Boxwell Hall.

"And Lady Boxwell, as well?" asked the butler.

Reed shook his head. "No, the dowager viscountess has decided to remain in town as she usually does. She is at a house party in Bath now and will return to town once it concludes."

Reed himself escorted Vanessa upstairs to what would be her suite in the future.

"Obviously, Constance hasn't been here since she learned of our engagement so her things are still here. I will see that they are moved to a different bedchamber so that when she returns, she can settle in there."

"Do you think that will cause trouble, Reed? I don't want her to feel displaced."

"Constance had her time as Viscountess Boxling. Now it is your time."

"But won't I share your bed here as we do in the country? If so, it would be simpler to give me a bedchamber to store my things and allow me a place to dress without inconveniencing Lady Boxling."

"No," he said firmly. "You are my viscountess and deserve the rooms meant for you. Frankly, I feel after speaking with Constance that she may not be long here."

"What do you mean?" Vanessa asked.

"I believe that she will go into future social affairs with the intent of finding herself a new husband. If she does, she will move in with him. No more arguing with me, love. Next time we come to London, these rooms will be yours. Not hers."

He led her down the hall and showed her his rooms and pointed to a room across the hall. "This can suffice for you now. Have Bertha unpack your things in this guest room. I have business in town with my solicitor now."

Reed kissed her and said, "I assume you will take charge of the packing to be done while I am gone."

"The girls have asked for you to take them to Gunter's. Would you be able to do so tomorrow?"

"I should if my business has concluded. If not, you would be able to do so. Gunter's is unique in that you can either eat your ices from your carriage or go inside. It is the one place in town where a single lady may be escorted by a gentleman without causing a stir. You would raise no eyebrows taking Camilla and Nicola there yourself."

"Very well. Then we will see you for dinner?"

"I hope to be back by teatime," he shared. "I hoped you might wish to go to the theater tonight. I have a box. Would you care to go and then partake of a late supper afterward?"

"Oh, yes, Reed!" she exclaimed. "I have never been to the theater and have always longed to do so. I am an avid reader of plays."

"I don't know what tonight's performance will be. I may stop by my club and find out there." He kissed her again and left.

Vanessa spoke with the butler and explained where her trunk was to be taken.

"Yes, my lady. Lord Boxling has instructed us to move his stepmother's things. We will be prepared for your future visits."

She returned to the bedchamber she would use, Bertha accompanying her. Soon, her trunk arrived and the maid unpacked everything for the short visit.

"Your things are all in place," Bertha said.

"Good, now let us go to the girls' rooms and see what all they have."

They went there and spent a good portion of the afternoon deciding what to take and what to leave behind. The girls chimed in with their own opinions, setting aside gowns they had outgrown, which they would give to the servants.

"Tomorrow, you can choose materials for my gowns," Vanessa told her maid.

Camilla volunteered, "Mama has a favorite modiste and she has scads of materials. Nicola and I love going through the bolts and helping her to choose. Could we do the same for you?"

"We might do so when we return to town next spring and I have a new wardrobe made up for the Season," Vanessa said. "For now, I am leaving things in Bertha's hands. She can select the materials she needs."

"Mama has an account there," Nicola offered. "Bertha can simply charge everything to Reed."

"I think things are in good hands here," said Miss Grey, who had arrived a few minutes before and watched the proceedings. "We can get in a few lessons now since I know you are going out with Lady Boxling tomorrow."

The governess whisked her charges away.

For the next two hours, Vanessa and the housekeeper toured the townhouse. It was quite large, much larger than her parents' townhouse had been. When they reached the ballroom, she thought how they might even host their own ball in it next Season. She hoped it would not be awkward, standing at the head of the receiving line as all of the people who went through it officially met her for the first time, people who had ignored and scorned her long ago. Things were different now, however, because Vanessa had friends. Good friends. The Three Cousins would always stand with her and she looked forward to meeting the other two wives who were a part of their circle. She also had made friends at the house party and would know those women, as well. More importantly, this time, she would have Reed continually by her side to her through any social event.

They finished going through the townhouse and Vanessa talked over a few things she might wish to change. The housekeeper readily agreed with her and said she would have the butler draw up a list of tradesmen who might do some of the work, as well as merchants who could provide the goods Vanessa was interested in replacing within the house.

By that time, Reed arrived home and found her, saying he had asked for tea to be sent to his study.

"Shall I summon the girls?" Vanessa asked.

Reed shook his head. "No, I wish for some private time with you."

Vanessa's cheeks heated, thinking he might want to make love in his study and the thought appealed to her greatly.

She was mistaken, however. Once their tea arrived, her husband became all business and she poured out for the two of them.

"I wish to tell you what I have been up to this afternoon."

"You said you went to speak to your solicitor."

"I did. About you."

"But . . . all the wedding settlements were drawn up," she protested. "Owen looked them over and said they were most generous."

"I wished to speak to him about your first marriage and those contracts."

Her belly roiled at the thought. "What did he advise?"

"I went to my club before I saw him and learned the name of Horace the Horrible's solicitor. We went to see him."

"Was he forthcoming about the matter?" she asked nervously.

"Not at first," Reed said. "In fact, he was most reluctant to share anything with us." He paused. "But I am a most persuasive man, as you know. Since you are now my wife, it is my right by law to be able to pursue this kind of investigation."

He stopped to take a sip of his tea and Vanessa pressed him.

"What did you learn, Reed?"

"That you did have a settlement. Monies owed you upon Horace the Horrible's death and that the current Lord Hockley denied them to you." Fire flashed in his eyes. "When I think of how he succeeded in pulling a fast one and sent you off to go earn a living, it makes me ill." He took her hand. "It would have been enough for you to either purchase a small cottage or rent a small place in town. You were not left penniless as you were led to believe."

Anger surged through her, partly aimed at Milton the Muddleheaded, but she also knew she shouldered some of the blame.

"I must admit that I believed everything he told me. I had no reason not to do so. It did not surprise me that Stillwell and Horace the Horrible had not thought about what would happen to me when I became a widow. That is why I never questioned what he told me."

She took his hand and squeezed it. "But I cannot fault what happened because it led me to you. If I had been awarded what was due me, I would have lived a quiet life. I doubt that our paths would ever have crossed."

He cradled her cheek and softly kissed her. "I will admit that you are right about that. If you hadn't been forced from the dower house and told to make your way to London, we would never have met. I cannot imagine what would have become of my life without you in it, Vanessa."

His thumb caressed her cheek. He dropped his hand and said, "I am not about to let Hockley get away with this, however. Now that I know the terms of the contracts, I am going to do whatever it takes to pursue the matter. Hockley's solicitor will no doubt tell him of my visit and warn the earl just how angry I am."

"Most likely, he is in town still, though he installed his mother-in-law in the dower house, Milton the Muddleheaded always did prefer town over country. I assume his bride would go along with whatever he suggested. Will you confront him while we are here?"

"Now that I know of the likelihood he is here, I will send word to a judge I know. Perhaps he, my solicitor, and Hockley can meet tomorrow and iron out this disagreement amicably without any scandal. If not, I will tear him limb from limb, both physically and financially."

CHAPTER TWENTY-FOUR

V ANESSA EXITED THE carriage, gazing at the Drury Lane
Theater. A few patrons were entering and she and Reed
joined them.

"This is nothing to what it is like during the Season," he told
her. "Carriages line up for blocks. The crowds swell at the many
theaters which operate during the Season. I am assuming tonight
will be half-full at best."

"Why do they continue to perform if the *ton* has left town? Is
there any money to be made?"

"Thanks to the Licensing Act, only Drury Lane and Covent
Garden hold performances during the winter months. Both have
royal boxes so any member of the royal family can see a
performance no matter what time of year."

As they entered, she said, "I remember reading about this
theater burning just after I arrived in town for my come-out."

"Yes, it was in February of 1809. This theater opened three
years later and was designed by Benjamin Dean Wyatt. He based
his design in part on a theater in Bordeaux, supposedly because it
contained the best acoustics in Europe."

Reed led her through the lobby and up the stairs to his box.
Once seated, Vanessa looked out over the theater.

"It's so large. How many does it seat?"

"A little over three thousand, which is about five hundred less than the previous one that stood here."

"What will we see tonight?"

"Ironically enough, tonight's performance is *Hamlet*, the same play which opened this new theater. The lead will be the same actor as that opening night, Robert Elliston."

"Good evening, Boxling," a familiar voice said.

Turning, she saw Viscount Thadford there, along with Lady Jayne.

The women quickly greeted one another with an embrace.

"I did not know you were in town," Lady Jayne said, "until Thadford said he had seen Lord Boxling at White's today." She turned to Reed. "Thank you for inviting us to your box this evening, my lord. I am so pleased to see the both of you again."

Vanessa and Lady Jayne took seats next to one another and her friend said, "You do not need to tell me how married life is going for you. You are positively glowing."

"We are very happy," she said. "Boxwell Hall is a beautiful place and we have Camilla and Nicola with us. They will be staying there permanently though we will bring them to town with us next spring so they can visit some with their mother. We came yesterday to pack up the girls' things and take everything back to the country."

"They are sweet girls. They will make their own come-outs before you know it," Lady Jayne said.

"Yes. They are fourteen and fifteen and a delight. I think by being at Boxwell Hall they will receive the attention they have cried out for. I am teaching them to ride. But how are the plans for your wedding going?"

Lady Jayne chuckled. "I never really thought much about my own wedding. My goodness, a lot goes into planning one."

"We received your invitation and look forward to attending the ceremony next month," Vanessa said. "Are you and Lord Thadford remaining in town until it takes place?"

"Yes, it is easier to see to the details if I am here."

"Will you take a honeymoon?"

Lady Jayne nodded. "We are going to Spain. Thadford has been there before and said I would enjoy the land and architecture, not to mention the food and wine."

Reed, who had sat next to Vanessa, said, "I would love to hear more about this trip and my half-sisters, no doubt, would enjoy hearing details of your wedding. Camilla, in particular. She is much more interested in fashion and anything having to do with the *ton*. Would you care to come to dinner tomorrow evening? We will be leaving the next morning and won't be back in town until your wedding."

Thadford sat next to his fiancée. "We would be delighted to come to dinner. Things in town have slowed with so many retreating to the country."

The orchestra began up and they fell silent. Vanessa sat in rapture, seeing Shakespeare come to life for the very first time. When intermission came, she curbed her disappointment at the break.

"Would you care to visit the retiring room with me?" Lady Jayne asked.

"Yes, I believe I would."

Reed and Thadford accompanied them from the box, joining friends they saw in the hall as she and Lady Jayne moved down the corridor. They were stopped three times, with Lady Jayne making the introductions and Vanessa receiving congratulations from people who had seen hers and Reed's wedding announcement in the newspapers.

The retiring room was crowded and so they agreed to meet one another outside. Vanessa emerged first and stepped near a wall so as to be out of the way. She gazed up at the architecture of the building, marveling at the place.

"So you managed to hook yourself a rich viscount?"

Cold fear filled her belly as she turned. "Stillwell," she said stiffly. She noted how disheveled he looked and how he smelled of spirits. Some things never changed.

"I came to see you. Hockley said you had left for London,"

her brother said. His fingers latched tightly on to her elbow. "I need money, Vanessa. You are going to get it for me."

"I will do no such thing," she told him through gritted teeth. "The mess you are in is one of your own making. It is not for Boxling to extricate you from it. The debts are yours, not his."

His fingers tightened, causing her to wince. "I am your flesh and blood, Vanessa. You owe me."

"I *owe* you?" she hissed. "Not that I ever did, but I paid any debt to you long ago when you sold me to Lord Hockley. I was young and innocent and you handed me over to a monster. No, Stillwell, I owe you nothing."

"Lady Boxling, are you all right?" Lady Jayne asked, her eyes narrowing as she studied Stillwell.

Her brother released her arm and stepped back. He glared at her for a moment and then strode off.

"That was Lord Stillwell," Vanessa said. "My brother."

Understanding lit Lady Jayne's eyes. "Ah, the one Milton the Muddleheaded mentioned when we ran into him at Blackburn. The brother who came to you for money."

"Yes," she said tersely, not wishing to discuss it.

"He must know you have wed. Did he wish for Lord Boxling to help with his debts?"

"He did."

"You must tell Boxling. Your husband needs to know of this threat," Lady Jayne warned.

"I will," she told her friend.

"Did you tell him about encountering your stepson in Blackburn?"

"No," Vanessa admitted.

"You should do so. Lord Boxling needs to know about both men," Lady Jayne urged.

She felt eyes on her and saw that Stillwell now watched them from a distance. "Come, let us return to our box."

Vanessa slipped her arm through Lady Jayne's and they returned upstairs. She met a few of Reed's friends, once again receiving congratulations on their nuptials.

Once inside the box, she found the rest of the performance ruined for her because she couldn't stop thinking about her wastrel brother. Suddenly, people were applauding and she realized the performance had ended. She began clapping.

Reed leaned close. "Is something wrong?"

"I just have a bit of a headache," she lied. "Perhaps we can return home so I can get some rest. I have a big day planned with the girls tomorrow. I would not want to let them down."

"All right."

They said their goodnights to Lady Jayne and Lord Thadford, who agreed to come at seven o'clock the next evening. She placed her head on Reed's shoulder in the carriage and they were quiet the entire way home. After Bertha prepared Vanessa for bed, she crossed the hall to join Reed.

He was already in bed and she climbed in, curling up against him.

"Go to sleep," he urged.

She listened and within a few minutes, his breathing evened out.

For the first time in their marriage, they had not made love before sleep.

THE NEXT MORNING, she awakened early and teased Reed from sleep, needing him to make love to her. She promised herself when they finished that she would share that she had seen her brother and what he wanted.

Basking in the aftermath, though, she refused to ruin the happiness that surrounded them. By this time tomorrow, they would almost be ready to leave London. She decided not to bother Reed now. She would share with him down the road about her brother approaching her last night.

They breakfasted with Camilla and Nicola. She had suggested to Miss Grey that the girls be allowed to do so, thinking them too old to be eating in the schoolroom each morning. The packing would continue through today and they would leave for Sussex sometime tomorrow morning.

"Are you taking us to Gunter's, Reed? Nicola demanded.

"No, Vanessa will be doing that with you. I have another business matter to deal with before we return to Boxwell Hall."

Vanessa could not wait to be back in their carriage and on the road again. It was bad enough that she had seen Stillwell last night. She prayed her brother would not turn up here today, causing a scene and pestering Reed for money, simply because she had married a wealthy man and Stillwell thought she owed him. Her brother was no brother to her and, frankly, an embarrassment to their family name.

"Why don't you do your morning lessons," Vanessa suggested. "Then at noon we can go to Gunter's."

"Could we also go to the bookshop? Afterward?" Camilla asked. "You will love it, Vanessa."

"I do love books. Yes, Gunter's and then the bookshop." She looked to Reed. "I hope we will return by teatime and that you will be able to join us."

"If I don't, I will be home in plenty of time to get ready for when our guests arrive for dinner."

Nicola perked up. "Who is coming to dine with us?"

"Friends from the house party we attended," Vanessa told her. "Lady Jayne and Viscount Thadford. They are now engaged and will wed at St. George's in mid-October."

"Oh, are we still able to come to dinner?" Camilla asked. "I love to talk about weddings. I cannot wait for my own."

Nicola snickered. "Camilla has already planned out her entire wedding, from the color of her gown to the flowers she wishes to wear in her hair and the food to be served at the breakfast."

Camilla snorted. "At least I think about these things, Nicola. You never do. I do not wish to be unprepared."

Her sister sniffed. "Well, I may not wed," she declared.

Camilla's mouth formed an O. "Not wed? Are you mad? Every young lady of good breeding weds."

"I will wed if I feel like it," Nicola told them. "It will take a very special man for me to change my mind, however."

"Since you are only fourteen, Nicola, that is far into the future," Reed said, ending the discussion. "I must go now. You two head up to see Miss Grey for your lessons. Enjoy your outings this afternoon."

Vanessa kissed him goodbye and returned to her room, where she rang for Bertha.

"The girls are engaged in lessons with Miss Grey so I thought now would be a good time for us to go to the dress shop for materials."

"You have changed your mind and wish to go with me, your lady?"

"Yes, I might as well get out and about and meet this modiste."

Reed had told her he would leave the carriage for their use today and so she called for it to be ready and gave the coachman the dressmaker's address. She worried the modiste would be a bit snobbish, considering the age of the gown Vanessa wore, although Bertha had spruced it up quite a bit.

Instead, she found Madame to be delightful. With the Season completed, no customers were in the shop and so Madame spent a good two hours with them, talking about clothes and helping choose materials for gowns that Vanessa would wear in the country.

"I already have a few ideas of how to dress you next Season, Lady Boxling. Perhaps I might do a few sketches and send them to you at Boxwell Hall if you would not mind."

"No, I would be delighted to see your work. It has been many years since I have been in town and I do look forward to making a good impression upon Polite Society now that I have remarried."

"Lord Boxling is a handsome, kind man," Madame said. "You

could not have made a better choice for your husband. I look forward to seeing you in the future and hope you will like my designs for you."

Vanessa and Bertha returned to the townhouse and footmen carried in the numerous bolts of material for them. Bertha said she would see about finding an extra trunk in the attics and placing the bolts in them.

"You will be ready for us to leave tomorrow morning, Bertha?"

"Yes, my lady. I have the girls' things organized and much of it can be loaded onto the carriage this afternoon."

"I appreciate both your efficiency and organization," she told her maid. "I am so happy you came to us."

"You are a dream to work for, my lady. I will admit—naming no names, of course—that I have been employed by others who have never said a kind word to me. Boxwell Hall is a happy place, all because of you."

Tears misted Vanessa's eyes and she thanked the servant for her kind words.

The girls found her, ready for their outing to Gunter's, and Vanessa rang for the butler and asked that the carriage be readied for their outing. A quarter-hour later, they stepped from the front door into the square, the vehicle waiting.

As the girls were assisted into the coach, she sensed eyes upon her and turned. She found a bald, portly man across the street staring at her, which made her uncomfortable. Vanessa entered the carriage and watched out the window as it pulled away.

The man continued to study her as they passed and then he mounted a horse. A chill ran through her. Her gut told her that Stillwell had sent him.

And things were far from over.

CHAPTER TWENTY-FIVE

"**A**REN'T YOU LISTENING, Vanessa? We're here."
She looked up to see Camilla frowning at her. "Oh, I am sorry. A little woolgathering, I am afraid. Well, what do you wish to do? Reed said we can eat here in the carriage or go inside."

"I want to go inside," Nicola said. "I like it there. And we can get more than just ices if we dine inside."

"Very well."

She called out and the footman opened the door, placing the stairs down before taking her hand and helping her from the coach. She glanced about, worried that man had followed them but she did not see him in sight.

Until she did.

Dread filled her. Why was he following her? Was he one of Stillwell's employees, tasked with discovering her location? Would her brother approach her in public, as he had last night, demanding money? Perhaps they should have their ices in the carriage and go straight to the bookshop afterward.

But she saw Camilla and Nicola already crossing the street. Nicola called over her shoulder for Vanessa to hurry and she did so, crossing it and joining them as they entered the sweet shop. She couldn't disappoint the girls. Perhaps it had been her imagination. That the stranger just happened to be going in the same direction they had been.

"Quit lying to yourself," she muttered under her breath.

"What's that?" Camilla asked.

"Nothing," she said, mustering a smile.

A young woman appeared and handed them pages with the day's offerings. The girls discussed some of the ices that they had ordered before, as well as favorite tea sandwiches. When the young woman returned, they placed their order for both sandwiches and lemonades, as well as their ices, which would come out after they had eaten.

Vanessa had bitten her nails as a girl and longed to tear her glove off and do so again as the nerves built inside her. Thankfully, neither Nicola nor Camilla picked up on her mood and chattered away.

When their sandwiches and drinks came, she forced herself to eat half of one, washing it down with the lemonade.

"Aren't you going to eat any more, Vanessa?" Camilla asked.

"I am saving myself for my dessert. I don't want to be too full and not be able to eat it when it comes."

They talked some of books and what they might purchase as they ate, her eyes continually drifting to the entrance each time the bell tinkled with a new arrival or departure.

Finally, their ices were delivered to the table. Nicola had chosen chocolate, while Camilla had selected lavender. Vanessa went with chocolate and found it to be rich and decadent. It was easier going down than the sandwich had been and she was able to finish almost the entire thing.

"You only have a few bites left," Nicola said.

"I am full," she declared. "You may have them if you'd like."

Both girls took Vanessa's dish and dipped their spoons into it, finishing off the sweet, as Vanessa arranged to have their bill placed upon Reed's account.

"Are you ready to go?" she asked. "I know you wish to spend quite a while looking for books. Then we must get back for tea."

"Will you help me decide what to wear this evening?" Camilla asked as they left Gunter's. "Dining with a duke's daughter has me a bit agitated."

"Lady Jayne will set you at ease," Vanessa promised. "She is charming and quite a bit of fun."

"I suppose I never thought of a duke's daughter being full of fun," Nicola said.

"Well, you are both daughters of a viscount. Does that make you any less fun?" she asked. "Lady Jayne is a lovely woman."

"And we will talk about the wedding, won't we?" Camilla pressed.

"Reed mentioned your interest in weddings to Lady Jayne when we were at the theater last night. She is more than willing to talk about the upcoming ceremony at St. George's."

They climbed into the carriage, with Vanessa looking guardedly about, spying no one resembling the bald stranger. The driver drove them another mile and halted the carriage again and they entered the bookshop.

Finally, she relaxed. Her fears were for naught. They had not been followed.

The girls immediately went their separate ways. Nicola wanted to look at books on history and architecture, while Camilla went in search of novels and ones on gardening. Vanessa roamed the aisles freely, merely browsing. Boxwell Hall had so many books that she would not purchase any for herself today and merely choose one from the library.

Then she thought how she had not gotten Reed anything for his birthday and thought she might find him something while they were here. In getting to know him, she learned he had a great interest in horses and war. She found a section that included books from ancient wars, such as the Peloponnesian War, to more modern engagements. One book focused solely on the Battle of Trafalgar. It contained intricate diagrams and tables with all kinds of facts and figures. She decided Reed would enjoy this.

Turning so she could leave it with the clerk until the girls made their final selections, she found the aisle blocked.

"Excuse me," she said and then looked up, meeting Stillwell's gaze.

"You!" she accused. "Get out of my way."

Instead, he stepped forward, forcing her back until she was cornered with nowhere to go. Panic filled her—before a calm descended.

She was Viscountess Boxling. She did not have to put up with any nonsense from anyone, least of all her worthless brother. If she caused a scene, so be it. Most of Polite Society had vacated London since the Season was over. If the newspapers reported anything that occurred here and now, hopefully few would see it.

"Get out of my way, Stillwell," she demanded loudly.

"Keep your voice down, Vanessa," he warned.

"I will not!" she cried, her tone sharp and the volume loud. "I do not want to see you. I wish to have nothing to do with you. You have placed a stain upon the Hughes' family name and the title which might never wash out."

His jaw fell, no words coming out, giving her a chance to continue.

"You are on a sinking ship, Stillwell. One in which *you* were the one to blow a hole in its bow. You are now sinking because of your heavy gambling debts and God only knows what else."

"You can't do this to me," he declared, his chest puffing up.

"After what you did to me?" she countered. "Oh, yes, I can."

Desperation filled his eyes. "This is urgent, Vanessa. There are . . . people. People who are after me. People who wish great harm to me because of what I owe them."

She shook her head. "If you were foolish enough to turn to disreputable men for a loan, of course they want their money back—with interest. Heavy interest, I assume."

"They are going to hurt me," he pleaded.

"They won't kill you," she said succinctly. "They cannot get money from a dead man."

She saw movement over his shoulder and supposed their loud conversation was beginning to draw a crowd.

"I am miserable," he admitted. "I have sold off everything not nailed down or entailed. I've had to let most of the servants go. You have married well, Vanessa. Surely, you could convince Boxling to give—" He paused and corrected himself. "To *loan* me the appropriate funds."

"I will not," she vowed. "You are a miserable example of a human being, Stillwell. Reckless. Thoughtless. Uncaring. Unfeeling. You ignored me our entire lives. Sold me to a stranger to pay off some of your markers. How do you think I felt going to a stranger? I survived a wretched marriage and came out of it alive. I am wed now to a man I love."

Vanessa looked at him, shaking her head. "The truth is that you are nothing to me, Stillwell. Nothing. In fact, you are dead to me. Never approach me again else I will turn Boxling loose upon you—and then you will wish you were truly dead."

She pushed past him, seeing half a dozen people gathered at the end of the aisle, including the bald man, who she assumed worked for Stillwell and had followed her here, and Camilla and Nicola. Camilla was wide-eyed; Nicola was smiling triumphantly.

"You were magnificent, Vanessa," Nicola praised.

"Come, girls," she said brusquely. "We can look at books another day."

They followed her from the bookshop, past others whose mouths gaped. One redheaded woman who looked to be in her late-thirties smiled at her and said, "Bravo, my lady. I am Lady Martin. I admire your bravery and will make certain Polite Society knows your side of this ugly story." She glanced in Stillwell's direction. "No one likes him a bit anyway."

Vanessa paused. "Thank you, Lady Martin. It is lovely to make your acquaintance."

Lady Martin nodded. "Perhaps we might see more of one another next Season."

"I look forward to that."

She marched from the bookshop and the footman handed her up. The girls quickly followed, a dozen questions spilling from their lips. She shushed them.

"I will only say this once to you and will take no questions."

They nodded solemnly.

"That was Lord Stillwell. My brother has never shown me any kind of interest or affection. His gambling debts mounted and on the night I was to make my come-out, Stillwell promised me to Lord Hockley. My dowry and I were to cover debts he owed the earl. I wed Hockley, whom I called Horace the Horrible, the next morning. It was a terrible marriage and I will never speak of what went on between us. But I never was introduced into Polite Society. I never danced at a ball. I was banished to the country and told I was no good."

She paused, taking a deep breath. "But I am strong. I outlived Horace the Horrible. I had the great fortune of becoming friends with Lady Danbury, who invited me to her house party. And it was there I met Reed. He has changed my life."

"You two are so in love," Camilla said dreamily.

"We are," Vanessa agreed. "I will never take him for granted. I thank the heavens every day for him coming into my life and bringing laughter and love."

She sighed. "We are now closing the door on today's incident. I never wish to hear of it in my presence."

But she knew they would tell Reed everything.

They arrived home and she went to her bedchamber, rinsing her face in cold water. She no longer trembled from anger—and none of the trembling had been from fear. She had stood up to her bully of a brother and doubted he would come calling.

Deliberately, she was late to tea. As she entered the drawing room, she saw Nicola waving her arms, her face animated as she no doubt recalled the conversation in the bookshop. Camilla quickly nudged her sister and Nicola fell silent, glancing guiltily at Vanessa.

"They brought some of those lemon cakes Reed loves," Camilla said as she joined them.

"Forgive me for being tardy. I was checking with Cook regarding dinner for our guests," she fibbed.

Camilla poured a cup of tea and handed the saucer to Vanessa.

"Thank you. We should have the both of you practice pouring out from now on. It is a skill which will be important to possess."

She sipped on her tea and then set the saucer down. Reed slipped his hand around hers.

"I hear you have had an eventful day," he said, his eyes gleaming in mischief.

"Yes, Bertha and I went to select bolts of material for new gowns. Then the girls and I ate at Gunter's and spent a short time at their favorite bookshop."

Nothing was said about Stillwell.

Several hours later, Vanessa helped welcome Lady Jayne and Lord Thadford. Camilla and Nicola were obviously taken by the viscount's good looks and they basked in the attention Lady Jayne gave them, peppering her with questions about her upcoming wedding and what a house party was like.

Dinner was a pleasant affair and then Reed sent the girls up to bed while the four adults planned to retire to the drawing room.

Reed rang for his butler and asked him to escort his guests to the drawing room, telling them that he needed a moment alone with Vanessa on an important family matter.

When the butler left with the Lady Jayne and Lord Thadford, Reed embraced Vanessa and whispered in her ear, "The meeting with Hockley was a smashing success."

Vanessa pulled back and gaped at him. "What do you mean? What has happened?"

Reed smiled and said, "My solicitor and the judge met with Hockley this morning. Milton the Muddleheaded knew he was in serious trouble. His own solicitor had already informed him of what was coming. He needed to avoid any scandal, so he immediately agreed to hand over the entire settlement amount . . . plus interest from the day your husband died."

Vanessa was astonished that Reed had been so efficient at making this happen so fast. "Thank you, my darling. I'm so lucky to have you. What will you do with the money?"

Reed chuckled. "*I* won't be doing anything with it. The settlement and interest has already been recorded in my bank in your name. The money is rightfully yours and yours alone. *You* get to decide what to do with it. I want nothing to do with it."

He could see that she was getting ready to protest. He kissed her softly and said, "The money is yours, Vanessa. End of discussion. Now, let's join our guests. They are waiting for us."

Reed took her hand and they walked to the drawing room in silence. When they arrived, Lord Thadford turned with a magnificent smile on his face.

"It seems you made quite a splash today, Lady Boxling," Lord Thadford said. "Talk spread quickly through my club regarding you reading the riot act to your brother. In public, no less."

"Oh, dear," she said.

"No, it is a good thing," Lady Jayne said, covering Vanessa's hand with her own. "Stillwell's reputation is nasty. This lets the *ton* know you and Lord Boxling want nothing to do with him. I think many will salute you for dressing him down so."

"A Lady Martin was there," Vanessa said. "She was quite kind to me."

Lady Jayne's eyes lit with interest. "Ah, Lady Martin. She is one to have in your corner. If she approved of your actions, the rest of the *ton* will, as well."

They conversed for another hour and then their company departed, with Vanessa saying, "The next time I see you, you will be coming down the aisle at St. George's, ready to become Viscountess Thadford."

She embraced her friend. "You will adore marriage," she said softly.

Lady Jayne winked. "I already enjoy certain aspects of it. Let me say that Thadford and I are well suited. In every way."

They looked at one another and then burst out in laughter.

"I better get this one home," Viscount Thadford said. "She is probably causing trouble. Boxling, you better watch your wife or she will be doing the same."

Reed's gaze met hers. "I hope she causes trouble for me every night, Thadford." He slipped an arm about Vanessa.

They walked their guests to the door and then once it closed, her husband swept her into his arms and raced up the stairs. He did not stop until they were safely ensconced behind closed doors, where he gave her a lingering kiss, still holding her in his arms.

Breaking the kiss, he said huskily, "I thought I would always be your knight in shining armor but you certainly rescued yourself today, based upon what the girls told me."

"I don't want to talk about Stillwell," she said seductively. "I only want to talk about us. Or not talk at all." She smiled up at him.

"Perhaps our bodies should do the talking for us," Reed suggested and then seized her mouth with his in a hard, possessive kiss.

He continued kissing her as he brought her to the bed and placed her upon it. As her husband slowly undressed her, Vanessa fell in love with him all over again.

And knew she would every day until her last breath.

EPILOGUE

London—October 1816

V ANESSA AWOKE, HER belly queasy. She was rarely ill and hadn't been since three years ago when she had suffered from a brutal summer cold, the worst kind of cold to get.

Her belly seemed to rumble and flip and explode all at the same time and she knew she had to get out of bed. Now.

She lifted Reed's arm gently and slipped from the bed, setting it back down where she had lain a moment ago. With her hand pushed hard against her mouth, she ran from the bedchamber, going through his dressing room and making it to hers. There, she fell to her knees and vomited in the chamber pot.

Immediately, she felt better. She rose, still a bit shaky, and went to her own bedchamber. Pouring water from a pitcher into a basin, she bathed her face and rinsed the sour taste from her mouth. Then a thought came to her.

Her courses had not come.

Joy exploded within her.

She was with child. A babe she and Reed had made together grew within her. Vanessa smiled, placing her hands over her flat belly. Smiling, she thought of Adalyn. How her friend now rested in bed, awaiting the birth of her twins. Her letters to Vanessa were full of mirth as she did her best to keep her babes inside her as long as possible. Adalyn explained to her that babes usually came in nine months' time, give or take a couple of weeks, but that carrying twins was a little different. They would have a better chance of survival the longer they remained within Adalyn's womb.

She would have to write Adalyn—actually, all her friends—and share the news with them.

Before that, she would tell Reed. He would be so happy. Quickly, she counted the months and arrived at an approximate date.

Vanessa crept back to their bed and as she lifted his arm and slid against him, he awoke.

"Is something wrong?"

"No. Everything is absolutely perfect."

He smiled sleepily at her. "I agree that waking up with you makes every day a perfect one."

His lips found hers and, soon, Vanessa was in paradise, thanks to her husband's loving touch. Afterward, she was nestled in his arms, the sound of his heartbeat beneath her ear as she rested against his massive chest.

"What time is the wedding?"

"Ten o'clock," she replied. "We should leave for St. George's by nine, I would think. After all, there's sure to be a crowd with a duke's daughter marrying there today."

"Why don't we have breakfast sent up to us?" he suggested. "We never do so. I feel lazy today. Besides, with the girls in the country, it is only the two of us. We have no need to make an appearance downstairs in the breakfast room."

"All right," she agreed, happy to remain safe and secure in her husband's arms.

Reed rang for his valet and told him it would be breakfast for two, followed by sending Bertha up to help dress her mistress for the wedding.

"What shall we do to pass the time?" her husband mused. "I know. I can kiss you."

He did just that, leisurely exploring her mouth—and beyond—until a knock sounded at the door.

A maid brought in their breakfast tray and they sat up in bed, feeding one another. Halfway through the meal, her belly twisted again.

"No more for me," she said brightly. "I'm off to dress."

Vanessa barely made it to the chamber pot this time, losing all of her breakfast. If she hadn't been certain before, she was now.

She rang for Bertha and then used her tooth powder to rinse away the foul taste. Her maid dressed her and then styled Vanessa's hair in a simple chignon.

"There, my lady. You look lovely."

"You certainly do."

She turned and saw Reed standing in the doorway. Bertha quietly left the room.

Rising, she went and slipped her arms about his waist. "I have something to tell you. Something absolutely wonderful."

He cupped her cheeks. "Whatever it is, I agree—it is wonderful."

"We are going to have a baby."

He looked confused for a moment and then he smiled brilliantly. "We are going to have a baby," he repeated.

"Yes. I think he or she will come mid-June but I will need to see a midwife to confirm that."

"A babe," he said, wonder in his voice.

"A babe," she agreed. "Hopefully, the start of many to come."

Reed bent, his mouth touching hers in a reverent kiss.

Vanessa's heart exploded with love for this man.

And for the child they had made.

About the Author

Award-winning and internationally bestselling author Alexa Aston's historical romances use history as a backdrop to place her characters in extraordinary circumstances, where their intense desire for one another grows into the treasured gift of love.

She is the author of Regency and Medieval romance, including: Dukes of Distinction; Soldiers & Soulmates; The St. Clairs; The King's Cousins; and The Knights of Honor.

A native Texan, Alexa lives with her husband in a Dallas suburb, where she eats her fair share of dark chocolate and plots out stories while she walks every morning. She enjoys a good Netflix binge; travel; seafood; and can't get enough of *Survivor* or *The Crown*.

9 781958 098646